She didn't know how long she'd slept or what instinct caused her to awaken. What she did know was the heat had seeped into her bones and chased away the chills. Last night's goose bumps were replaced by a sheen of sweat.

A sound in the distance caused her to sit up and throw off the blankets. She listened. Maybe her imagination was playing tricks on her. She stood, shaded her eyes, and strained her ears.

The sound of a vehicle. Her elation was rapidly replaced with panic. What if Vargas had returned to find them? She searched for a weapon. Sand, only sand and dried brush. A Jeep approached through the shimmering waves of desert heat.

She rummaged inside her purse and wrapped her hand around the fingernail file. She would not go down without a fight. She sat next to Mitch, shielding his body with hers, and waited in breathless fear.

Sun spots danced in front of her eyes, making it difficult to see. She shielded her eyes with one hand and clasped the fingernail file in the other. If it could open tin cans, then it could surely pierce a heart, or gouge out an eye.

A hand reached toward her.

She drew back her arm, ready to fight to the death.

"Laura?" It was a deep, slow voice.

The man went down on one knee. Her vision cleared, revealing two more men who knelt, their hands reaching for Mitch.

Praise for Loretta C. Rogers and...

***LADY ADEL'S CAPTAIN*:**

"An exciting Historical Romance. A delicious romp though England and [Ireland] with a lady, a three-year-old child, and two servants to an unknown destiny. ...A sweet romance, with honorable and delightful characters. ...Fast paced and filled with passion, a bit of mystery, a soldier's sacrifice, and lots of love. ...The characters are realistic, with realistic issues, and the storyline was very engaging."

~Tarenn, My Book Addiction and More (4.5 Stars)

~*~

"I enjoyed the rich historical details of this story set in England, Ireland and India in the 19th Century. Loretta Rogers creates realistic characters who suffer hardships and learn to overcome the worst circumstances that life has to offer. I highly recommend *LADY ADEL'S CAPTAIN* for fans of historical romance."

~Melissa Beck, Fresh Fiction Reviews

~*~

"A fine historical romance, and the twists and turns will keep you guessing."

~Clare O'Beara, Fresh Fiction for Today's Reader

~*~

***FORBIDDEN SON*:**

"This book is a keeper."

~Barb, Night Owl Reviews (4.5 Stars)

~*~

"Loretta C. Rogers has done it again in a story that is actually about the hero and heroine and what they go through during the years."

~Melinda B., Fallen Angel Reviews (5 Angels)

Shadowed Reunion

by

Loretta C. Rogers

Sequel to Murder in the Mist

This is a work of fiction. Names, characters, places, and incidents are either the product of the author's imagination or are used fictitiously, and any resemblance to actual persons living or dead, business establishments, events, or locales, is entirely coincidental.

Shadowed Reunion

Contact Information: info@thewildrosepress.com

Cover Art by *Rae Monet, Inc. Design*

The Wild Rose Press, Inc.
PO Box 708
Adams Basin, NY 14410-0708
Visit us at www.thewildrosepress.com

Publishing History
First Crimson Rose Edition, 2015
Print ISBN 978-1-5092-0322-2
Digital ISBN 978-1-5092-0323-9

Sequel to Murder in the Mist
Published in the United States of America

Dedication

To my readers
old and new:
thank you!

Other books by Loretta C. Rogers
available from The Wild Rose Press, Inc.

Murder in the Mist
Cloud Woman's Spirit
Lady Adel's Captain
The Witching Moon
Forbidden Son
Bannon's Brides
McKenna's Woman
Isabelle and the Outlaw

"It's a part of what we call the Shadow,
all the dark parts of us we can't face.
It's the thing that, if we don't deal with it,
eventually poisons our lives."

~Michael Gruber

Chapter One

Laura Friday peered through her sunglasses at the smiling waiter as she accepted the frosty piña colada. After savoring a long sip, she looked at her aunt. "Isn't Hawaii glorious? I can't believe we're wearing shorts in December."

Phyllis Friday wriggled her bare toes. "I don't envy our friends in Maine. Cole Harbor is a ghost town this time of year. Poor Maudine, having to shovel snow at her age. I wish she had agreed to come with us."

"Thank you, Aunt Philly."

Phyllis lowered her sunglasses to peek over the rim. "Whatever for? I'm the one who should be thanking you. You've made my long-awaited dream vacations come true. Paris in September, and now basking in the sun here in this tropical paradise with my favorite niece."

Laura laughed. "I'm your only niece."

"Ayuh, and you are a keepah."

Silence stretched between the two women as if each were lost in her own thoughts. It was Phyllis who broke the interlude. "Have you given thought to Bryan's proposal?"

"I swear, sometimes I think you're psychic." Laura kept her voice casual. "He's handsome, caring, and kind, a senior park ranger, his future is secure—but we've only know each other a few months. It hasn't been a year since Jolly's death, and I'm still traumatized over being kidnapped and nearly killed by Benjamin Noone. I need time, Aunt Philly. That's why being here with you is so special."

"Ayuh, you've had your share of grief, that's for certain. Nonetheless, Bryan loves you."

Laura harrumphed. "Love? I don't even know what that means. I loved Jolly like a brother. I love you, I love my job as a reporter, and I love the lobster rolls from the Silly Lobster. I have feelings for Bryan, but I don't think what I feel is *love*. Aren't you supposed to experience euphoria, and giddiness, and want to dance on air?"

Phyllis laughed and waved. "Yoo-hoo, waiter. Two more piña coladas, and with an extra splash of rum. Bill it to our room. Suite 2312." She turned back to Laura. "You make a good argument. All I can say is sometimes friendship grows into an even stronger affection. Remember what Mitch kept telling you—give it time. If you're not ready, don't let Bryan pressure you."

Mitch Carter. Laura didn't want to think about him, and decided to change the subject. She offered a mischievous smile. "C'mon, let's go freshen up. I'm looking forward to the luau and watching the hunky male hula dancers swiveling their sexy hips."

After an evening of over-indulging in food and fun, Laura and Phyllis returned to the hotel. "Laura, I can't remember the last time I felt this alive, totally exhausted, and a wee bit tipsy."

Laura kissed her aunt on the cheek, quietly slipped into her bedroom, and shut the door. Uttering a sigh of relief, she kicked off her silver orthopedic slippers and let her feet sink down into the soft lush carpeting. She changed into an oversized T-shirt and climbed beneath the silken duvet.

The past several weeks had a dreamlike quality about them. Could it already have been four months since Deputy Sheriff Mitchell Carter had rescued her from a demented psychopath? She closed her eyes. Too much had happened since the beginning of the year. She found it all slightly overwhelming.

It was still incomprehensible that she'd let Mitch walk out of her life. Yet hadn't they both agreed the timing wasn't right for them? He was returning to El Paso to run for sheriff and, too, to bring down the men who had murdered his wife and wounded his mother. As for herself, she had given up her job as a New York investigative reporter, purchased Cole Harbor's only newspaper, the *Harbor Gazette*, and was still trying to recover from post traumatic stress disorder, plus coming to terms with being a cripple for the rest of her life. She had made it clear she wasn't ready for a relationship, and she certainly wasn't leaving Cole Harbor except for vacations. And then there was Bryan.

It was true, Mitch had often told her to set the rules, to go slow and easy. Maybe that's what bothered her about Bryan. As much as she resisted his proposals, he pushed, always declaring his love for her. There was, as yet, no formal announcement of an engagement, but everyone in Cole Harbor expected a spring wedding.

A solitary tear dislodged itself from the corner of her eye and slowly slid down her cheek to finally fall unheeded on the pillowcase. So here she was on a beautiful breezy night in Hawaii, her hip and leg aching, and feeling a little sorry for herself.

An even bigger sigh escaped her lips as she stared up at the ceiling.

****

Just for an instant, unable to separate dream from reality, Laura believed herself back in her own bed in Cole Harbor.

“Laura!” The voice cut through the silence in the room like a knife. “Wake up.” The voice was resonant and forceful.

She wanted to shrug off this intruder. Brilliance from the bedside lamp, and the persistent hand shaking her shoulder, caused her to force open her eyes. She yawned. “Aunt Philly, what’s wrong?”

Her aunt’s voice quavered and broke. “I don’t know—how to tell you.”

Laura looked at the clock. She scooted to a sitting position. “It’s one in the morning.” Every muscle in Laura’s body tensed at the pinched, drawn look on her aunt’s face. “What’s happened? Are you ill?”

Phyllis stood at the edge of the bed, hands knotted together, her voice a pitch higher. “There’s been a terrible accident. We’ve lost everything! Oh, by Godfrey, Laura, what are we going to do?”

Laura swung from the bed and gripped her aunt by the shoulders. “You’re not making sense. Take a deep breath, and start from the beginning.”

“I-I actually think I might faint. I feel all swimmy-headed.”

Laura steered Phyllis toward a chair and helped her sit down. “I’ll get you a cold cloth.” She limped to the bathroom and dampened a washcloth, then returned. “Did you have a bad dream about an accident? Can I get you a bottle of water from the refrigerator?”

Phyllis shook her head as she placed the cool cloth to her face. She drew a shuddering breath. "If only it were a bad dream. It's seven p.m. in Maine. Maudie didn't realize the time difference. There was a gas leak in the underground lines. Something happened. I don't know what or how. Maudie was near hysteria and yelling into the phone. I could hardly make sense of what she was saying. Oh, by Godfrey! This is terrible…terrible."

"Aunt Philly, inhale, then exhale, and try to calm down. Tell me about the gas leak."

Tears stained her aunt's cheeks, her shoulders shaking as she sobbed, but she did as Laura suggested: inhaled, exhaled. "Apparently, unbeknownst to anyone in the town, gas has been leaking and accumulating underground for quite a while. There was an explosion." She placed her hands over her face and shook her head before refocusing on Laura. "The bookstore, the newspaper office…the entire block went up in flames. The Silly Lobstah is gone, and the gazebo, too. Maudie said it looked like a bombed-out war zone, buildings blown apart and houses burned to the ground."

Laura's heart pounded against her chest. She had difficulty getting the words out. "Was anyone hurt?"

"Maudie said ten people were killed, and about twenty-six injured. She wasn't sure. Thank goodness most everyone leaves for warmer climates before now, and they don't return until after Easter."

Laura reached for her cell phone. "We'll catch the first flight out."

Phyllis grabbed Laura's arm. "No, we can't. Maudie called from Bangor. She's staying with a cousin. Cole Harbor was evacuated. She said gas leaks formed all around the town, and the gas has to be burned off slowly."

Trembling visibly, Phyllis attempted to stand, but her legs gave way, and she fell back in the chair. Her face tightened, and she became more pale. "Laura…I-I'm so sorry."

Laura gulped. "You're scaring me. Who was killed? Please, not Nadia or Amy?"

Tears glittered in Phyllis's eyes. She spoke between sobs. "There was a second explosion. As a primary responder, Bryan went to assist after the first blast, and his father went, too. Oh, if only they had stayed on the mountain! I can't imagine how Daphne is coping with the loss of two loved ones on the same day."

Her skin turning cold and damp, then hot, Laura sat motionless. Stunned. The entire room seemed out of focus. "Bryan?" Her voice came out in a squeak. It couldn't be, she thought to herself. It just couldn't be. "Maybe Maudie was mistaken. With all the confusion, how could she be sure it was Bryan?"

Her voice sounded fragile. Phyllis shifted to the bed and clasped Laura's hands. "She saw when the second blast hit, right where she'd just seen him. I'm sorry, Laura."

Blood pounded in Laura's ears. It took all the inner strength she possessed to keep from screaming. She stood and limped across the room to stare out the large picture window. A thousand lights gave Honolulu a celestial appearance. From where she stood, she felt as if she were precariously perched atop a world that was crumbling around her.

She clutched her hands to her breast and moaned, "Oh, God."

Phyllis loosed a heavy sigh. "Perhaps you're right. We should go back. We could book rooms at the Hahbah House in Boothbay. It's hours before morning. Let's try to get some rest."

"Yes, of course. There will be paperwork and legalities needing our attention." Laura curled her arms around herself. "Aunt Philly, I think I'm jinxed."

Phyllis appeared taken aback by the statement. "Why on earth would you say such a thing?"

"B-because it seems that everyone who loves me dies."

Phyllis shot a worried glance at her niece. "Stop it this minute. You are not jinxed. I know what you're thinking, but you didn't pull the trigger on the gun that killed your cameraman, and the gas pipes under Cole Hahbah are as ancient as the town itself. If anyone is to blame for the explosion, it's Mayor Shipley, who refused to listen to the town council. We've been telling him for years the pipes needed replacing." The timbre of her voice softened. "As for Bryan, he was in the wrong place at the wrong time. Don't place his death on your conscience. Hear me?"

"Yes," Laura whispered, and the tears flowed unheeded down her cheeks.

Chapter Two

El Paso, Texas

Long after the minister's words, the rifle salute, and the good wishes from lawmen, friends, and family, two lone figures remained at the gravesite. "It wasn't a blood clot that killed your mother. No, sir, it was the bullet that sonafabitch Navarre Àron put in her spine. Two years of sittin' in a wheelchair… She hated every day of not being able to ride a horse." Wyatt Carter turned to look at his son. "I promise you one thing for sure: if I ever get the bastard in my rifle sights, he's a dead man."

The ache in Mitch Carter's heart felt like barbwire ripping through his soul. He couldn't imagine what his father was feeling. Outrage, hatred, devastation? Those were a given. His father had often expressed his aggravation that Texas' most powerful drug lord had managed to remain elusive. It was what would come later that worried Mitch. How would his father cope with the eternal loss of the woman who'd been by his side every day for fifty years?

Frustration gnawed at Mitch. Four months had passed since he'd pinned on the sheriff's badge, and every lead he'd followed toward Àron led to another dead end. "We'll get him, Dad. One way or the other, we'll find a snitch willing to rat out the bastard." He placed a hand on his father's shoulder. "C'mon, the temperature is dropping. There's folks at the house waiting on us. Plus, we need to let the cemetery workers finish up here so they can go home."

Wyatt stared at the spray of Texas bluebells atop the coffin. "They were her favorite flowers." His voice hitched. "I hate leaving her here, Mitch. All alone."

In the fading light, it seemed to Mitch that the wrinkles on his father's weathered face hung heavier, and the broad shoulders slumped even lower. It was as if this once-vibrant man was aging before his eyes. He searched for words of comfort. "She's not in the casket, Dad. Mom is in your heart. She'll be with you…with me, every day for the rest of our lives."

Although the words gave Mitch little solace, he hoped they helped ease his father's grief. "I hear you, son, and I thank you. Mebbe you're right. I don't know. Right now, I find it hard to believe." The older man removed a handkerchief from his pocket and wiped his nose. "Every night since I carried her across the threshold some fifty years ago, when I turned out the light, your mother and I held hands. All that'll be there tonight will be an empty space."

Those last words poked a deeper hole in Mitch's heart. He steered Wyatt toward the black-and-white police SUV. Sitting behind the steering wheel, he buckled his seatbelt, then leaned forward and tuned the radio before starting the ignition. A melodic voice belted out "O Holy Night." Mitch switched the radio off.

His father's voice cracked when he said, "Helluva way to spend Christmas Day."

The tears he had successfully held at bay now

blurred Mitch's vision. *Damn Navarre Àron.*

The twenty-mile drive to the Double C Ranch seemed to stretch on forever.

****

Laura and Phyllis wended their way through Maine's Augusta airport lobby. "There, Aunt Philly." She pointed to a stout man wearing a red Santa Claus hat and holding a sign that read, "Friday."

"Hi, I'm Laura Friday. This is my aunt, Phyllis Friday."

"Fred Tiddle. You goin' to the Hahbah House in Boothbay?"

Laura glanced at her watch. "If you don't mind, we have a memorial service to attend. It was unexpected. Can you get us to St. John's Church in Bangor before one o'clock? I hope you don't mind."

Tiddle shrugged his shoulders. "Ayuh, I get paid either way. Lucky for us there's no snow on the roads. Ayuh, I can get yuh to the church on time."

He guffawed and slapped his beefy thigh. "Get it? Get you to the church…" Maybe it was the expressions on their faces that caused him to say, "Aw, never mind. It's twenty-two degrees out. You ladies wait here while I go get the cab and pull it curbside. I'll have it nice and toasty for yuh."

Once on the highway, Laura was certain all the energy had left her body. She leaned her head back against the seat. Phyllis reached over and clasped Laura's gloved hand. The rest of the trip was made in silence.

The cab pulled up in front of the church. Tiddle looked in the rearview mirror. "You ladies need a ride to Boothbay aftah the service?"

Laura heaved a sigh. “No, we’ll stay the night in Bangor.” She opened her purse for the fare. “I’ll call the company for a cab when we’re ready to leave.”

Tiddle said, “I got nothin’ but time. When you call, ’preciate it if you’d request me. My cab is numbah one zero seven.”

Laura offered a sad smile. “Yes, we’ll do that.”

“If you ladies tell me whey-ah you plan to stay, I’ll drop your luggage so yuh won’t have to mess with it durin’ the services, and whatever usually comes after.”

Phyllis reached into her purse, then extended her hand. “That’s very nice of you, Mr. Tiddle. A little something extra for your generosity. We’ve made reservations at the Bangor Inn East.”

He opened the door and held it wide. “I’d wish you ladies a Merry Christmas, but under the circumstances that don’t sound quite right.”

As soon as Laura and her aunt had stepped up on the curb, the cab pulled away.

Inside the church, an usher escorted Laura and Phyllis down the aisle. Laura exchanged a polite embrace with Daphne Cole before being seated.

The minister spoke of two devoted men, a son and a father. “On this Christmas Day let us not focus on the departure of our loved ones; rather, remember they are with you always.”

Laura wanted to disagree with the rhetoric. Memories didn’t fill the void in your heart, memories didn’t tell silly jokes, and memories certainly didn’t fill a room with laughter.

After the service, a church elder invited family and friends to convene in the social hall. What Laura really wanted was to change into a pair of warm pajamas, climb into bed, curl into a knot beneath the covers, and empty the tears she'd been holding back for hours.

She glanced around at the brightly lit room, the festive holiday decorations, the tall white Christmas tree decorated with cascading red ribbons, red glass balls, and a large angel perched on top, mingling guests with plates laden with food, sudden bursts of laughter, and Daphne Cole dressed in black. Tall and reed thin, she reminded Laura of a blackbird among a flock of cooing doves. She admired the woman's calm demeanor and wondered how, having lost a son and a husband on the same day, she could remain so stoic. Somehow, the entire scene seemed utterly contradictory.

Someone touched her on the arm. "Laura, I can't imagine how you feel. What with planning a spring wedding, you're a widow before becoming a bride."

Laura looked into Maudine Perry's teary eyes. She wanted to protest that she and Bryan had never set a date, and were, in fact, not officially engaged. She hadn't accepted the ring he'd purchased. "Thank you, Maudie. I'm certain after witnessing the…" Her throat hitched. "After seeing Bryan…" She couldn't bring herself to say it. *Witnessed his death.* "What about you? How are you coping?"

"I'm faring. Horrible thing to see. If you and Phyllis need anything, I'm staying with my sister right here in Bangor. Don't hesitate to ask." She patted Laura's arm, again. "There's Phyllis. Talk to you later, dear."

Laura felt as if her smile had permanently glued itself to her face. Fatigue from lack of sleep and the difference in time zones was beginning to take its toll.

Though she didn't feel close to Bryan's mother, she meandered through the crowd to speak to her.

Daphne Cole touched a crisp white handkerchief to the corner of her eye. Her slim jaw set, her deep brown eyes puffy from tears, she spoke to a couple of well-wishers. "Neither of my men wanted to be put in the ground. When the time is right, I'll follow their wishes and scatter their ashes."

Laura stepped forward. "You'll let me know when?"

A pause.

Daphne's eyes slanted. "No, Laura, I will not. You may have fooled Bryan into thinking you loved him, but never me. You toyed with my son's emotions. He adored you, worshiped you, but in the end, you would have crushed his feelings."

"Mrs. Cole, I-I assure you that—"

"Oh, stop it, Laura. There's no need to deny what we both know."

Pressing her lips tight, a hot flush seared through Laura. "I understand your grief, but you have no right to insult me. I had a deep affection for Bryan. I'm as devastated as you by his death."

Phyllis intervened. "Daphne Cole! You were an outsider when you married Furman. It didn't take long for the entire town to conclude that you married him for his wealth and his political connections, so how dare you attack my niece with your vile accusations."

Daphne Cole pressed the lacy handkerchief to her nose as she turned away in a huff.

Surprise evident in her voice, Laura smiled. "Thank you, Aunt Philly. I thought Mrs. Cole and I were friends."

“Humph. Maybe I could have found a more tactful way of telling her to kiss-off. At the moment, I didn’t have the energy to figure it out. I’ve called the cab company and requested Mr. Tiddle. I’m ready to leave. What about you?”

“You don’t have to ask twice. Lead the way.”

A chilling wind greeted them as they walked down the church steps toward the waiting cab.

For a long moment, Laura sat lost in thought. “Once Cole Harbor is cleared for reentry, do you plan to return and rebuild the bookstore, Aunt Philly?”

“I could ask you the same—do you plan to return and rebuild the newspaper office?”

Chapter Three

El Paso, Texas, six *months later*

She stood with her back to him. When had she come to Texas, and why hadn't she let him know? Stunning, absolutely stunning, Sheriff Mitch Carter couldn't help thinking as he stood in the shadowy doorway of the private hospital room staring at the woman talking softly to the patient in the bed. Small-boned yet with a lush figure that her pale blue silk blouse and slim charcoal slacks couldn't disguise, she still wore her ash-blonde hair short, though she had tamed the spiked look to a softer style.

He was here to do a job, not gawk at a beautiful woman. A woman from his past. But, at thirty-five, Mitch wasn't often stopped in his tracks by a female who could make the tempo of his heart ratchet up several beats.

His gaze shifted to the reason he was here, the woman lying in the hospital bed looking as pale as the starched white sheets.

Phyllis Friday had answered a knock on the hotel door, and the intruder pushed his way in and proceeded to attack her. The doctor had just told Mitch that Phyllis had a broken arm—the kind of fracture most likely to result from being severely twisted behind her back—two cracked ribs, several bruises, and a swollen cheek from a nasty punch to her face.

What could this mild-natured, elderly woman have done to warrant such a beating, Mitch wondered. According to notes taken by the first officer on the scene, the suite had been thoroughly ransacked. Had the thug been looking for valuables to steal? Or searching for something in particular?

Sensing his presence, Laura Friday straightened. Eyes the color of the blue waters in the cove at Cole Harbor, where he'd served less than a year as a deputy sheriff, met his assessing gaze.

Although the male in Mitch would like to question Laura alone, preferably in a quiet place, the lawman in him was more interested in the woman lying in the hospital bed. The officer's report indicated that, though hurting badly, Phyllis had mumbled that the man beating her had kept asking where the bitch was. However, no matter how hard he hit her, she wouldn't tell him anything. Why would the trespasser be interested in Laura, Mitch asked himself. Unless… He shook away the notion that Laura's background as an investigative reporter and her involvement in last year's New York drug bust had anything to do with this case. That was old news. The key players, Elio Casper and his boss, drug lord Mario Gombiani, were both dead.

He stepped inside the hospital room and watched the worry in Laura's eyes deepen. Deliberately he moved close to the bed and gave Phyllis a reassuring smile.

"You and Laura are the last people I expected to see in El Paso, Phyllis." His voice was gentle as he made note of the several purpling bruises on her neck. "Do you feel up to answering a couple of questions?"

"I'm sorry, Mitch. We should have contacted you earlier." Laura moved closer to her aunt's other side and hovered protectively. "She already told the deputy at the hotel everything she knows."

"But she did ask my deputy to contact me."

"Of course, and, just so you know, the attacker had his hands around her throat. It hurts when she talks."

Phyllis managed to speak in a croaking rasp, reaching toward her niece. "It's all right, Laura."

Phyllis Friday was a slender woman with sharp blue eyes and salt-and-pepper hair worn short and curly. Rimless glasses sat low on her nose. Despite her many bruises, she squared her shoulders against the mound of pillows and seemed unafraid, as if to say she was no one's victim. This time Mitch's smile was one of admiration.

"I don't want to cause you more discomfort," he told her. "Why don't you just shake or nod your head by way of answer?"

Phyllis nodded. Laura again protested.

"Is it necessary she do this *now*? Can't you wait until she's feeling better?" She narrowed her gaze toward Mitch.

"No, no," Phyllis rasped. "I want to help catch the pissah."

Phyllis Friday had been one of the first citizens in Cole Harbor to make Mitch feel welcomed. He had always admired her spunky spirit, and today his feelings toward her were no exception. "Did you recognize him?"

Phyllis shook her head. "Ski mask," she croaked out and gave a short cough. She grimaced at the pain in her throat but gamely continued. "Long black ponytail, black pants and shirt." Her cough increased and was more strenuous. "Tattoo…right hand, or maybe his left. I don't remembah."

"What kind of tattoo, Phyllis? I know your throat is hurting, but it's important."

She didn't quite get the entire word out when her voice gave out.

"Dragon? Is that what you tried to say?"

Phyllis gave him a weary smile, and a thumbs up.

"No more questions for Aunt Philly today. She needs to rest," Laura told Mitch.

He took the elderly woman's hand and patted it. "I happen to know you'll get the VIP treatment here. The chief of staff is my uncle." He winked as he looked at Laura. "Let me buy you a cup of coffee while you fill me in."

"Thanks, but I'd rather not leave her."

Both women looked pale and drawn, their eyes shadowed with fright. "Don't worry. She's in good care."

Laura glanced back at her aunt, who gave a nod of approval. "Try to get some rest. I won't be gone long."

****

Leaving the room with Mitch close behind her, unease filled Laura. She knew Mitch would do everything in his power to find the man who had committed this foul injustice against her aunt, and that persistent questions would be part of the process. She wouldn't allow Phyllis to be upset further, though. Despite her show of bravado, the older woman was more fragile than she seemed. Laura's memories of her own horrific ordeal of being kidnapped and nearly killed had flooded back, shaking her more than she realized, since she'd received the phone call at work about the attack on Phyllis. Her hands continued to tremble as she allowed Mitch to escort her to the elevator. Glad for the others who stepped inside the confined space, she glanced toward him, crossed her arms over her chest, and took a moment to study his profile. It was as if she were seeing him for the first time. He was tall, several inches above six feet, causing most people to crane their necks when looking at him. His height probably came in handy when he needed to intimidate suspects.

His face was tan, angular, square-jawed, his dark blue, somewhat hooded eyes appearing nearly black. His shoulders, under the olive green shirt open at the throat and his black lightweight sport coat, seemed wide as a football quarterback's. His hands were big, the palms callused. Clearly the hands of a man used to outdoor work. The clean, pressed jeans he wore hugged powerful thighs and long, long legs. He appeared relaxed, as if unaware she was taking inventory, with the usual high intensity of his gaze deflected at the moment. Right now he looked slightly amused as he waited for the elevator doors to open.

The walls of the hospital cafeteria were sunshine-yellow, and the tables and chairs alternated between peachy and sea green. Laura's spirits almost lifted when she walked into the light, bright, colorful room.

Neither of them spoke until after Mitch had seated her at a table and returned with a tray holding two large cups of steaming coffee and two slices of blueberry pie. "Not nearly as good as Miss Maudie's." He forked a piece into his mouth. "By the way, how is she?"

Laura laughed. It sounded a bit rusty, and filled

with shadows. She picked up her fork and toyed with the pie crust, and then gave him a brief sketch of the underground gas leak and the explosion that had destroyed half of Cole Harbor and displaced the majority of the township. "Aunt Philly and I rented a place in Bangor until the fire marshal and the insurance investigators were satisfied there was no duplicity involved and that the leak was a result of antiquated pipes."

His dark eyes drifted to her left hand. He ran his thumb across her finger. "No engagement ring? How is my ol' buddy Bryan?"

She withdrew her hand and placed it in her lap. He watched the myriad of emotions playing across her face. The furrowed frown, the way her chin quivered, eyes that suddenly teemed with tears. He wanted to fold her into his arms and kiss away whatever the pain she was suffering.

His voice was low and soft, compassionate. "I guess it didn't work out between the two of you. I'm sorry."

She blew out a deep sigh as she shifted her eyes to look at him. "Bryan and his father were killed in the explosion." Laura's voice was equally as soft but strained as she explained about being in Hawaii when they received the news. "His mother had the bodies cremated. The memorial service was on Christmas Day." She offered a contrite smile. "I'm sorry. With everything that's happened, I didn't think to call you."

He tried to absorb the shock of her words. Miraculously, he found the self-restraint to remain seated when what he really wanted to do was scoop her into his arms. He'd wanted this woman, wanted to make her his. It seemed the timing was never right—not in Cole Harbor, and certainly not now with the unexpected announcement of Bryan's death. Mitch regarded Laura in silence for a few moments. "Perfectly understandable. No need to apologize. Seems we both suffered a heartbreaking Christmas."

Mitch told her about his mother's death and her funeral. There was a grim tone in his voice when he spoke. "You're here, now. Were you not going to contact me?"

His cell phone rang just as she pursed her lips to answer his question. He looked at the caller ID, and swore under his breath as he pushed back his chair to stand. "Excuse me. I have to take this."

After a few minutes he returned to the table with an apologetic smile. "Sheriff's job never ends." Looking over the rim of his insulated paper cup, he said, "What brings you to El Paso?"

She leaned forward, her elbows propped on the table. "When Aunt Philly decided not to rebuild the bookstore, and said she had no interest in building a house in Cole Harbor, I called my former editor in New York to see if he had a position open. He did. Everything she and I owned was in our suitcases, which made moving easy. Max gave me the choice between online specialist or beat reporter. With my hip, I opted for the online specialist position. It's like being a behind-the-scenes investigative reporter." She loosed a small chuckle. "I get to dig up the dirt without having to face the enemy."

"And how does that fit with you coming to El Paso?"

Mitch didn't miss the faint tic under her left eye,

nor the split second she took to glance away. In the course of his years in law enforcement he had studied body language, a skill that helped him determine a person's unspoken thoughts. She was hiding something, and he'd bet his sheriff's badge it had everything to do with why she was in his neck of the woods.

She was about to answer when a voice filtered through the hospital's intercom system. "Paging Laura Friday. Please return to Room 414."

Laura stiffened. She used her hands to push away from the table. "Aunt Philly needs me."

Mitch stood and placed his hand in the small of her back. He drew in a deep breath and wished he hadn't as the lightly floral fragrance of her wrapped around him. He managed to keep his hands to himself, though not easily.

As they entered the elevator, Mitch said, "I'll need to go through the hotel room as soon as possible. I'd like you to be there to let me know if anything is missing."

Laura glanced at her wristwatch. "I want to stay with my aunt for a while longer. I can meet you at the hotel at four."

He nodded his understanding. "Do you have a car?"

"No. I'll call a cab."

"I'll drive you."

Laura's expression tightened. "Why?"

Mitch prayed for patience. In Cole Harbor, he'd learned Laura was a hard-nosed reporter with an often testy personality, but he figured his next statement might rock her tough inner core. "The first deputy to arrive on the scene wrote in his report that Phyllis told him the man in the ski mask kept asking, 'Where is the' "—he cleared his throat and choked out the word—" '*bitch.*' Could you be the woman the perpetrator was looking for?"

The blood drained from Laura's face as she reached to steady herself by gripping the safety bar in the elevator car. She straightened and licked her dry lips. "We've been in El Paso all of five days. I have no idea."

Mitch almost smiled. He knew he wouldn't win any points if he pushed too hard. "The report states you're staying at the Carlton. Acts of violence don't just happen in an upscale hotel."

"No more than they did in a quaint coastal community." Her words were clipped and angry. "Stop with the innuendo, Mitch. We're the victims here, not the criminal."

With that, she exited the elevator and walked quickly back to Phyllis's room, and he followed. When she entered, her aunt pointed to a vase of yellow begonias. She held up an envelope and rasped, "Read the card."

Laura exchanged curious glances with Mitch as she removed the small white card from its envelope. It contained one scrawled word—*Beware*. "Mitch, how did…I mean who…Oh, God. It's like déjà vu. Remember the white rose buds from Benjamin Noone?" She clasped Phyllis's hands. "We saw him die. This can't be happening. Not again."

Mitch stepped out of the room and down to the nurse's desk. "Can you tell me who delivered the flowers to Room 414?"

The nurse shrugged as she smiled at him. "I don't

know. They were on the counter when I returned from answering a call to one of the other patients. Is there a problem?"

"No."

He returned to the room. "Is there a florist's name on the card?"

Laura flipped the card over. "None."

"Whoever sent these was probably smart enough to wear gloves. Nonetheless, I'll take them back to the office for my fingerprint guy to dust."

****

After stopping at the precinct to make a few calls, Mitch climbed behind the steering wheel of his SUV. In a reflective mood, he drove toward the hotel to meet Laura.

For as long as he could remember, he'd wanted to follow in the footsteps of his uncles, Morgan and Virgil, both Texas Rangers. His father was one of five brothers. Sam was the chief of staff at the hospital, Patrick, Director of Homeland Security, and his father, Wyatt, a retired Hollywood stuntman, rodeo champion, and now one of the largest cattle ranchers in Texas.

Although he'd spent his early years and college summers working on the ranch, Mitch knew he wasn't cut out for that kind of work. At least not permanently.

He also knew his dangerous line of work had worried his mother. Fortunately she'd tucked her concerns aside, and his risky career was rarely mentioned. All he'd heard was her gentle nagging about when was he going to get married and add more grandchildren to the family, like his sister and brother had. The happiest day of his life was when his bride, Susie, had walked down the aisle, looking like an angel.

Married less than six weeks, her beautiful existence had been snuffed out like a candle. Two women he loved more than life itself, now dead because of his job.

Where had all this introspection come from? Laura Friday was a woman alone, living with an elderly aunt, and neither one had any family left. Mitch thought about the weekly dinners and holiday get-togethers at his parents' big cluttered ranch house, everyone seated at the long dining table, talking at once, with all the laughter and lots of good food. That was the thing he'd missed most while in Cole Harbor, the camaraderie, and maybe that's why he was taking the attack on Phyllis Friday personally. She'd given him unqualified acceptance.

Which brought him back to wondering just exactly what it was that brought about the assault. Mitch pulled into the hotel's front lot and parked next to a cruiser belonging to one of the deputies guarding the room.

Walking down the fifth-floor hall, his boots barely made a thud on the thick Persian carpeting. A man with white hair stood in the doorway of his room, a housemaid pushed a cart laden with linens and cleaning supplies down the hall, and openly curious onlookers eyed him. Crime scenes always interested people.

The yellow crime scene tape was still stretched across the open door. Mitch stepped over it. He wondered at Laura's earlier reaction to him. Had she calmed down, or did she still wear her armor of self-protection?

Mitch spoke to a young deputy seated in a straight-backed chair. "Evening, Wes. How's it going?"

The officer scrambled to his feet. "Pretty quiet, Mitch. A few nosy spectators gawking, is all."

"I'm expecting one of the occupants soon, Ms. Laura Friday. I'll wait for her inside."

"Yes, sir. The hotel manager said he'd send a repair man to install a new safety latch once we give the all-clear."

Mitch nodded. He checked out the shattered security bolt and wondered why no one had noticed a guy clad in all black messing with Laura's door, and why Phyllis hadn't looked through the peephole before opening the door. The woman was too gutsy for her own good.

Inside, he stopped, hands on hips, looking around. What a mess. Cushions yanked off the couch and tossed on the floor, sheets stripped from the bed, the mattresses shoved on the floor, feathers strewn across the room from the slashed pillows, the desk drawers methodically upended and emptied. The man had left no space untouched.

Then the fingerprint guys had come through dusting every surface with fine black powder. With her investigative background, a crime scene was old news for Laura, but it was different when you were the victim. He wondered how she would react.

Chapter Four

"Is the yellow tape necessary now?" Laura asked Mitch. "Hotel management would probably appreciate it if you took it down."

Mitch held the door wide. "Wes, you can remove the tape."

Laura looked around, her lips thinning. Otherwise, she gave no sign of how upset she was inside. "It looks pretty bad."

She wandered to the bedroom and then to the bathroom. Cosmetics and prescription bottles had been emptied onto the floor. Clothes had been pulled from the closets and strewn helter-skelter across the room. In the kitchenette, doors hung open, some plates and glasses smashed as if in an angry frenzy.

Since receiving the call regarding her aunt's attack, all she'd been able to think of was that her worst nightmare was beginning all over again. The question that ran through her mind was—who was after her and why?

Mitch seemed to be lost in reflection. Funny, she thought, how he managed to look even more masculine with one hand leaning against the kitchenette counter. One of the few men who could pull that off.

"Apparently he didn't find what he was looking for," Mitch mused aloud. He swung his gaze to Laura and saw her watching him. He looked her in the eye.

"Are there any important papers missing, an address book, any story you were working on?"

She was determined not to look away from those searing cerulean eyes. "I store all my rough drafts in a Cloud account, as well as my contacts, so no address book or physical papers."

"What about your laptop?"

She reached into her oversized purse, removed an iPad, and opened it to reveal the keyboard. "Much lighter, especially for anyone on the go."

Mitch glanced at his watch. "I'll gather your things in the bathroom while you pack the suitcases, and then we're out of here."

Laura's eyes widened. "Where to?"

"I'm driving you out to the ranch. You'll be safe with my dad and a dozen ranch hands working all over the property."

"Thanks, but no thanks. I'll ask the manager to move us to another room. I don't want to be a bother. Besides, I don't have a car. I'll need a way to get to the newspaper office until my current assignment is finished."

"As sheriff, I have a sworn duty to protect you and Phyllis. Because I'm your friend, humor me. I'll see to it you get to work."

Her frown deepened. "Maybe all this is a simple case of mistaken identity. Maybe the guy got the wrong room number."

"Where crime is concerned, anything is possible. Right now, I'm hungry, and being hungry makes me grumpy, so get your things together. We'll eat lunch, then head out to the Carter Cattle Company."

"What about Aunt Philly?" She moved a step

closer. “I researched the symbolism of the begonia. Mitch, it means exactly what was written on the card—*beware*. I won’t leave my aunt alone.”

Mitch scrubbed his face with one hand, his irritation apparent. “I don’t know what it is you’re not telling me, and it’s making me damned impatient.”

He removed his cell phone and punched in his uncle’s private number. Holding the phone to his ear, he mumbled something under his breath. “Sam, yeah…yeah, dinner as usual on Sunday. Listen, about the patient in Room 414, I’d appreciate it if you’d move her to where she’s visible from the nurse’s station. I’m also placing a deputy outside the door.” Mitch listened. “I’ll explain everything Sunday. Thanks, I’ll owe you one.”

A shiver wracked through Laura. She tried not to think that her own life was in jeopardy. Mitch looked at her with angry dark eyes. She sighed and tried to lighten his mood. “If being hungry makes you this grumpy, I’d hate to see what missing a couple of meals would do to you. Shall we go?”

El Paso in June was a huge contrast to Cole Harbor, Maine. Walking out of the hotel’s main lobby was like exiting a refrigerator and stepping into a furnace. While waiting for Mitch to open the SUV’s door, Laura was sure the skin was melting off her bones. “Is it always this hot?”

He chuckled. “Texas weather takes a little getting used to. Hotter’n Hades in the summer, mild winters, an occasional hurricane.” He helped Laura inside the vehicle. “How’s your hip?”

“Well, I won’t be running any marathons. Seriously, it’s about the same. Although it doesn’t seem to hurt as much in the warmer weather."

He slid behind the wheel and turned the ignition. Laura wanted to lean in to capture the cool air flowing from the dashboard vents. Instead, she smiled and said, "I suppose we're going to your favorite cop hangout for a beer and pretzels."

He arched an eyebrow. "Stop being a cynic. Rosario Gonzalez owns Rosie's Café and makes the best tacos in town."

Laura fastened her seatbelt and leaned back. She breathed deep and willed her body to relax. She felt a twinge of guilt as she cast a peripheral view toward Mitch. There were things she needed to tell him. Dangerous things. His soft Texas accent touched a chord of memory, and her melancholy increased.

Deep in thought, she missed his question until she heard Bryan's name. "I'm sorry, Mitch. I guess my mind is elsewhere. What did you ask about Bryan?"

He waved a dismissive hand. "Nothing important. Making conversation, mostly. Damn shame about Bryan. He was a good man."

"Mmm."

"Mind my asking if he proposed?"

Her throat tightened. "He did. He even bought a beautiful engagement ring, which I didn't accept. I tried taking your advice, Mitch. Remember? You said to set the rules and to go slow and easy. It didn't work. Bryan was persistent to the point that he became pushy. I was deeply fond of him, but I didn't love him. And now…" As her voice trailed off, she fiddled with her fingers.

Mitch finished the sentence for her. "And now that he's dead you feel guilty because you didn't love him."

"Yeah, something like that." She turned her head

away. Hearing the words and admitting to them caused an unaccustomed emotion to clog her throat. She told him about the accusation Bryan's mother had flung at her during the memorial service. "Perhaps it was Daphne's motherly intuition that knew I didn't love Bryan. What she didn't know is that was the very reason I couldn't bring myself to accept the ring. Even though I did say yes when he proposed, I couldn't bring myself to commit to setting a date for the wedding. I thought if enough time passed, I would grow to love him."

"Would you have eventually given in and married him?"

"Since his death, I've asked myself that same question. Truthfully, I don't think so. The horrible thing is his dying let me off the hook, and that only exacerbates my guilt."

Mitch wheeled into the parking lot of Rosie's Café. He shut off the ignition and turned to Laura. "Stop beating yourself up. None of us can control our destiny any more than we can cheat death. Getting on with your life is easier said than done, Laura. I know from experience. All we can do is put one foot in front of the other and try to put the tragic loss of our loved ones behind us."

He opened the door and walked around the front of the SUV to her side. She allowed herself a small smile as she looked into his ruggedly handsome face.

She wanted to recall those rare moments of sentiment they had shared back in Maine. Except for the poignant farewell he'd written to her on the day he'd left Cole Harbor, neither of them had ever allowed their emotions for each other to grow beyond friendship. She wanted to reach out and touch the deep cleft in his chin. Her mind was reeling with confused emotions.

Taking his hand, she allowed him to help her out of the vehicle and lead her inside the brightly decorated restaurant. It took a moment for her vision to adjust from the bright outside glare to the cool and dimly lit interior. Clearly Mexican décor—colorful serapes, sombreros, and a variety of musical instruments—adorned mustard yellow adobe walls. Red vinyl tablecloths covered the tables, and mariachi music played in the background.

A short, chubby-cheeked woman with black braids came from behind a high counter that separated the kitchen from the dining area. Her arms widespread, she greeted, "*Buenas tardes, mi amigo*. Who is this beautiful *chica*?"

"Hello, Rosie. Meet my friend Laura."

Rosario Gonzalez wrapped her flabby arms around Laura. "*Bienvenida*. Welcome. Any friend of Mitch's is my friend. Now come and sit yourself down. Are you off duty, Mitch? What about a pitcher of ice cold cerveza?"

"Sorry, Rosie, no beer, I'm working. Make it two colas, and two of your taco specials."

In Spanish, the short stout woman shouted the order to the cook as she made her way back to the kitchen.

Mitch spoke to several people seated at tables. Others called out, and he waved as he guided Laura to a booth in a rear corner of the room. It was out of the way, and where he could keep his eye on anyone entering or leaving.

"You seem pretty popular. Especially for a lawman."

"I've known most of these folks my entire life. At different times, a few of the men worked at the ranch."

He thanked the waiter who set a bowl of tostado chips and dip on the table. He helped himself. "Warning, the salsa will set your mouth on fire. I can ask Jose to bring a milder sauce."

She raised her eyebrows. "And let you think I'm a wussy? No way." She scooped an ample portion and popped it into her mouth. Almost immediately she gasped, grabbed the glass of cola, and chugged down a large gulp. Her eyes watered, and she coughed as she placed an ice chip in her mouth. "Holy crap. That's like eating liquid fire."

Mitch laughed. "I warned you. Don't worry. The tacos are only as spicy as the sauce you put on them. For you, I'd recommend the mild."

It felt good to relax. She was safe from an unknown enemy. For now.

Several couples entered the restaurant. Within a few minutes, the place was a hub of laughter and chattering voices, which made carrying on a conversation difficult. She leaned forward, and spoke over the noisy din. "Is it always this loud and this busy?"

Mitch plopped the last bite of taco in his mouth. "Pretty much."

Yelling wasn't good. She wanted to tell Mitch the reason she was in El Paso. She wanted to tell him about the research she'd uncovered. And she wanted to tell him about the headless bodies turning up in the most unusual places in New York. No, yelling in a crowded restaurant wasn't good. What if the wrong person overheard?

"What's bothering you, Laura? If it's your aunt's safety, I've got one of my best deputies posted outside her hospital room."

"I'm suddenly very tired." The statement wasn't entirely a lie. She looked at her empty plate. "The food was delicious. Thank you."

"C'mon, let's get you to the ranch."

After paying the bill and accepting a goodbye hug from Rosie, Mitch escorted Laura to the SUV.

She waited for him to open the door, then slid inside, locking the seatbelt in place. "Staying with your family feels…" She spread her hands wide as if searching for an appropriate way to finish her thoughts.

For a long moment they gazed into each other's eyes, until he spoke. "Feels like what, Laura?"

Why was it the mere sound of his baritone voice sent her emotions into a tailspin?

"I'm a stranger, and don't wish to impose. It feels…awkward."

He winked as he put the vehicle in gear. "I'd consider it a huge favor if you and your aunt would stay at the ranch for a while. I never realized how big the house was until my mom died. Now, it seems overly large and very empty. It's been six months, and it's like my dad has lost interest in life. He hasn't ridden his favorite horse in all this time, or looked at the ranch receipts or the books. Honestly, I think having a couple of women in the house will do him good."

Laura offered a cockeyed glance. "If you say so. At least I won't have to worry about leaving Aunt Philly alone." After a second of silence, she added, "You just wait until I get my hands on the bastard that hurt her."

"Yeah, what do you plan to do?"

She swore softly. "I'm going to wring his balls off and stuff them down his…"

Mitch almost choked on his laughter. "Whoa. Remember I'm the sheriff, and what you're proposing is a definite crime…against manhood. But, then again, I might be convinced to take a bribe and look the other way."

Laura cut him a smirk. She settled against the seat.

Shaking off the memories of her aunt's bruised and battered body, Laura scanned the terrain ahead. The endless sweep of June-brown range stretched to the horizons in every direction. Carter Cattle Company would be her home for the next few weeks, or until she finished her assignment and returned to New York.

She scanned the empty, rolling grassland on either side of the road. The highway seemed to stretch clear to eternity, a faded black ribbon bisecting the flat land until perspective narrowed it to invisibility. An unexpected sense of loneliness invaded her heart.

Mitch drove with one wrist cocked over the steering wheel and his other arm draped across the back of the seat, and she wondered what he was thinking. He turned right and drove under a large arched sign that announced Carter Cattle Company. "Almost there."

She gazed out at the long stretch of white fencing that lined both sides of the graveled drive. Distance gave the scene a surreal look. In one pasture, a dozen or more horses cropped grass. On the other side of the driveway, cattle milled. She didn't know one breed from the other. These were black with white faces.

Then, like a scene from an old western movie,

opening before her eyes was the view of a sprawling ranch house adorned with a wraparound porch, backed by a collection of barns and numerous corrals off in the distance. Reminding her of fly specks, black cattle dotted the shoulders of hills rising far beyond the buildings.

"I hadn't expected to see this type of wild beauty," she murmured, unfastening her seat belt as Mitch halted the vehicle. "It's beautiful."

Without intending to, she found herself slipping out of the truck to absorb the impact of the setting, and regretted not having her camera.

The magical spell was broken when a long-legged brunette walked from the barn. Dressed in form-fitting jeans, boots, and a red plaid shirt, with her hair pulled back in a ponytail, the woman might have been a model for a western magazine.

"Howdy, Mitch. You going to the dance Saturday night?"

Something deep and unexpected tugged at Laura's heart. Compared to this beauty, she felt like a dowdy frump.

"Afternoon, Angie. I'd like you to meet Laura Friday. She and her aunt are my guests for a while. Right now Phyllis is a patient at the hospital. She had a…ah…an accident."

The woman offered a wide grin. She stuck out her hand to shake Laura's. "Nice meeting you, Laura. Mitch doesn't usually invite guests to the ranch, especially women. Consider yourself privileged." She looked over Laura's shoulder to waggle eyebrows at Mitch.

Turning slightly, Laura didn't miss the frown

Mitch didn't bother to hide.

"Dr. Angela Culver is a veterinarian. She's filling in for her dad while he's at a convention in Florida." He offered a friendly smile. "What brings you to the ranch?"

"Your brother called to say you had a filly down. 'Fraid it's colic. I've tubed her, and one of the hands has her on the hot-walker. Soon as the laxative works, it'll relieve the gas pains. I'll be back to check on her in the morning." She ran her fingers up the buttons on Mitch's shirt, her voice sultry. "That is unless you need me tonight."

Laura didn't know if the gruffness in Mitch's voice was flirting or irritation when he said, "Mind your manners, Angie."

Before leaving, Angie reached for Mitch's hand and laced her fingers with his. "Now, about Saturday's dance?"

Laura thought she saw Mitch's shoulders tense as he untangled from the woman's grip and hooked his thumbs into the front pockets of his jeans. "I never make promises I can't keep."

Angie opened the door to her white dually pickup. She stepped on the high running board and called over the top of the truck, "Just so you know, Laura, I have first dibs on our hunky sheriff."

Laura simply nodded an acknowledgement, and was surprised at the strange zing in her heart. Jealousy? Never! She and Mitch were just friends and nothing more.

Chapter Five

"Don't let Angie rattle you. She was born with a silver spoon in her mouth and, as an only child, spoiled rotten. Even though she's crass, she is a damned good veterinarian, and she doesn't take any guff off any of the hard-nosed ranchers she has to deal with."

Laura cocked her head to one side, and gave Mitch a questioning smile. "Does she have first dibs on you?"

She could feel him watching her, intent and somber. His voice was low and soft, but a tone of indictment ran like steel through his every word. "Angie's good for a lot of things. None of them include putting a brand on me."

As if needing to shift the subject away from his personal life, Mitch placed his hand in the small of Laura's back. "Though it's been renovated and modified over the years, five generations of Carters have been born in this house. My great-grandfather came west with little more than the clothes on his back and an oxcart filled with tenacity. C'mon, let's get you settled. I'll ask one of the hands to bring in your luggage."

"Do you live here?"

"When I'm not sleeping in one of my jail cells." He harrumphed. "Now that my mother is gone, it only seems right that I'm here to help look after my dad. Garret, that's my brother, has taken over as ranch manager. My sister, Jill, is our chief financial officer, and her husband is the foreman. They all have homes on the property. Having them close by is a comfort, especially when duty keeps me away for several days."

"Thanks," she said as she walked through the open doorway and entered the roomy cathedral-ceilinged great room. A massive chandelier made of entwined deer antlers hung from a high beam. The interior reminded her of an oversized log cabin with a floor-to-ceiling stone fireplace situated in one corner and, to the rear of the room, a wall of windows that looked out on an outdoor living space complete with an Olympic-size swimming pool.

She paused and looked up at him. She was trying not to let him see the effect his nearness had on her.

"For what?"

"For inviting Aunt Philly and me to stay here," she said.

"You're welcome." He hesitated. "The bedrooms are all upstairs, though I don't think the steps are as steep as the ones in your aunt's apartment above the bookstore."

As if his words acted as a reminder, she rubbed the ever-present ache in her hip. "I don't mind."

Tall, slender, and favoring her brother, Jill Carter Conroy came bounding down the stairs just then. Running past her were two rambunctious little boys who yelled in unison, "Uncle Mitch, can we turn on the siren in your car?"

"'Fraid not, boys. Why don't you run out to the barn and check on the sick filly? Make sure she's not laying down." He grabbed both of them by the arms. "But first, mind your manners and say hello to Ms.

Friday. She's a reporter from New York. She and her aunt will be our guests for a few days. You can show her around when I'm not here."

The youngsters offered Laura freckle-faced grins and continued to look around the room. "Howdy, ma'am. We don't see no 'nother lady."

Laura bent down to the boys' level. "That's because she had an accident and is in the hospital. What're your names?"

One pointed to the other, and said, "He's Kit, and I'm Carson. We're 'dentical twins."

Jill scolded, her voice stern, "Boys—what have I told you about pulling that prank? Apologize to Ms. Friday."

The boys offered contrite smiles. "Sorry." The one in the green plaid shirt said, "I'm Kit, and he's Carson. We were named after the famous lawman, Kit Carson." He looked at his mother. "Can we go now?"

Jill made a shooing motion with her hands, and they ran out as she said to Laura, "They're only five, and already a handful."

A frown furrowed Laura's brow. "Clue me in. How do I tell them apart?"

Jill sighed as she tucked a wayward strand of honey-brown hair behind her ear. "There are days when I'm not sure, and I'm their mother. Anyhow, Kit has a cowlick, and Carson doesn't."

Mitch laughed. "Don't worry, Jill. With all the uncles and a grandpa to help guide the boys, they'll grow into fine men."

Before his sister could offer a rebuttal, Mitch's cell phone rang. "'Scuse me." And he walked out to the porch.

The door slammed behind him when he re-entered the room. "Laura, you up to riding with me? That was my deputy. We've got a body."

It seemed like yesterday that she'd heard him say those same words in Cole Harbor. Instead, it had been nearly a year. "Count me in."

He looked at his sister, "Jill—"

"I know, don't wait supper. I'll fix both of you plates and put them in the warmer."

Outside, he opened the SUV's door, and in his need to get on the road quickly, he placed his hands around Laura's waist and lifted her into the vehicle. She reached over the seat and grabbed her camera case.

Mitch started the engine. Throwing the automobile into gear, he headed toward the long drive that led to the highway. A rooster tail of gravel spewed up behind the vehicle as it lunged forward.

Back on the highway, he headed northwest. She watched him concentrate on his driving as the siren blared.

A half hour later he pulled onto a wide gravel road leading through an open gate with an overhead sign announcing the Twisted Oak Ranch. The SUV vibrated when it rolled over the metal bars of a cattle gap, and dust boiled up behind them as Mitch raced down the road.

His manner was matter-of-fact. "You'll need to brace yourself for a grisly sight. My deputy said the body looks as if it was mauled by a bear."

Laura shuddered. "Does such a thing happen often in the wilds of Texas?"

"Last attack was about four years ago. Normally, I'd chalk it up to a hiker or ranch hand being in the wrong place at the wrong time. Not this time."

"What makes this one different?"

Though she couldn't see his eyes behind the sunglasses, she sensed his expression matched the grim tone of his voice. She didn't miss the jerk in his jaw muscle. "This body is missing its head."

She tipped toward him in curiosity. "The only bears I'm familiar with live behind bars in zoos. Do bears normally eat people's heads?"

"There's always a first time."

After a short period of silence, a chill that had nothing to do with the air conditioner slithered down Laura's spine and lodged in her midsection. For a split second she sucked in air to keep from disgorging the bile in her throat. "Mitch, I just had an insanely horrible thought. I pray I'm wrong."

The annoyance in his voice added to her chill. "By the expression on your face, does this horrible thought have anything to do with you coming to El Paso?"

She'd be damned if she apologized for doing her job and for not contacting him to say she was in town. She spoke through clamped jaws. "In recent weeks, headless bodies have turned up in Central Park, down by the pier at Coney Island, and at three other tourist attractions. The police think it's a new gang trying to make a statement."

He glanced at her. "What do you think?"

"Personally, I'm convinced it is gang related, but not as in hoodlums infringing on each other's turf. While doing research, I stumbled across information about a drug cartel whose signature is beheading their victims."

"Don't tell me. This gang is from Mexico, and with

El Paso being a border town, it makes perfect sense. You know the name of this bunch of goons?"

"*Los Cuchillos*."

"Damn. In English *cuchillo* means knife. What do you know about them?"

"My research indicates they're from South America. In a sense, I guess it is a turf war because Los Cuchillos want to take over the Mexican territories, which also includes Texas, New York, and California."

"Is that why you came to El Paso?" He added curtly, "To do research, and maybe get yourself killed for poking your reporter nose where it doesn't belong? Seems you've been down this road before."

She resented the innuendo. Guilt over her camera man's death still nagged at her. Laura shifted uncomfortably. The stress of riding in the confinement of a seatbelt was causing her hip to hurt. Her voice quiet and succinct, she said, "For your information, apparently the *El Paso Gazette* has, for several years, experienced financial difficulties and seen a drastic decline in readership. The stockholders sold the paper to Sentential Corporate. *EP Gazette*'s editor-in-chief took an early retirement to keep from getting fired. There was talk of embezzlement and possible criminal charges. I asked Max if I could come here, take a look around, and if interested, maybe apply for the position. I didn't contact you because if it didn't work out, then I'd planned to quietly return to New York."

What she didn't say was that she was afraid of igniting feelings she'd kept buried all these months. Why build false hope for either of them if the position didn't pan out? She was still trying to come to terms with the absolute fact that she had resisted setting a wedding date with Bryan because she secretly loved Mitch. This sudden surreptitious self-revelation was like a shock wave rippling over her. By his own admission no woman would put a brand on him.

"Leave…just like that…without a hello or goodbye or kiss my foot? I thought we were friends, Laura."

Before she could refute his words, she braced her feet against the floorboard and screamed, "Look out!"

Mitch slammed on the brakes and fought to control the vehicle, all to keep from plowing into a black-and-white-pied longhorn standing in the middle of the dirt road. Wrestling the steering wheel into compliance, Mitch brought the van to a halt.

He laid on the horn. "You okay, Laura?"

"Yeah, I think so. With all this open land, why is a cow in the middle of the road?"

"Bull. Not cow." He laid on the horn again.

"Cow, bull. What's the difference?"

Mitch looked upward as if pleading for patience. "Never mind. I'll explain later."

The animal turned to face the SUV.

Mitch rolled down the window and leaned out. "Hehya….hehya…get on outta here." He banged the side of the door.

Suddenly irate, the animal snorted and pawed the ground, sending a cloud of dust over its shoulder, and then, letting out a loud bellow, lowered its head.

"Oh, shit. The damn beast is going to ram us." Mitch yanked the gear into reverse. "Hold on."

As Mitch sped backwards, the animal charged, missing the front of the SUV's grill by inches. Thrown off balance, the bull went down on its knees; recovering swiftly, it came up and lowered its head again.

"Holy crap, Mitch! What's the matter with it? Does it have rabies, or mad cow disease?"

Concentrating on the lean-muscled animal's stance, Mitch inched the vehicle backwards. "There's probably no meaner critter in Texas than a longhorn bull. The slightest provocation will turn him into an aggressive and deadly enemy. He's letting us know we're intruding on his territory and he's not one bit happy about it."

"And I thought living in New York was dangerous."

Slinging its head from side to side, the bull blew noisily through its nostrils.

Laura didn't know why she was whispering when she asked, "Why is he doing that?"

Mitch revved the engine and inched forward. "He's offering a challenge. Sort of like playing a game of chicken."

"I think my blood pressure is about to skyrocket through the roof."

Mitch laughed. "Don't worry, as long as he's out there we're safe." Mitch shifted into reverse, and goosed the van backwards putting a couple more feet between him and the animal. "Brace yourself, Laura. I don't have time for games. It's gonna get bumpy."

Spinning backwards, the tires roiled clouds of dust. With enough distance between him and the animal, Mitch plunged the gear into drive. The vehicle leaped forward as he floored the gas pedal.

The bull accepted the challenge. Mitch jerked the steering wheel to the left and sped past the animal. A sharp thud sounded as if a boulder had exploded against the passenger's door, followed by an ear-splitting nailson-chalkboard screech. For a moment, Laura was certain the SUV had lifted and would topple on its side.

Again Mitch wrestled the steering wheel as he left the dirt road to plow through windshield-high weed-covered ruts. Laura gripped the armrest. She held her breath and dared to open her eyes, not realizing she had squeezed them shut. "H-he's not following, is he?"

Settling the van back onto the road and maintaining a safe speed, Mitch looked into the rearview mirror. "You can relax now. He's standing in the middle of the road and probably wondering what the hell just happened."

"Sheriff Carter, this is Luis. What's your twenty? Everything okay?"

Mitch reached forward to lift the microphone from the radio. "Heading your way. Ten minutes max. Had to play a game of chicken with a territorial bull."

The deputy laughed. "See you in ten."

Chapter Six

Laura set the filter on her camera. “Okay if I roll the window down, Mitch?”

Without making her wait, he accommodated the simple request. The camera clicked away as Laura shot scene after scene of foliage. Mitch pointed to a clump of scraggly trees. “Those are mesquite trees. Some of the ole-timers call them devil trees because the roots absorb all the water, so the surrounding plants and trees wither and die, which allows more mesquite trees to move in and take over. Plus they have wicked thorns capable of putting out an eye or causing some other serious wound.”

She looked out at the desolate rolling hills of the Twisted Oak Ranch and wondered why anyone would want to live here. A few minutes later horses, men, and vehicles lined her vision. Again, she lifted her camera.

The SUV rolled to a stop, and without waiting for Mitch to assist her, she opened the door and slid to the ground. The deep groove that ran from the front door all the way to the back fender was evidence of the pied bull’s attack on the vehicle.

In one fluid motion, Mitch stepped down, came around beside her, and put his hand to the small of her back to ease her toward the group.

He greeted one of the men. “Howdy, Buck. Bear attack?”

A lanky silver-haired man gave Laura a curious glance, then spat on the ground. He nodded his acknowledgment toward Mitch, then removed a pouch from his back pocket and stuffed his mouth with chewing tobacco. “Can’t rightly say. Seen some gruesome sights in my day. Never nothing like this.”

A burly Hispanic man hustled toward them. “Glad you’re here, Mitch. Doc Baker is ready to bag the body.”

Mitch made the introductions. “Laura Friday, meet my deputy, Luis Espinoza, and this is our neighbor, Buck Sorrenson.”

The deputy tipped the brim of his hat. “Ma’am.” He cut a peripheral glance toward Mitch. The tension in the deputy was evident by his stance. “It’s bad…real bad, and all my stomach can take looking at the remains.”

The rock-solid deputy drew in a breath, visibly trying to get himself together.

Buck Sorrenson agreed. “Near lost my breakfast. Couple of my riders did.”

“You find the body, Buck?”

“Nope. Those two trespassers found it.” He pointed at the young couple standing off by themselves. In spite of the heat, the woman hugged herself and leaned against the man as if for support. Buck spat again, then dragged his sleeve across his mouth. “Said they were hikers and thought they were on federal park land. Reckon they can’t read the No Trespassing signs posted all up and down my fence lines.”

Mitch heaved sigh. “Let’s get this over with. Friday, you might want to sit this one out. Albert Baker is El Paso County’s coroner and takes all of his own photographs. He's 'bout as thorough as they come."

Even with no breeze the decaying odor of death permeated the air. Without announcing the possibility that she was the next editor-in-chief of the *El Paso Sentinel*, she hoped Mitch understood her hint when she said, "I might as well consider this initiation day. Do you mind if I take a few shots of the deceased?"

Her throat constricted as she swallowed, then placed her hand over her mouth to contain the retch. He laid a hand on her shoulder. "Okay by me, and consider yourself forewarned."

For no known reason, Laura was certain the pain in her hip had escalated. Not wanting to appear weak, she tried to lessen her limp as she walked forward.

Mitch spoke to the doctor. "Al, Ms. Friday is a reporter from New York. I've given her the go-ahead to photograph the body."

The country coroner nodded. "You're the boss."

"Without a formal autopsy, what can you tell me?"

Adjusting the sunglasses on the bridge of his nose, Albert Baker simply shrugged. "Male. Head detached and missing. Age unknown at this time. Due to advanced stages of decomposition, I'd put the death about a week ago. I can be more accurate once I study the insects inside the intestines."

After one glance at the dirt-covered, ravaged body, its sinew and bones exposed, Laura once again placed her hand over her mouth and nose. "Excuse me." She walked away without seeing the smirk on the doctor's face.

Mitch heard her gagging, and wanted to wrap her in his arms, but this wasn't the time nor the place. He swallowed the bile that rose in his throat and accepted the handkerchief his deputy handed him. He tied it around his face against the overpowering stench.

Misery filled Luis's voice. "We haven't touched anything, Mitch."

Mitch looked down at the devastated remains of a man who'd probably been alive and laughing not so long ago. He squatted on his haunches and forced himself to study the body, what was left of it.

Luis was right. The man had been torn apart, his chest ripped by teeth and claws, his entrails ripped out, his clothing shredded.

"Something's not right here." Mitch stood. His voice was muffled from beneath the bandana. He twisted around to look at the others. "Here's a puzzler for you. If a bear ripped this guy apart, why would it do that without devouring him? Except for the severed head, there are no major body parts missing."

Mitch looked at the man's feet, and nearly dry heaved. "Look at his feet." The victim's feet and legs were nearly mangled beyond recognition. The ankles were almost gnawed through. Mitch continued to breathe lightly into the handkerchief. "Why would a bear do that?"

Luis said, "We found pieces of his boots. It appears they were ripped off the vic's feet and chewed to bits. Maybe we're dealing with a case of rabies."

Mitch pulled on polyurethane gloves before he leaned forward and gently removed the threads of rope embedded in the man's wrist.

"What's that?" Luis asked, staring down at the frayed cord blackened with dried blood.

Mitch showed him. "Doesn't make sense."

"What, Mitch?"

"Our victim's wrists were tied. Why anyone would want to do this to another human being. I mean, what's the point?"

Luis shrugged. "Someone without a soul…a monster."

Mitch stood up. "Al, can you give me an educated guess as to whether a bear killed this guy?"

Albert Baker had been a coroner for twenty-seven years. He forced out the words. "I'll need to test for saliva to rule out bear attack. Looks like every critter around has feasted at one time or another. But, if it's an educated guess you're after, I'd say decapitation is cause of death. Won't know until I get the cadaver cleaned and on a slab. You want me to call in the medical examiner?"

"By the book, Al. Go ahead and bag it."

There was a hint of sarcasm in the coroner's voice. "Right. I'll notify the ME."

Mitch chose to ignore the disdain. "Luis, did you do a sweep of the area?"

"Sure did. No sign of the head. Did find this." He pulled a plastic bag from his pocket that contained a cigarette butt. As the deputy stood talking with Mitch, Laura scoured the ground for anything out of the ordinary.

Mitch called out a warning, "Friday, if you hear buzzing, like a whirring rattle, stand perfectly still. Never can tell if a rattlesnake is coiled under a rock or a bush, and stay away from the mesquite trees."

She waved her acknowledgment. About twenty-five yards out, she turned and zoomed in to snap several shots of Mitch, the two hikers, the entire crime scene. When she took a step backwards, a rock rolled under her heel, and she stumbled. Looking down as she caught her balance, she spotted it. A partial heel print with a crisscrossed pattern. She zoomed in and out to shoot different angles of the print. "Mitch, over here."

He sprinted to where she stood. She pointed. "Look."

His grin was all the approval she needed. "Most all our locals wear western boots. This looks like the heel from a working brogan or hiker's shoes. Could be from one of them."

He called out to instruct the deputy to take measurements of the print. She followed as Mitch walked over to the waiting couple. After a few minutes' interrogation, he checked their boots and ruled out the heel print being a match on either one of them. His questions elicited the information that the pair was from the UK and hiking their way across the United States. Mitch told them, "My deputy will drive you to town."

"Are we under arrest, Sheriff? I mean, we did notify 911 as soon as we spotted the…the…you know."

Buck Sorrenson had mounted up, and now he rode over. Mitch looked from the couple to the old rancher. "Unless Mr. Sorrenson wants to press charges for trespassing, the only thing I need from you and the young lady is a signed and sworn statement about finding the body." To the rancher, he said, "Up to you, Buck."

"Oh, hell." He fairly snarled at the couple. "Underneath 'Private Property—Keep Out' the sign plainly says, 'Trespassers will be prosecuted.' Seeing as how you're foreigners and things might be different in your country, and seeing as how I got cattle to look after and don't have time to fill out a bunch of gall-dang papers, consider this your lucky day. Get 'em outta here, Mitch."

Laura watched Mitch pull the hat further down on his forehead and wondered if he was hiding a smile. He said, "Luis, I'll come to the office as soon as I drop Ms. Friday by the ranch." He nodded toward the couple. "See to their comfort. You know the drill. Don't turn 'em loose until I get there."

"Understood, Sheriff."

Mitch opened the SUV's door for Laura and assisted her up onto the high running board. An odd sensation fluttered again in her stomach at his touch. A sudden lack of energy left her limp. A reaction from the heat, no doubt.

He studied her for a long moment, as if debating whether or not she would pass out from either the temperature or the shock of seeing a gruesomely mangled body, or both.

Mesmerized, she caught herself staring at him and jerked her gaze away. She drew in a deep steadying breath. With a sigh of frustration, she shook her head. "This heat makes me long for Cole Harbor's cool ocean breezes."

He cocked his hat back far enough that a shock of blond hair swung down over his forehead, but there was nothing boyish about this man. Well-muscled arms glistened with perspiration; his broad shoulders blocked the view out her door. "Yep, that was one thing I liked about the place."

She buckled her seatbelt and waited for him to slide behind the steering wheel. She was ready to soak up relief from the air conditioner. "Instead of the ranch, I'd rather go by the hospital to check on Aunt Philly."

The vehicle bumped down the road behind the ambulance. After five minutes of silence, Mitch cleared his throat. "I'm taking you to the ranch, Friday. No arguments. I have a heinous murder to investigate. It's late. You need to rest, and your aunt is probably asleep. I'll check on her myself and let you know."

"I—"

Mitch held up his hand. "With this morning's attack on Phyllis, moving out of the hotel, being rammed by a loco bull, and experiencing a murder scene, you've had a busy day. Until you decide whether you're staying in El Paso or returning to New York, let's keep it friendly but professional. No arguments. I'm taking you to the ranch."

She stared at him curiously. "Professional? Sure. Absolutely."

He concentrated on navigating the ruts. That same muscle ticked along the side of his jaw.

Laura stared at him in disbelief. Another mile or so of dust and brown landscape passed before she spoke. "So what do you do out here in your free time?"

"Work. Running a ranch is a year-round, day-to-day-job operation. When I'm not chasing bad guys, I'm doing whatever it takes to help out my family."

The SUV vibrated across the cattle gate. Laura looked around. There was no sign of the cantankerous black-and-white-pied bull. "Okay, so tell me the difference between a bull and a steer."

Mitch cleared his throat and tried to look serious. "A bull has a full set of dingle berries, and enjoys courting the heifers. A steer, on the other hand, has been castrated, and the only thing he's interested in is standing under a shade tree."

Laura cast an incredulous glance. “What are dingle berries?” Then as if the definition had smacked her between the eyes, she said, “Ooh, gotcha. No further explanation is needed.” And then she laughed.

The sun was a fiery orange ball sinking behind the horizon, and Laura felt a twinge of homesickness. Not for New York but for Cole Harbor. She longed to trade the flat land, the miles of nothing, and the heat for some cool breezes off Cole Harbor’s bay and some green grass. Even the monotonous clanging of the channel buoy would be better than this. She leaned her head against the seat and closed her eyes.

Mitch interrupted her musing. “I suppose you’ve already written the headlines for the morning paper?”

She smiled. “You know me too well. Any details I should omit?”

“Same old drill. Just stick with the facts, ma’am.”

“Okay if I post pictures?”

“Of the body, sure. The heel print—let’s keep that under wraps. At least until we rule it out as evidence.” After a few moments of silence, he said, “Tell me about the headless bodies in New York.”

While he drove, Laura filled him in, sparing no details. “None of the remains were as decomposed as this one, or ravaged by wild animals. Maybe there is no connection.”

“Were the heads ever recovered?”

“Not to my knowledge. However, all of the victims were male, estimated twenty-five to fifty years of age. And, Mitch, every single victim had the first joint of the middle finger in his pocket. I’m sorry, I should have remembered that fact sooner.”

“What kind of hellish sick-os are we dealing with?

Don't worry about it, Friday." He reached for the microphone and called in the code. "Luis, yeah, Mitch. Listen, hot-foot it over to Al's office and tell him to check the victim's pockets."

"Ten-four, but what am I looking for?"

"The first joint of a middle finger."

"Damn, Sheriff. Are you serious? I mean, yes, sir, okay. You comin' in tonight?"

"In about an hour."

The rest of the ride was in silence.

Mitch looked very somber when he escorted Laura inside and to the kitchen. True to her word, his sister had left dinner in the warming oven.

"Mitch, how will I get to the office in the morning?"

"You won't. You're safer here. Besides, that's what emails and cell phones are for. And before you say anything—I'll check on your aunt."

"Yes, but—"

She'd never seen such commanding force in his expression. The tone of his voice matched the steel in his blue eyes. "Friday, if you were halfway across the world, how would you send in a news story?"

For a split second she wanted to spit in his eye. Impetuousness had sent her down this road once before, and it had cost the life of a dear friend and left her with a permanent limp. "I hate it when you're right."

He smoothed a thumb down the side of her cheek and then he was gone, taking his plate of food with him. He settled on a tall stool at the breakfast table.

Instead of Laura, he'd reverted back to calling her "Friday," just like in Cole Harbor. A flood of disappointment filled her. She sat at the table and surprised herself when she devoured the mashed potatoes, gravy, and cubed steak. There was even sour cream pound cake for dessert.

The house was eerily quiet, and feeling like an intruder, she wondered if she would be totally alone in the dwelling or if the elusive elder Carter had retired for the evening.

The note on the table had said hers was the guest room upstairs at the end of the hall. After he'd washed both their dishes, Mitch escorted her upstairs. Inside the spacious area were two twin beds, with an attached bathroom. She was happy her aunt would share the room with her. At least she wouldn't feel alone.

"Rest well, Friday." And then he was gone.

Later, showered and dressed in her favorite oversized T-shirt, and settled in bed, she thought about the day's events. She understood what Mitch had said about keeping their relationship professional. They were both strong, determined people. Both were bruised from the loss of loved ones. Yet she could already feel a shimmer of undeniable attraction rekindling between them.

She reached for her laptop and created two different files: ranch photos and one titled *Los Cuchillos* (Knives). After uploading the photographs to the respective files, she forced herself to look at the pictures of the body, and then of the footprint she'd discovered. Was today's discovery connected to the bodies found in New York? Either way, she grimaced and shuddered.

She researched bear attacks on humans, and then recent bear attacks in El Paso, and did bears eat or drag off the heads of their victims. Finding nothing conclusive, she researched drug trafficking along the border. Using a special password, she accessed the newspaper's morgue files, looking for any articles that might link to the current death.

Her eyes glazed from all the scrolling, until a headline seemed to flash like a flickering neon sign: Deputy Sheriff's Wife Murdered. Tears blurred Laura's vision as she read the detailed account of the shooting that killed Mitch's wife and left his mother crippled. A revenge shooting was what the reporter had dubbed the crime. Although never proven, Navarre Àron had disappeared after openly admitting to ordering the hit.

Laura used the corner of the sheet to wipe the tears from her eyes. "Oh, Mitch, how perfectly awful for you and your family." She recalled the day in Cole Harbor when he'd given her a brief sketch about his wife's death. Hearing about it wasn't the same as reading the details in print.

Taking time to collect her thoughts, she wrote an article about the headless body and spared few details about the victim while omitting information key to the case. She uploaded the report and emailed it to the night editor. Within minutes her email alert sounded.

The message read: "Good stuff. Front page news!"

A long soak in a jetted tub helped soothe away the tension in her body. She telephoned her aunt to learn that Mitch had visited.

"The doctor is releasing me tomorrow, and Mitch will drive me to the ranch."

"That's great news, Aunt Philly."

Unable to sleep, Laura used the moon's light to guide her across the bedroom to the double French doors. Easing them open, she stepped onto the balcony.

Hot air greeted her. Looking down, the pool seemed to invite her to relax in its shimmering waters.

As she turned to reenter the room, a distant flash drew her attention. She leaned against the balcony railing and watched. Another flash, like a quick wink. For what seemed an eternity, she watched for an answering spark. Nothing.

She shut the doors, and even though the bedroom was on the second floor, she clicked the lock in place. Easing back the sheer curtain, Laura once again peered toward the horizon, and wondered who was out there?

****

In another life, he was Fernando Ramirez de Ayala. Not anymore. He stood outside in the darkened corner of the barn, silently watching the house. A gust of sultry wind blew against his back as if trying to force him to move from the shadows. He needed to get some sack time. Work on a ranch began before first light, but the woman inside the upstairs bedroom kept him rooted in place.

She moved now and then past the windows, sometimes looking out as though searching for something. Her slender form drew him now just as her blue eyes had drawn him the first time he'd seen her inside the courtroom, and then each night on television as she reported news of his brother's trial.

The sneer quivered his top lip. He shoved his hands deeper into the pockets of his jeans. Yeah, she might call herself Laura Friday. He knew better. The bitch was none other than Laura Schofield, miss high-and-mighty New York investigative reporter, and she had no idea of the danger she was in. He knew she wouldn't remember him from their five-minute encounter eight years ago. She'd taken away his only sibling. It was the luck of the stars that brought them together in this place. He raised the gold crucifix that hung around his neck and kissed it.

There was just one problem. He liked the Carters. A down-on-his-luck hungry kid, he'd tried to rob a gas station. Instead of throwing him in jail, Mitch had brought him to the ranch to work off the debt and then hired him. Now, after three years in their employ, he was trusted by the Carters. But the memory of what Laura had done to his baby brother was permanently branded in his brain. As much as he liked the sheriff, he hoped Mitch wouldn't try to play the hero when it came time to seek revenge on Ms. Laura Schofield.

In the shadow's heat, he watched her step out on the balcony. He studied her, knowing he needed to get on to the bunkhouse before one of the ranch hands spotted him and started asking questions. Sweat trickled between his shoulder blades, and the heat fueled his need for revenge. He had memorized the words she'd spoken into the camera the day his brother had been sentenced to life in prison.

"Another lowlife off the mean streets of New York. Although Romeo Ramirez de Ayala deserves the electric chair, he will spend the rest of his life incarcerated on Riker's Island, placing yet another tax burden on our law-abiding citizens."

She had called Romeo a sociopath, an incorrigible baby-faced killer. He didn't know what those words meant, just that they were lies, all lies. And his brother had died because of her lies.

He forgot about the heat as he thought of what he would do to her. For years he'd planned every detail of how he would punish her for the death of his *hermano*. He frowned, remembering. Even now, he flexed his hands to release the tension in his fists as he thought of all the painful ways he planned to make her suffer.

She stepped back as if to return to the room, and then stopped. He wondered what had caught her attention, and then he saw it, too. The flash of light, and then another quick spark.

He forced his mind to clear. Carter and Sorrenson land ran along the border. Maybe that burst of light was a signal. Maybe there was new activity along the border, and maybe if he played his cards right, Miss Laura Schofield-alias-Friday's death could be pinned on illegals crossing the border. Night signals usually meant drug trafficking. He'd heard rumors of *Los Cuchillos* wanting to seize territory from Navarre Àron.

"Hey, Frankie, what the hell you doin' out this time of night? We're up at dawn to move cattle down from the hills to the west pasture." Travis Conroy's baritone voice cut through the night shadows.

The ranch foreman's unexpected appearance startled him out of his vengeful fantasizing. "Couldn't sleep. Thought I'd check on the colicky filly to make sure she wasn't laying down."

"Four thirty comes before the cock crows. Be saddled and ready to ride out by five."

"Count on it, boss man."

He ventured one last look at the window. Light no longer lit the room. A smile quirked his lips. With a little bit of luck, he'd avenge his brother and let one of the cartels take the fall. Yeah, fate had made the plan come together.

Chapter Seven

Mitch sat at his desk. The office was quiet, and he hoped it stayed that way. He picked up his mug and grimaced at the cold coffee. Shoving back the chair, he stood, then walked across the room to freshen the brew, and to make another pot.

His mind drifted to Laura. In her own way, she had made it clear there was no room in her life for settling down. The words she had said that day in Cole Harbor remained crystal clear in his mind. *"I'm thirty-two, and underneath this blonde from a bottle lies a beginning crop of gray hairs."* She had laughed. *"In the olden days, I'd be considered an old maid. Joking aside, Mitch, I'm not looking for love. If it happens, he'll have to be someone pretty darn special."*

And now she was in Texas. With not so much as a social call to say howdy. That sent a strong signal. He hated to think it, but Laura haunted him. He of all people should know the "keep your distance" signs. Yet her perfect features, her stunning blue eyes, her kindness to others, her quiet nature, and the way she went after a story without ceremony all combined together to draw him to her.

He remembered their first meeting. It was more like he and Laura were sparring partners. She was impertinent and he was, well, arrogant. The thought caused him to smile. The smile drifted into a cheerless frown. He was haunted enough as it was. His wife, dead almost two years, had also been beautiful. And she had used her genteel beauty to capture his soul.

His mood darkened as he reread the typed report written by his deputy. Just as Laura had informed him about the New York bodies having the first joint of a middle finger found in their pockets, so did today's victim. The same method of operation suggested that whoever was working in New York had moved into his territory, and this didn't sit well with Mitch.

He opened the computer to the Sheriff's National Database (SND) and typed in *Los Cuchillos.* For a long time he sat scrolling through information. A South American crime syndicate based in Columbia. Suspected political ties in the USA. Narcotics and human trafficking, racketeering. Key players, unidentified.

Mitch rubbed his tired eyes. At this point he didn't intend to call in the FBI. But he did plan to discuss the case and this information with his uncles. Two pieces of data stuck in his craw. One thing he despised was a dirty politician. Was such a person involved, and was that the reason no top commando names appeared in the SND?

He glanced up at the large round wall clock. After midnight, and all was calm. He decided to catch a catnap in a cell reserved for himself and his deputies. His drift into nether land was interrupted by loud voices, followed by even louder profanity. Mitch was brought to full alertness.

In two strides, he crossed the room, opened his desk drawer, grabbed his 9mm Smith & Wesson, and holstered it. At that moment Deputies Wes Rojas and

Luis Espinoza virtually carried a scrawny, handcuffed thug into the processing cell.

The guy shouted in languages that sounded like a mixture of Spanish and Asian. Once the cell door was locked, Deputy Rojas heaved an tired sigh. “For a little fellow he was a handful.” He and Luis Espinoza bumped fists—a sign of victory.

Luis said, “I’ll process the paperwork.”

“Thanks for watching my back, bro.” Wes Rojas removed his hat. He flexed his shoulders and sat in a chair facing Mitch’s desk. “Sheriff, meet Phuong Soto. Luis and I answered a robbery-in-progress call. Our model citizen, here, was beating a female convenience store clerk with a spring stick. We called an ambulance and had her transported to the hospital.”

Mitch handed the deputy a cup of coffee. “How bad was she hurt?”

“Pretty messed up. Damn, the woman was old enough to be my grandmother.”

Disgust filled Mitch as he thought about his own mother, and Phyllis Friday. “Our friend seems to have a penchant for hurting women. Does Mr. Soto have any priors?”

Wes blew to cool the liquid. “Yep, as long as your arm. Interesting thing; he has a tattoo on his left hand between the thumb and the forefinger.” He arched the brow over his left eye.

Mitch leaned forward. “Tell me it’s a dragon?”

“Yep. Plus Soto fits the description the elder Ms. Friday gave us, right down to the long black ponytail and black pajamas.”

Elation feathered Mitch’s insides. “We’ll let Mr. Soto cool his heels in a cell for the night, then question him in the morning. By the way, my Spanish is pretty good, but damned if I understood what he was saying. Does he speak English or just cuss in English?"

Wes suppressed a yawn. He flexed his right arm and rubbed his shoulder. "Probably as good as you and me. His records state his mother is Mexican, father Vietnamese. My guess is his gibberish is a mixture of the two languages, which even I can't understand."

Wes had answered a domestic dispute call and ended up taking a bullet to the shoulder. That was ten months ago. Mitch asked, "How's the arm?"

"Getting better. It's not holding me back from doing my job."

"Didn't think it was. I'm just asking."

Wes tipped the cup to his lips and finished off the coffee. He situated the hat on his head. "Duty calls."

The following morning, Mitch opened the bottom drawer to his file cabinet and pulled out a fresh shirt. Keeping a supply at the office was more convenient than driving out to the ranch after shifts that required him to pull an all-nighter.

"Morning, Mitch. Ham, scrambled eggs, biscuit." Alma Duckworth set a to-go box on the desk. "When Sheriff Juh was here, he never ate at his desk. Said it was bad for a man's constitution. If you ask me, that's good advice. You orta at least walk over to the café. Get some fresh air, clear your lungs, stretch them long legs of yours, and get in a little politicking while you're at it."

Mitch smiled at the woman who had served as secretary to three sheriffs, and he was the fourth. "Alma, I love you like an aunt. I'll take your words under advisement."

She harrumphed. “You’re gonna miss me when I retire. Got it circled on my calendar. Yep, last day of December. Six more months.”

He lifted the lid and stabbed a forkful of eggs. After several thoughtful chews, he pointed a plastic fork toward her. “How long’s it been—a hundred years? That’s quite a pension check you’ll draw.”

She poured a cup of coffee and set it in front of him. “Don’t be impertinent. I’ve known you since you were in diapers. And for your information, it’s been forty-five years. Started long before cell phones and computers.” She harrumphed again. “In my day, clouds were puffy white things floatin’ in the sky. Now they’re cyber accounts for storin’ stuff that used to go in filing cabinets.” She then offered him a smile and a wink. “You’re gonna miss me when I’m not here to keep you on your toes and bring you breakfast.”

With that, she turned and left him to finish his meal. She called over her shoulder, “I’ll hold the calls till you’re finished eatin’.”

There weren’t many women like Alma Duckworth. She and his mother had been best friends since grade school, and she’d kept his mother socially involved rather than allowing her to stagnate in the wheelchair. Yep, the woman was a treasure.

Wes Rojas, senior deputy, fluent in several Mexican/Spanish dialects, had a way of getting prisoners to talk. Now he rapped on the office doorframe. “Phuong Soto is in the interrogation room.”

Mitch tossed the empty breakfast container into the trashcan and wiped his mouth with a napkin. “In the event Mr. Soto decides his lingo of choice is Vietnamese, do we know anyone who can translate?”

"There's not a big culture here. Maybe somebody in the language lab at the university."

"Can't say that makes my day. Let's hope he's not smart enough to lawyer up."

"Good cop, bad cop?"

Mitch shrugged. "You know the routine. I'll be in the viewing room. We'll give it an hour. If he doesn't break by then, I'll come in."

"Let's rock and roll."

Alma hurried into the room. She handed Mitch a document. "Don't leave just yet, Wes. Hot off the press. Crime lab pulled a DNA sample from the strand of hair at the hotel."

The two men exchanged smug smiles. Mitch said, "Alma, you have any teabags in your stash of goodies? I'm thinking our guest might like a couple of donuts and a nice cup of hot tea to help wash 'em down. And lower the temperature in the interrogation room."

Alma shot a conspiratorial wink toward the two men as she rubbed her hands together. "I surely do. Give me a sec to heat water in the microwave."

While Mitch and the deputy waited, they discussed the subject of the headless victim. "I've been on the job nearly fifteen years, and I'm telling you, Mitch, this is a new one for me. Luis said he nearly tossed his cookies at the sight. You think a bear really attacked the vic and made off with the head?"

Mitch related what Laura had told him about the bodies in New York. "I think it's likely we have a new breed of criminals on our hands. Beheading is what terrorists do. Whoever *Los Cuchillos* are, they are without conscience, and highly dangerous."

Alma came in carrying a small tray with a steaming

mug, a couple packets of sweetener, and two glazed donuts. “I was careful to handle the cup with a napkin.”

Wes relieved her of the tray. “What’ll we do when you retire, Alma?”

She playfully swatted him on the arm. “You’ll regret not being nicer to me, that’s what.”

****

Mitch stepped into the viewing room where the one-way mirror allowed him to observe and listen to a suspect being questioned. He watched Wes enter and slide the tray in front of the suspect.

In English he said, “‘Morning, Phuong. It’s a little chilly in here. Thought you might like a cup of hot tea. Even kicked in a couple of donuts, in case you didn’t get breakfast this morning.”

The man offered the deputy a sullen glance. He didn’t speak or move.

Wes pointed at the tea and made a drinking motion. “Go ahead. It’s fresh made.”

A reluctant hand picked up a donut. The confection disappeared in two bites. Likewise, the second one. He licked the sugar off his fingers, then wiped his hands down the front of his black shirt.

Behind the glass, Mitch muttered, “Come on, pick up the cup and drink.”

He listened to Wes say in English, “Is your name Phuong Soto?”

Silence.

He then spoke in Spanish. “Do you live at 4545 Sunland Avenue?”

Mitch knew the address was part of the worst slums in El Paso.

Still the suspect didn’t answer.

Wes left the room. He was gone less than ten minutes. He returned wearing a jacket. Mitch smiled. "Getting a little chilly in there. Good."

Wes continued with the simple line of questioning. "Phuong, were you at the Carlton Hotel on the morning of June 15th, and did you force your way into room 512?"

The wiry man rubbed his hands up and down his arms. He gave a pleading look toward Wes.

"Air conditioner's thermostat is broken. If I were you, I'd drink the tea before it gets stone cold and can't take the chill off you. 'Course, I could bring you a blanket, but, nah, on second thought, I'm not exactly inclined to be nice to a jack-off who enjoys beatin' up on elderly women."

Wes pulled out the chair on the opposite side of the table and sat. "You know, Phuong, I think you speak real good English, and real good Spanish, so why don't you stop wasting my time and tell me if you were at the Carlton Hotel on the morning of June 15th, and did you force your way into room 512?"

The suspect spoke. The dialect sounded Asian. Mitch assumed Vietnamese.

Wes leaned forward and spoke in Spanish. "Listen up, pal, don't pull this 'no speakady English or no *comprende* Spanish' crap. If I have to, I'll bring a translator in from the university who is fluent in every village dialect in Vietnam. You savvy that?"

Behind the mirror, Mitch silently cautioned the deputy to keep his cool. About that time, Wes shoved back the chair and stood. He leaned forward to take the tray, and when he did Phuong Soto grabbed for the tea. He wrapped both hands around the cup as if to garner the heat, and then he gulped like a man dying of thirst. When finished, he set the cup back on the tray and heaved a sigh, as if satisfied.

Though the glance and the nod toward the one-way window was subtle, Mitch didn't miss it. Wes spoke in Spanish. "Excuse me, Phuong, while I take the tray back to the snack room." Then in English said, "Can I get you anything else: purple elephants, dancing ducks, a bar of lye soap, maybe?"

Just as he was shutting the door behind him, Phuong Soto's whisper was audible to Wes and Mitch. "Fuck off, bastard."

Mitch stepped out of the viewing room. "Our friend speaks pretty good English."

"Yep. I'll get this to the lab boys, stat. Should we leave the little weasel to freeze?"

"We'll let him sit it out for another thirty minutes before adjusting the temperature. Let's hope the DNA is a match."

An hour later, Alma entered Mitch's office. "I'm reasonably sure this will make you happy."

"DNA report?"

"Yep, and a match as close as you can get without being totally perfect. I told Wes to meet you in the interrogation room."

"Thanks, Alma."

Inside the enclosure, Mitch said, "Phuong Soto, I'm Sheriff Mitch Carter. We heard your nasty expletive toward Deputy Rojas, so you can cut the crap about not speaking English. Understand that I am placing you under arrest for exacting bodily harm to a female victim residing in room 512 at the Carlton Hotel. You have the right to remain silent, you have the right to an attorney, if you cannot afford an attorney—"

"Cut the crap, man. I've heard it all before. You ain't got jack-shit on me."

Mitch shoved the document forward. "A long strand of black hair must have fallen from beneath your ski mask, because our forensics team found it. The saliva you left on the cup of tea was a perfect match. Who sent you after Laura Friday?"

"Man, I don't know nothing 'bout no bitch by that name."

Wes kicked the chair leg, nearly upsetting the man from the seat. "Watch your mouth and answer the question."

A knock sounded at the door. Wes opened it to find Alma. "I need you and Mitch to step out."

The furrowed frown on her face concerned Mitch. "What's happened? My dad…?"

"No, no, nothing like that. The hospital called. That poor woman from the gas station just died. Cause of death: brain hemorrhage due to extreme blunt force trauma." Shaking her head, Alma turned and walked away. Mitch blew out a deep breath as he looked at his deputy. "Damn."

The two lawmen reentered the room.

Mitch crossed his arms over his chest, and the wide stance was enough to indicate his anger. "As I was saying, Mr. Soto, if you can't afford an attorney, an attorney will be provided for you."

"Aah, cut the bullshit, man. It ain't like the ole lady died. I just slapped her around and twisted her arm."

Mitch placed his hands on the table and leaned forward so that his face was inches from the suspect's. He spoke through clenched teeth. "As a matter of fact, she did. About twenty minutes ago. Phuong Soto, you are under arrest for the murder of Jimena Santiago." He straightened. "Take him down to booking, Wes. Might want to contact the DA's office, too."

A puzzled look clouded Phuong's face. "Who the fuck is Jimena Santiago?"

Mitch fought back the urge to place his hands around Phuong Soto's scrawny neck. "She's the woman from the convenience store. The one you beat with a spring stick." Mitch thumped him in the middle of the forehead. "Wes, get this asshole outta here before I lose my temper."

Wes grabbed the skinny man by the arm and hauled him toward the door. Phuong Soto pleaded, "Hey, wait. If I give you the name of the person who hired me to find Sandra Piedmont, you'll cut me a deal, okay?"

Mitch and Wes exchanged confused glances. Mitch said, "Who is Sandra Piedmont?"

Soto sighed as if exasperated. "Her old man thought she was screwing around on him. He hired me to put a scare in her, and maybe rough her up a bit. 'Cept, he said room 512. Instead it was 215. How was I s'posed to know? Anyhow, roughing up the old bitch wasn't nothin' personal. It was business."

Mitch's anger deepened as he growled, "What about the yellow begonias with the card saying, 'Beware'?"

Soto reminded Mitch of a little bantam rooster, cocky and always ready for a fight. "That was Piedmont's idea. He thought I'd done the job and that his ole lady had checked into the hospital under a fake name. He paid me to deliver the flowers without being seen. So I did. Simple as that. Now, what about my deal?"

"Wes, get this piece of trash out of my sight before I commit an irrational act. Then take over from here. I'm off in ten minutes. You know where to reach me."

The deputy pulled Soto's hands behind his back and put the cuffs on him. As he hauled him out of the room, Soto yelled, "I want a lawyer. I have rights, you know. Get me a lawyer."

Keys in hand, Mitch stopped by Alma's desk. "Did you take care of that errand for me?"

"I sure did, and let me tell you, it was a pleasure meeting Phyllis Friday. Damn shame, her being an innocent bystander and taking a beatin' like she did. Anyhow, she was appreciative of the new outfit. You taking her home today?"

"Only if my uncle says she's well enough." He bent over and placed a kiss on Alma's cheek. "You know, Dad and I can never thank you enough for all you did for Mom."

Alma waved her hand as if brushing aside the remark. "Horse feathers. She would have done the same for me. Now get on with you. Your shift was officially over two minutes ago."

Chapter Eight

Mitch glanced at the woman sitting next to him. "You're awfully quiet, Phyllis. Are you in pain?"

Although her broken arm was in a cast and rested in a sling, Phyllis Friday cradled it in her good one, across her midsection. "Truthfully, being beaten within an inch of my life seems to have taken some of the wind out of my sails. I shudder to think I could have wound up like that poor woman from the convenience store." She pushed the gold-rimmed glasses further up on her nose. "Let's change the subject. I enjoyed meeting Alma Duckworth. She did a fine job of picking out this spiffy new outfit. Even though she wouldn't tell me the name of my generous benefactor, I have a suspicion his name is Mitchell Carter. Would I be correct?"

"My lips are sealed."

"I'll reimburse you."

"As far as I know, it was a good Samaritan who wishes to remain anonymous."

"You are a frustrating man." She leaned her head back against the headrest. "Okay, have it your way. Will I get to meet your family today?"

He offered her a gentle smile. A warm and sincere woman, in some ways she reminded him of his mother. "Even though she's my secretary, I've known Alma my entire life. She's like a second mother to me. And, yes, except for my brother Garrett, you'll meet them today. My mother had a tradition that once a week the whole family has at least one sit-down dinner together. Every Sunday for as long as I can remember, no matter where we were or what we were doing, we didn't dare not show up. To do so was to suffer the wrath of Marilee Mahoney Carter's Irish temper. Since her death, my sister is trying to keeping the tradition alive. It's tough. My oldest brother—that's Garrett—is in the Navy, currently stationed in Japan. Two of my uncles are Texas Rangers, one in Houston and one in San Antonio. You met Uncle Sam Houston Carter at the hospital, and the other uncle is with Homeland Security in D.C. My sister and her husband live on the ranch. We also invite one of the ranch hands to eat with us. We try to treat everyone as family."

Phyllis cut a curious look toward Mitch. "Was your uncle named after the famous Sam Houston of Texas?"

"Yep. My grandpap, Thaddeus Carter, was a Texas Ranger. He named all of his sons after well-known western heroes. My father is Wyatt, and we have Virgil and Morgan—all after the Earp brothers—and the brother in D.C. is Pat Garrett Carter."

"That's quite a legacy to live up to. I'm guessing your parents didn't follow the tradition?"

"Nope. My mother said she didn't want her children coming home from school with bloodied noses and blacked eyes because of trying to live up to a name."

"Sounds like a sensible woman. How's your father handling her passing?"

"Truthfully, I'm worried about him. He seems to have lost the will to live. Most days, he just sits in his room and watches television." Mitch reached over and squeezed Phyllis's hand. "I think you might be just what the doctor ordered."

"Me? Pffft. I'm an old gal past my prime, and with a busted wing, to boot."

Mitch steered the SUV expertly around the circular drive to park in front of the front porch.

"Good Godfrey, Mitch, who are all those people?"

"The welcoming committee." He laughed. "Mostly family, a couple of ranch hands."

Phyllis let out a happy squeal. "Oh, there's my Laura." She wiped away a tear. "Mitch, shame on me for saying this. As much as I'm heartbroken over Bryan's untimely death, I'd always hoped it would be you and Laura."

Before he could respond, Laura hurried forward and opened the door. "Aunt Philly, am I ever happy to see you."

Mitch slid out and sprinted around to help Phyllis from the vehicle, then reached into the back seat to get the plastic hospital bag containing her bloodied and torn clothing. He whispered in Laura's ear as he handed her the bag.

She nodded her understanding.

It was an unexpected pleasure to see his father, the patriarch, standing with the rest of the family. Pale and looking a little more frail, he reached out and shook hands with Mitch. "Good to see ya, son."

"Dad, this is Laura's aunt, Ms. Phyllis Friday. She'll be our guest for a while. Maybe when she's up to it you might show her around the ranch." It wasn't a question, or a command, more like an expectation from Mitch.

His father nodded. "'Spect I can take care of that. Welcome to the Triple C, Ms. Friday."

"Ayuh, and I'd prefer you call me Phyllis."

Mitch thought he caught a glimmer of a smile from his father. He made the other introductions. "My youngest brother and sister-in-law, Rob and Claire; my sister and her husband, Jill and Travis Conroy." He placed his hands on top of the heads of the boys. "And these two whirlwinds are my nephews, Kit and Carson."

The twins, both missing their two front teeth, offered engaging smiles and spoke in unison. "Did it hurt when your arm got broke?"

Phyllis smiled, but her eyes were serious. "Ayuh. You betcha."

The twins scrunched up their faces. "Uncle Mitch, she talks funny."

Travis reached forward and grabbed each boy by the ear. "Mind your manners, or you'll be shoveling manure until you're old and gray. Now go inside and get ready for lunch." He removed his Stetson. "Sorry, ma'am. They're old enough to know rudeness is unacceptable."

"No offense taken. I suppose we Mainers do talk a tad funny."

Phyllis wobbled a bit, and Mitch and Laura both steadied her. He said, "Let me help you inside."

Jill held the door open. "If you'd like to rest, I'm more than happy to bring a tray upstairs."

Phyllis blinked and inhaled deeply as if to shake off the sudden fatigue. "Not on your life. Mitch has told me about your Sunday gatherings. Aftah staring at four white walls with only a television for company, I'm looking forward to some spirited conversation."

He led her to the dining room and seated her. Laura sat next to her aunt. Wyatt and Rob sat at each end of the table. Mitch and Travis faced her, with the twins next to their father.

"Sorry I'm late."

Mitch offered a smile and motioned for the ranch hand to take a seat next to Laura. He made the introductions. "This is Frank Romeo. Like most of our hands, he works wherever needed."

"Nice meetin' youse ladies."

Laura placed the napkin in her lap. "You are not from Texas, are you, Mr. Romeo?"

"Nah. 'Riginally from Noo Yawk. Reckon we don't never lose our accents."

The conversation drifted around the table about the colicky filly, the price of cattle, and the arrest of Phuong Soto for murder, with everyone offering an opinion on every subject. And so it went until Wyatt intervened. "I s'pect this kind of talk is a mite boring for two refined ladies. What is it you do for fun back in Maine?"

Phyllis brightened. "First, I'd like to compliment the cook for this excellent meal. I don't know when I've had a bettah steak. Actually, I find the talk quite interesting. Now, as to your question, in my day I did a fair amount of horseback riding. I also enjoy sailing, hiking, and bird watching, and as the former owner of a bookstore, reading is my passion." She pulled a frown and held up the sling. "I'm afraid horseback riding is out."

Wyatt said, "Mitch told me about the fire. Do you plan to rebuild?"

Phyllis cast a look at her niece. "Laura and I have kicked the idea around. At my age, and after doing a bit of fun travel, I can't say we've come to any definite decisions about returning to Cole Hahbah on a year-round basis. Maybe a small cottage, just for summah visits. The wide-open spaces are nice, but there's no place like home."

Jill and Claire returned from the kitchen with a large platter of pecan pie cookies and bowls of vanilla ice cream topped with caramel sauce.

As he munched on one of his favorite desserts, Mitch took pleasure in listening to the exchange between his father and Phyllis. "There's a rodeo next Saturday. In his day, Dad was a champion bull rider. Won the national championship three years in a row. Why don't we plan to go? Travis, you entered in any events?"

"Yep. Me and Rob are in the head-'n'-heeling competition, and then bull-dogging. Say, you used to be pretty fair at bull ridin'. 'Course, sittin' behind a desk and ridin' one of them roll-around chairs most of the time, I'll wager you can't stay on for eight seconds anymore."

"Nah, don't think so."

All the family members chimed in with chicken clucking sounds. "Bak-bak-bak. Yeah, c'mon. Carters don't wear feathers."

Laughter followed the good-natured teasing.

Mitch rose to the challenge. "You've got yourself a bet. Loser washes next Sunday's dinner dishes."

The two men spit in the palms of their hands and shook. The twins spit in their palms, too, and yelled, "Yippee!"

Frank Romeo excused himself. “If youse ladies need anythin’, let me know.” He thanked Jill and Claire. “Can’t say when I last had food that makes me want to lick my chops for mo’.” Then, grabbing his cowboy hat off the hall tree, he let himself out through the front door.

Likewise, Laura stood. “As soon as I get Aunt Philly settled, I’ll be down to help with the dishes.”

“Filly?” The twins giggled. “She’s not a horse.”

Jill rolled her eyes upward, as she rubbed her belly. “Lord, help me. I pray this baby is a girl and that there’s only one of them.” Then she put her hand to her mouth and said, “Oops, I was waiting until I told Travis first.”

Her news set off a round of hugs and questions about the due date and lots of laughter. Wyatt fairly gushed when he said, “Travis, break out the good bottle of bourbon. This calls for a toast.” He pointed at his daughter. “Orange juice for you.” He winked. “We’ve got enough buckaroos around here. I’d like to have me a little fair-haired granddaughter.” His voice then cracked with emotion and dropped to a near whisper. “If it is a girl, reckon we might name her Marilee?”

Jill hugged her father and kissed his cheek. It was evident she struggled with her own feelings. “I think that would make Mama very proud.”

Mitch’s heart swelled with affection for the people he loved. Nostalgia tugged at his heart. He wanted to build his own family and have this same kind of devotion. And he wanted to share it with only one woman.

****

Inside the guest bedroom, Laura helped her aunt into a nightgown. “Aunt Philly, how do you suppose a guy from New York ends up on a ranch in Texas?" She shivered. "I wonder if he's from Spanish Harlem? His accent sounds more like the East Side."

Phyllis lay with her arm supported on a pillow. "What does it matter? The same can be asked of us." She yawned. "The pain pill is beginning to kick in. My eyelids are really heavy." What she mumbled next was unintelligible. Something about Mitch and Bryan.

Laura walked out to the balcony. Feeling like an outsider, she was not comfortable at the ranch. Besides, being around Mitch upset her emotional equilibrium. She looked beyond the swimming pool and beyond the endless pasture, her mind filled with questions: stay in El Paso or return to New York?

Chapter Nine

Eight seconds.

Eight heartbeats of eternity stretched between him and not having to wash Sunday's dinner dishes. A silly bet. Mitch silently swore he could endure anything for eight seconds.

He straddled the top rail of the chute as the bull shifted restlessly from side to side. Mitch turned for a moment to scan the crowd until he located the family's booth and spotted Laura. Even now, knowing he was short on time before the ride, he continued to stare at her. What was that expression on her face—a mixture of fear and adoration? Seeing her almost broke his concentration.

Hearing the announcer call his name, Mitch jerked his gloves on. As he did, the cantankerous bull slammed its massive body sideways, rattling the metal pen. Mitch centered his attention on the creature that had the strength to stomp him into the ground. He threw his leg over the chute and eased down to straddle the colossal animal and grip the flat, braided rope. The bull bellowed and hauled back on its haunches, then with a quick twist tried to horn Mitch.

Rob yelled, "Watch your legs, Mitch." He'd already pulled them up to keep his feet from being pinned between the animal's sides and the metal bars. The steadying hands of his father and brother at his back helped him stay upright as the bull continued to ram the sides of the chute.

Rob reached down and grabbed a horn to jerk the bull's neck around. "Settle down."

Mitch eased down to straddle the bull so aptly named Butcher's Blade. The animal seemed to have a sixth sense about how to outsmart the rider on his back. He was mean and powerful, and earning the reputation of being a killer.

Above the noise of the crowd and the rodeo announcer, Wyatt yelled in Mitch's ear. "You all set, son?"

Mitch nodded once and used his fist to pound his clenched fingers to grip the bull rope tighter. He moved his legs forward and squeezed with his lower body while trying to relax his upper torso. Two thousand pounds of muscle and rage rippled beneath him.

Wyatt patted Mitch on the back. "Don't forget, that first jump out of the chute is the most important."

Mitch nodded his understanding. How long had it been since he'd competed? Too long.

Eight seconds.

Adrenalin rushed through him as he shouted, "Outside!"

The tall metal gate swung back and the brindled Brahma with a massive horned head leaped sideways out of the chute, coming down with front feet and shoulders first as he exploded into the arena.

Butcher's Blade twisted his hind end to the right, then abruptly to the left. His rear legs came up high, missing the back of Mitch's head by inches.

Stay centered. Focus on balance.

The dance began between man and beast.

Keep the right arm high. Make it look good.

Mitch braced himself against the twists and the up-and-down jerks that rattled his teeth and jarred his bones.

The bull switched ends by coiling to the left, then whipping immediately to the right.

Good try, BB—round one goes to me!

Mitch lost his momentum and slid sideways. He struggled to adjust his weight to re-center himself. Not to be outsmarted, the bull lifted his haunches and kicked upward, landing on his forelegs again, then touched down in back and went into a spin.

Yeah, come on, you ugly slobbering brute, let's give the crowd everything we've got!

Like rolling thunder and lightning strikes melding into a powerful storm, Mitch and the bull became a united force to see which of them was the more powerful. Mitch started the countdown in his head and held fast like a tick on a dog.

As the buzzer sounded, Butcher's Blade reared its horned head upward. Rider and beast hung suspended in the air for what seemed a lifetime, and then it was over. Eight seconds of eternity had ended.

Mitch reached down with his free hand to jerk the bull-rope loose from his riding hand. He waited until the beast was spinning away to propel himself as far away from the locomotive action as possible.

He hit the ground on his knees. The odors of sweat, dirt and manure rose up to greet him.

Victory!

The audience came to their feet and roared as he stood. He lifted both arms, fists clenched in a gesture of triumph, feet dancing, torso twisting.

A force slammed him in the right shoulder. His first thought was that the bull had turned away from the rodeo clowns and gored him. The impact threw him to the ground. He struggled to breath. The fresh, hot, coppery scent of blood assailed his nostrils. Blood. Lots of blood. He was certain a horn had pierced his lung. He lay there, gasping, as the faces in the crowd spun out of control.

It took a minute for him to realize that he'd been shot. It wasn't the first time. He tried to move, and couldn't get up. Black dots danced in front of his eyes. He thought he blinked to clear his vision.

He heard a voice that sounded far away. Someone rolled him over, and said, "Gawd almighty." And then, "Mitch, stay with me, boy. The ambulance is on its way." The voice coaxed him to hang on.

"Shot," he gasped, and then a sudden wave of nausea and pain caused a blanket of darkness to close in on him.

****

A kaleidoscope of images flashed before Mitch: His first horse, an old mare about twenty years old. He was three. Trophies from the bulls he'd ridden. Susie, the day of their wedding, her dimpled smile. Her mouth moved, her beautiful mouth. He didn't understand the words as she reached for him. Their fingertips touched. She disappeared. A black car with darkened windows, the scat of gunfire. His mother lying on the pavement. Blood...lots of blood. Iraq! His men taking on fire. The whoosh of an RPG. Yelling and more yelling, in Kurdish, or was it Arabic?

The crazy swirl of remembrances slowed and dimmed as Mitch fought against the dense gray fog holding him prisoner.

His eyes fluttered open. He was cold, and the bright lights hurt his eyes. For one terrifying moment, he thought he was back in Fallujah, in a field hospital. He only knew he wasn't where he had been. The constant beeping annoyed him.

Memory drifted back to him. Feeling a spurt of fear, he forced himself to think, to remember. A ripping throb pulsated in his shoulder. It pounded so hard it was difficult to focus, and then he remembered. He saw himself in the middle of the arena, his arms lifted in victory, remembered hearing a pffft sound, and then hearing his flesh tear. He'd tried to dodge the bullet by whirling to one side, but he wasn't fast enough.

He heard a movement to his right, turned his head quickly, and groaned with the slicing pain in his shoulder.

Dr. Sam Houston Carter bent over him with a stethoscope to his chest. "Welcome back to the living. For a while there, I was afraid we might lose you."

Mitch blinked through a haze to bring his uncle into view. "Wasn't the bull, was it?"

"Nope, you were shot."

Mitch licked his parched lips. "Yeah, now I remember. How am I?"

A nurse came over and slid a sliver of ice between his lips to help moisten his mouth.

His uncle frowned down at him. "From the scars on your back, you really took some hits when you were in Iraq. It's a wonder you haven't died from lead poisoning."

Mitch asked in a raspy voice, "How bad is it?"

"You're lucky. The bullet missed your heart but

collapsed your right lung and tore up your shoulder. We're ballooning your lung now." He indicated a tube coming out of Mitch's side from under a sheet. "We've removed the bone fragments and debrided the area to promote healthy tissue growth. For now, we'll keep you on antibiotics and pain medication."

"When can I go back to work?"

Sam chuckled. "Funny man. You're fresh out of surgery and still in the recovery room. In a word, not anytime soon."

Mitch closed his eyes. "I feel like a bull stomped all over me."

"Stands to reason," his uncle sympathized. "You've been through major surgery. For now, your job is to rest."

"What about the bullet? Did you retrieve it?"

"Don't worry, I've got it. When you're out of ICU and up to it, I'll bring it to you. I've got you on a pain-pump. Right now, I want you to sleep. Doctor's orders."

"Get it to Wes to send to forensics."

Sam Carter nodded his understanding.

"What about Dad? I don't want him to worry."

"He's in the waiting room, along with a mighty pretty young woman and a whole passel of others. I'll let everyone know you're okay. We'll get you into a room as soon as we can."

"I'm cold."

The same nurse walked over and covered him with a toasty warm blanket fresh from the warming cabinet.

Mitch managed a wan smile. A second later, he was asleep.

When he awoke again, a nurse was bending over

him. "Good evening, Sheriff. I'll be done in a jiffy." She checked his pulse, temperature, respiration, and then the catheter. After making a notation on his chart, she asked, "On a scale of one to ten, how would you rate your pain, with ten being the highest?"

"Eleven."

She smiled as she inserted a needle into the IV tube. "The morphine pump was removed last night. You might feel a slight burn as the pain med enters your arm."

He felt an immediate jolt as the drug surged into his vein. "Is my dad here?"

"Your uncle sent him and everyone else home."

Mitch winced when he tried to scoot up on the pillow. "I need to see one of my deputies. Either Wes Rojas or Luis Espinoza. It's important."

"I'll make a note of your request."

"How long do I have to wear the catheter?"

"If the doctor gives the okay to move you out of ICU, then we'll remove it tomorrow." She gave him a kindhearted smile, and patted him on the shoulder. "Try to sleep."

"You do know the doctor is my uncle? I can call in favors."

She plumped his pillow, straightened the sheet, and smoothed the blanket. "Uh-huh. He said you'd probably try to use family influence to finagle special treatment. Except for your father and brother, no visitors until Dr. Sam says so."

She flicked off the light and walked out of the room.

When his uncle came in, Mitch was barely awake. "Can't a fellow get any sleep around here without being awakened just to get poked and prodded?"

His uncle frowned as he listened to Mitch's chest. "I don't like the sound of that rattle. It means you've got a lot of congestion. The last thing we want is for pneumonia to set in."

"When can I go home, Sam?"

Sam Carter pulled up a chair and sat down. "How long did it take for you to recover from the previous gunshot wounds? Be honest, because I can check your military medical records."

"Okay, so it took longer than a day or two."

Sam's serious expression deepened. "You're a lucky man, Mitch. Even though you've suffered a collapsed lung, the ballooning was a success." He crossed his legs. "However, you were shot with a high-powered weapon. The muscle damage is extensive. Healing will take time, and if you have pneumonia, I'm keeping you in ICU another day or two."

Mitch heard the words. His gaze sought his uncle's. "Give it to me straight. How bad is it?"

"Bad enough. You'll need physical therapy, and lots of it, to regain full use of your right arm and to keep the muscles from atrophying. In fact, for a while it'll be difficult for you to use your arm."

Mitch wanted to contest his uncle's prognosis. "How long is—a while?"

"Depends on how quickly you heal and how conscientious you are with the PT. You need to know it's going to be a rough ride, and how you progress is up to you."

Mitch stared at the ceiling. "Damn. So when can I go home?"

"When your lungs are clear and there's no more

congestion. And when you do go home, if you overdo and relapse, your bullheadedness will land you right back in a hospital bed." Sam offered a lopsided grin. "Your dad's waiting outside. I'll send him in."

He stood to leave, then turned back to look at his nephew. "I seem to recall you were about twenty-five the first time the Army notified us you had been shot, and then two years later we got another call that you'd taken two more hits. You're thirty-five now. As we get older, it takes longer for our bodies to heal, which makes recovery time longer." He tweaked Mitch's big toe as he left the room. "We Carters are a tough lot. You'll be all right."

Wyatt wore a worried frown when he entered the room. He grabbed Mitch's hand and held it tight. "Hurts my heart to see you laid up like this. Brings back too many bad memories."

Mitch knew which memories his father referred to and felt worse than ever. He sank deeper into the pillow.

His father sat down and rested his white cowboy hat on his knee. "Sam filled me in on all the details. You won't be able to lift anything heavier than a fork for about a month."

Mitch pushed a free hand through disheveled hair. He wanted to stand under a hot shower to wash away the dingy feeling. He was already tired of the pain, and he wanted something to eat other than the plain broth and jiggly green congealed water he knew he could expect. And above all else, he wanted the damn catheter removed.

Wyatt's voice cut into Mitch's doldrums. "Wes and Luis are working the case." When Mitch grunted, his father spoke in a gentle voice. “If you’re not up to hearing this, I’ll save it till later.”

Mitch waved hisleft hand. “Go ahead, Dad. Better hurry, though, ’cause I’m fading fast from the pain shot. Tell me, what did they find?”

“The boys found a shell casing.”

Mitch’s eyes fluttered. He widened them as he fought to stay awake. “They’re good men with excellent training. What else did they find?”

“Luis used one of them laser pointers to ex…extra…damn, can’t think of that fancy word he used.”

“Extrapolate. It means to estimate or come to a conclusion.”

“Yeah. Anyhow, from where you were standing, and the angle of your wound, the boys placed the shooter in the rear parking lot, where the competitors park their horse trailers and RVs, and he was using an AR-15 semiautomatic. Luis is certain forensics will match the shell casing to the slug Sam dug out of you.”

Fighting through the fuzz collecting around the fringes of his mind, Mitch did a quick calculation. “That’s almost eight hundred yards, plus he’d have to have been standing on the cab of a truck, or the hood. Either our guy has sniper experience or he’s a damned good shot.”

“Yep, my guess is the jackleg used a silencer, plus with the noise from the crowd, the announcer blaring your victory over the loudspeakers, and the music, stands to reason why no one heard a shot. You’re lucky to be alive, son. That little victory dance you did probably threw off his angle and saved your life.”

Mitch closed his eyes, then jerked them open

again. “Dad, how would the shooter know I was at the rodeo and competing in the bull riding?”

Wyatt reached up and scratched his head. “Dang good question.”

Chapter Ten

Mitch spent the next two weeks complaining about sponge baths, tasteless food, limited television programs, and wearing hospital gowns. When the nurse helped him walk to the bathroom, he hunched forward and gritted his teeth. “My chest feels like it’s going to cave in, and I don’t know what hurts worse, peeing with the catheter in or without it. Damn!”

The elderly nurse smiled as she chastised him. “No swearing. It’s against hospital rules.”

A snarl curled his lip as he glared at her.

“Mitchell Carter, just because you’re the sheriff doesn’t mean you can give me *that* look. Remember, I can always re-order the catheter.”

He grunted his disgust. “At least get me a pair of pajamas. I don’t like my hind side flapping in the wind for the whole world to see.”

“Hmm,” she mused. “Thirty-five years ago, I put the first diaper on that skinny little butt. It’s not like I haven’t seen it before.” She helped him into the bathroom. “I’ll wait outside, and don’t fall. Not unless you want to extend your stay in this fabulous establishment.”

“You are a funny woman, Edith Crandall.”

A few days later Nurse Crandall arrived with the usual pink plastic tub filled with tepid water. “This is your lucky day, Mitchell. Checkout is at noon.”

Sam Carter greeted the nurse as he sauntered in pushing a wheelchair. He laid a pair of folded pajamas and a robe on the bed. “That’s right, nephew, I’ve issued your walking papers. We need the bed. Your dad and Ms. Friday are in the lobby. Soon as you’re dressed, I’ll wheel you down.”

Mitch screwed his face into a frown. “Pajamas? Where’s my boots and hat and uniform? And I can damn well walk out on my own two feet.”

Sam jerked a thumb toward the window. “Out there, you’re the boss. In here, I say what goes. Hospital rules: on release day, every patient gets a free ride in a wheelchair. In your case, no extra charge.” He explained the prescriptions and placed them with the release form on the bed. “If you have any excess pain or redness, especially around the wound area, call me. Doesn’t matter what time of day or night. Also, I’ve already scheduled your first physical therapy session for next week.”

When Mitch acted as if he was about to protest, his uncle added, “This one almost did you in, Mitch. I watched your heart stop twice, and that put a strain on my old ticker. You can take the next month or so to completely heal, or else find a new line of work. If memory serves me correctly, there’s not much demand for one-armed lawmen.”

Mitch heaved a sigh. His voice softened. “Give me a few minutes to rinse off and get dressed. By the way, what happened to the clothes I was wearing when I got shot?”

“I gave them to Wyatt, with instructions not to wash them in case they were needed for evidence.”

“’Preciate it, Sam.”

Once he was dressed, Mitch sat in the wheelchair in rare docility while his uncle wheeled him down the hall and toward the elevator.

He spotted her the moment the metal doors opened. The sun glinting off the large plate glass windows formed a halo around Laura. Her hair feathered about her face like a cap of spun gold. In that instant, he noticed everything about her. The sprinkle of freckles across the bridge of her nose. Pert breasts mounded beneath the pink scoop-necked top, and hiding inside black slacks were legs that seemed to go on forever. She offered a timid smile but didn't speak, and neither did he.

Sam broke the silence. "Don't forget PT next week. It's important."

"Yeah, important." Mitch was already trying to think of a way to avoid physical therapy.

Wyatt stepped forward and clasped Mitch's good hand. "Don't worry, Sam, either me or Laura will make sure he doesn't play hooky. C'mon, son, let's get you home."

Sam pushed the wheelchair out the automatic doors to the sidewalk. The blast of heat nearly sucked the air from Mitch's lungs. Wyatt stood next to the luxury SUV and held the door wide. Pearl gloss exterior with high running boards, the Carter emblem emblazed on the hood—Wyatt called it his Cowboy Cadillac.

Mitch stepped up on the running board and slid into the black leather front seat. His first thought was "Thank goodness for air conditioning," and the second was how bad it hurt when Laura pulled the seatbelt across his chest.

"Sorry." Her voice was soft as she fumbled to

make the strap less restricting.

He spoke through gritted teeth. “It’s okay.”

She closed the door and climbed into the back seat. Mitch flipped a salute to his uncle, who nodded and turned back to the hospital.

It took a couple of miles before Mitch let himself relax. He preferred being behind the wheel rather than in the passenger seat. He laid his head back and closed his eyes, thankful for the pain pill Nurse Crandall had given him before leaving his room.

The last thing he remembered was his dad saying, “I don’t know what was worse, thinking the bull had gored you, or realizing you’d been shot and then thinking, dear God, don’t let this boy die.”

Mitch rubbed a hand over the large bandaged area of his chest. It hurt, and it hurt to hear the anguish in his father’s voice.

Subconsciously, he knew the vehicle had stopped. He opened his eyes in time to see the twins rush down the steps. The door opened and the rambunctious boys clamored, “Uncle Mitch, you can lean on us.”

Laura rushed to his aid as he climbed laboriously out of the SUV. She winked. “I believe your uncle is a bit too heavy for you to support. Why don’t the two of you grab those plastic bags from the back seat and take them to his room.” She placed her arm around his waist, and Wyatt came around and lent his strength to Laura’s.

Mitch watched Kit and Carson scramble for the hospital bags. “Thanks, fellas.” He was trying not to notice how nice it felt to have Laura next to him. Even through the pain, the scent of her perfume curled around him, beckoning him to lean closer. Yet he was relieved when his brother replaced Laura. It was good to lean on Rob's substantial strength.

****

The morning sun poured into the bedroom. Mitch lay on his back, the pillow scrunched under his head, his hair mussed, his face shadowed with morning beard. He looked like a young boy, his face relaxed and carefree. Only there was nothing little-boyish about this man. His bare chest revealed broad shoulders, and a large bandage covered an angry red wound that had almost stolen his life. She was appalled by the sight. Images of holding Jolly's head in her lap and watching his life slip away left her weak-kneed, with her stomach in a tight turmoil.

Laura stood there, a myriad of emotions flooding through her as she thought back on all the times she and Mitch had spent together in Cole Harbor and of all the time she had spent holding him at arm's length. With a heart full of longing, she watched him sleep in the early dawn and wanted to rid herself of regrets as soon as possible. It was time to return to New York. She was running away, and she berated herself for being a coward. For not wanting to lose another man she loved.

Sighing, she eased from the doorway, pulling the door behind her to close it. Lost in her troubled thoughts, she almost missed hearing him say, "Don't go, Laura."

He patted the bed to indicate she should sit next to him. She said, "Are you in pain? Can I get you something?" She reached for the carafe of water and filled a glass, then opened the bottle of pain pills. He grimaced as he used his good arm to push higher against the bed's headboard. Downing the tablets, he closed his eyes for a moment to regain his equilibrium.

When he opened them again, she wondered what he was thinking as he studied her face. "What?"

He coughed to clear the morning rasp from his throat. "I did a lot of thinking in the hospital, and I want you to answer one question. Just one."

She met his serious gaze. "Okay."

"I care about you, Laura. Deeply. But before I allow my feelings to grow, I need to know if it's mutual. If not, I won't ask again."

She tried not to let him see the effect his nearness had on her. She searched his blue eyes for longer than she meant to.

"I'm not playing here. I'm dead serious. I need to know."

"It's not that simple, Mitch. I can't answer you right now; my life is too complicated, and…"

He reached to caress her cheek. His voice husky with emotion, he told her, "Life is filled with complications, Laura. You have to decide what's important, if we're important."

She moved away from him, unable to think clearly with him touching her. "I—"

Jill came bustling in carrying a tray, her voice jovial. "Good morning! I figured you'd like some real food after all your griping about the hospital's mystery meals." She set the tray on Mitch's lap. The silence caused her to glance from her brother's dark expression to Laura's troubled face. She clasped her hands together as she straightened. "Uh-oh. I seem to have interrupted a serious moment. My bad." She pirouetted toward the door. "Excuse me…sorry…I'm, uh…call me when you've finished eating."

Laura saw the hope in his eyes and hated

disappointing him. He could ask her to stand up to a grizzly bear, and she'd try, but this question… There was more involved here than both their feelings.

Mitch frowned. He saw the direction of her eyes and looked down at the arm cradled across his chest, and the unsightly raw flesh peeking from beneath a large white bandage. "I'm guessing it's memories of Jolly and Bryan that's put the frown on your face. I'm not them…I'm alive, Laura. You can trust that I'm not going to die, at least not anytime soon. Trust yourself to love again. To love me."

She backed away from the bed. "I'm jinxed, Mitch. Don't you understand that I can't love you?" She didn't want to have this conversation. "Don't ask for more than I can give right now, please; I need time."

It wasn't the answer she wanted to give him. She wanted to trust what he said as she watched him tamp down his impatience. He had no idea how much he meant to her. Yes, it was time for her and Aunt Philly to leave. "I'm sorry."

As she reached the door, he called her back. "Laura, it's written all over your face. There's no need to leave the ranch. Stay. Enjoy a different type of life before you return to New York. At least until I get on my feet again."

It was almost as if a sailing sloop's spar had slammed against her head. How did he know? Was she such an open book, to be so easily read?

With quiet reverence, she lifted the white linen napkin from the tray and gently placed it against his chest, then removed the lid from the plate of scrambled eggs, home fries, and bacon. She poured a cup of coffee, set it within easy reach, and took a step backwards. She swallowed hard. "Okay."

His smile melted her insides. "Okay what, Laura?"

She swallowed hard. "Aunt Philly likes it at the ranch. I won't make any promises I can't keep, and I don't want to wear out our welcome. Maybe we should find a place in town."

Mitch smiled and it lit his eyes. "Stop. You're doing it again—finding reasons to run away."

"I'm sorry. Running seems to be the story of my life." She glanced at her watch. "The paper goes to press on Mondays. I'll check on you this evening."

As she moved toward the door, Mitch called her name again. She turned, her voice quiet as she answered the question in his eyes. "We'll stay until you're up and about."

****

She'd said "we" rather than "I." Mitch chuckled deep in his throat as he polished off breakfast. At least Laura had agreed to stay.

He set the tray aside and shifted uncomfortably. With Laura gone and the house quiet, he reached for his cell phone and called Wes.

"Morning," he said. "I've been sprung."

Wes snarked. "Way to go, boss. Are you at the ranch?"

"Yep. Who shot me?"

"Luis and I are working on it," Wes assured him. "We think it may be tied to the two drug mules we sent up to Beaumont Federal a couple of months ago. Seems like there were some rival gang-bangers who didn't want to play friendly. The Alvarez brothers were taken out. Rumblings are Navarre Àron isn't happy his cousins bit the dust, and he blames you. By the way, the new Columbian cartel's boss is rumored to be Hugo Vargas's grandson. He and Àron are waging war along the border in Ciudad Juarez."

"Damn. The mayor there is Navarre's brother-in-law." Mitch shifted to ease the pain in his chest and shoulder. "This is not good."

"Yeah, and if you think the *Los Cuchillos* are bad, this Vargas calls his army *Las Serpientes Venenosas.*"

"Poisonous snakes? I don't get the connection."

"Intel informs us the MO for Vargas is to sew poisonous snakes in the mouths of their victims…while the victim is still alive. Àron and Vargas are each determined to take the other down. Whoever wins will be a crime lord with power like we've never seen before."

Mitch grimaced as he thought about his wife and mother. "These are evil men. If I wasn't sworn to uphold the law, I'd gun both of them down in a heartbeat."

The undercurrents of hatred in Mitch's voice was evident. "Can we prove Àron tried to take me out?"

"Not yet, but I've notified the Texas Rangers. Your Uncle Morgan said to tell you he and Virgil are working the case along with about forty others."

"Good enough, Wes." Mitch harrumphed. "The knife and the snake. Maybe they'll save us the time and money by killing each other."

Just after Mitch hung up, a knock sounded at his door. Phyllis peeked inside. "Thought you might like some fresh coffee." She placed the mug gently into his hand.

He blew to cool the steaming liquid. He tasted it and rolled his eyes. "I think I'm in heaven. I've missed your special brew. What's your secret?"

Phyllis smiled. "If I tell, it won't be a secret. Anyhow, I'm giving Jill a break from kitchen duties. Might as well make myself useful while I'm here. Anything special you'd like for supper?"

He drew a long sigh as he savored another sip. "Steak, and mashed potatoes piled high, with gravy and smothered onions."

"What about dessert?"

"If it's sweet, I'll sink my teeth into it."

She looked very somber. "Mitch?"

He waited.

"Thanks for convincing Laura to stay. In my heart, I know the two of you belong together." Then she offered a mischievous grin. "Besides, I kinda like spending time with your father."

When she left the room, Mitch smiled. Maybe Phyllis was just the medicine his dad needed to breathe vitality back into him. With some difficulty, Mitch got out of bed and managed to get to the bathroom. He felt dingy and wanted a shower, but instead he settled for his usual sponge-off from the sink. He managed to bathe and dress in fresh pajamas, and, with his left hand, managed to operate the electric razor without dropping it.

He spent the morning watching the western channel and dozing. It was the blood-curdling scream that brought him to a sitting position. Groggy from napping, he swung his legs over the side of the bed and nearly slumped to his knees as he moved to snatch the closet door open. He grabbed the pistol secured in a small chest on a top shelf. Adrenalin pumped hard and fast, pulsating the vein in his neck.

Thoughts invaded his mind, thoughts of Navarre Àron inside the house. He eased out of the bedroom and to the top of the stairs, where he shifted the revolver to his right hand. The weapon felt weighty and cumbersome. Pain watered his eyes when he tried to lift his arm. He was in danger of losing his grip and dropping the Beretta .9mm, so he switched it back to his left hand.

His profession demanded he keep his emotions in check. Years in the military and as a border patrol cop after leaving the Army had allowed him to see things most people never knew existed, all of which involved gruesome sights. As a matter of mental survival, he'd learned to shut down his emotions. Reeling in a calming breath, he peered over the banister and down into the great room.

Tension heightened his sister's voice as she scolded, "Kit…Carson…I'm so mad I could skin the both of you! How many times have I told you to never bring snakes inside the house?" She held each twin by the scruff of their shirts. "You know I hate snakes, and you caused Miss Phyllis to nearly have a heart attack."

Mitch stood behind a rustic redwood column to avoid being seen as he watched and listened in amusement and aggravation. For selfish reasons, he didn't want to give Laura and Phyllis any excuses to leave the ranch.

Kit pleaded his case. "But, Mom, it's harmless."

"Yeah, it's only itty-bitty." Carson spread his hands apart to demonstrate the length.

Wyatt entered the great room. It'd been a long time since Mitch had witnessed that angry scowl on his father's face. *Uh-oh. Boys, I wouldn't want to be in your boots right about now.*

Wyatt placed his hands on his hips. "How old are you boys?"

The twins answered in unison. "Six, tomorrow."

Their grandfather nodded. "Old enough to respect your mother's fear of snakes, and old enough to respect the guests in this house." He pointed to Carson. "And old enough to never say 'yeah,' to your mother. Am I right?"

Both boys nodded.

"That's not good enough. I want to hear you."

"Yes, sir."

Wyatt said, "Jill, Miss Phyllis, the boys have something to say." He frowned at his grandsons. "You better make it good, and say it one at a time."

Each twin hung his head for a moment before offering an apology. Phyllis thanked them and excused herself, claiming a headache. At the top of the stairs, Mitch touched her on the shoulder to express his understanding.

Wyatt's deep baritone voice boomed. "Where do you think you're going? I don't recall dismissing you, and I'm not done yet."

The twins stopped in their tracks and stood like stiff soldiers. Their mother wore a curious frown, and Mitch continued to watch.

His father's voice commanded attention. "First of all, one of these days you might mistake a rattler for a bull snake. If you don't get bit, someone in this house might. Do you understand a rattler's bite is deadly?" Wyatt didn't wait for the boy's answer. He forged on. "Secondly, tomorrow is a big day. You'll both be six."

Exuberant smiles lit the boys' faces.

"Wipe those smiles off your faces. As part of your punishment, there will be no party. Your mother will notify all your friends; the party is off. Now, what is it the two of you have begged for all year?"

The twins looked at each other and grinned. "Palomino Quarter Horses. Real horses. Not ponies."

"That's right. Go on out to barn number two and take a good look at them. They're in stalls six and seven."

Mitch didn't think he'd heard right. Had he pulled such a stunt, his father would have peeled the hide off him. Wyatt was letting the twins off with an apology and a cancelled birthday party?

"We're sorry, Grandpa. We won't bring no more snakes in the house."

"You're dang tootin' you won't, 'cause once you take a good look at those palominos, you and your brother are helping me load 'em in the trailer. I'm returning them, along with the brand-new saddles." Wyatt cast a look at his daughter that said, *Don't challenge me on this*. "There will be no birthday cake, no ice cream, no special supper."

Jill narrowed her eyes at her sons. "Wipe those tears. You heard your grandpa. Go on and help him load the horses."

Kit looked up at his mother. Carson sniffled and said, "We have to wait a whole year for a birthday party?"

Jill looked to her father. He remained stern. "Boys, we're Carters, and Carter men are honorable. We obey the rules, we respect the law of the land, and most of all, we respect and protect the women we love. Learn this lesson now, and by the time your seventh birthday rolls around, you just might have earned a party." He pointed toward the front door.

Pride swelled Mitch's chest as he made his way to the bedroom. He hoped to one day instill that same sense of honor in his sons. He returned the .9mm to its case and then collapsed on the bed. The pain in his shoulder and the weakness in his arm and hand had him rethinking his original decision to avoid physical therapy.

Chapter Eleven

Later that evening, Wyatt visited in Mitch's room. "Hope that ruckus this morning didn't disturb you."

Mitch smiled at his father. "I hid behind the redwood post and watched. Did you really return the palominos?"

"I did. I even had the boys explain to Buck the reason we were returning the horses. It wasn't like I was springing it on him. Your sister had called ahead to explain the situation."

"How'd Buck take it…having to return a couple of thousand dollars?"

"Oh, the two of us go back a coon's age. In fact, he gave his own lesson to the boys. Said the only reason he was taking 'em back is because he had a buyer looking for twin palominos for twin daughters. I think the idea of two girls getting the horses was worse than not having a birthday party."

Mitch joined his father in laughter.

Wyatt dropped his voice to a whisper. "This is between you and me. Not a word to your sister, but I went to the bank this morning and opened savings accounts for the twins. I'll add a little along and along to help out with college."

"You're a sly old fox, Dad. Used the refund money from the horses, did you?"

Wyatt winked at his son.

With a more serious tone, Mitch asked, "On a different note, what do you think of Phyllis?"

Wyatt furrowed his forehead as if thinking how to answer. "She's a right handsome woman. Makes the best pot of coffee I've ever tasted. Nothing against your mother."

Mitch nodded in agreement. "She's probably getting bored sitting and doing nothing. Especially when she's used to running her own business. I was thinking you might consider showing her around the ranch. She's already mentioned she used to like riding horses."

Wyatt stood. He placed his hands in the back pockets of his jeans and gazed out the window. Mitch knew it was a risky suggestion, as his father was still grieving. He waited.

Wyatt turned, and Mitch was certain his dad intended to reject the idea with an excuse about not feeling up to snuff.

Although there was a slight tremor to his voice, Wyatt said, "Horseback ridin' is out, what with her arm still in a cast. Reckon your mother wouldn't mind if I used the buggy to show Phyllis around. Tomorrow is as good a day as any, if she's up to it after today's snake scare."

"Don't worry, Dad. Phyllis has weathered a lot of storms."

"Reckon I'd better go ask Frankie to put the buggy horses on the hot walker, maybe walk a little feistiness out of 'em." He placed his hand on the doorknob. "Glad you're feeling up to joining us downstairs. I've missed having you at the supper table." With that, Wyatt quietly left the room.

****

Mitch was almost asleep when Laura walked onto the veranda with a tray. On it were sandwiches piled high with roast beef, a side of fruit salad, and a pitcher of tea.

He scooted upward on the chaise. “I thought you were at the newspaper.”

She set the two plates of food on the table, with silverware, and filled the glasses. “I went in earlier. We’ve sent tomorrow’s edition to press.” She offered a shy smile. “Do you need help getting to the table?”

Even though pain wracked his entire right side, he sucked it up with what he hoped was a convincing smile. “I can manage.”

“Uh, no, you can’t. Sit back and relax.” She rushed to adjust the chair’s cushion. Then she arranged his plate and utensils on the tray and set it across his lap. She moved the glass of tea to a side table within his reach. “There’s chocolate pudding for dessert.”

He took a bite of the perfectly seasoned roast beef. “Don’t remember when I’ve had a tastier sandwich.”

She sampled her own and chewed thoughtfully. “I confess that Jill and Claire are wonderful cooks, but I take credit for assembling the sandwiches and making the tea.”

When lunch was finished, and Mitch was savoring the last of the pudding, Laura said, “Your Uncle Virgil called to say he’d be here around three. I didn’t want to wake you. Are you sure you feel well enough to discuss business? I can always call him back.”

His face became somber. “If he needs to see me in person, then apparently he has a lead he can’t discuss over the phone. Yeah, I’m up to a visit. I want to find out who tried to kill me."

She nodded. "Your dad said if you hadn't done that little victory dance and moved when you did, the bullet would have hit your heart."

He was grim. "That means someone who knows his stuff."

"You mean like a professional hit man?"

"Yep."

She loaded the tray with the soiled dishes. "You look tired. Maybe you should rest before your uncle gets here."

He swung his legs over the side of the chaise and stood. Little black spots floated before his eyes. It took a moment to clear his vision and regain equilibrium. Damn, he hated feeling weak as a kitten. "When Virgil gets here, show him up to my room."

"Is it okay if I sit in to hear what he has to say?"

Mitch thought for a moment. He frowned. "On the condition that you don't stick your nose in this," he cautioned. "I don't want you in the line of fire."

Her eyes widened.

He glowered at her. "Don't play innocent, Friday. I'm serious."

She seemed to mull over his statement. "Hmm, I don't know which is the bigger story of the year, Sheriff Mitch Carter staying on a snorting, slobbering bull for eight seconds and winning a twenty-thousand-dollar purse, or Sheriff Mitch Carter getting shot by an unknown assailant." She shrugged and offered a nonchalant smile. "Besides, I've got the exclusive. You can't leave the house, because Jill has hidden your car keys and forbidden anyone, and that includes your father, to drive you anywhere until you are well enough for your PT sessions."

He burst out laughing as he shuffled toward the stairs. "That's not fair."

"Hey, I've got a nose for news, and when a scoop like this lands in my lap, I'm not about to let it pass."

He cocked his blond head and studied her intently.

Her smile faded. "Stop looking at me like that."

He liked the way her cheeks pinked. "Sorry." The blush added to her beauty. "But you're not printing one word until I give you the go-ahead. Nothing. Not even a teaser article."

She crossed her heart. "Scout's honor."

But he knew better. She didn't have a poker face. At least not a good one. "I'm serious, Friday. Whoever is after me makes those New York goons look like a bunch of gun-toting pansies. Besides, I won't have my family endangered because of headline news. They've suffered enough because of my job."

She averted her eyes as she headed for the kitchen. She pushed through the swinging doors, muttering to herself, "Way to go, Laura. He reads you like an open book."

Jill glanced at her as she entered the kitchen. "Are you talking to yourself?"

"Was I? I didn't realize. Geez, the men in white coats will be chasing after me if I make a habit of it."

Jill laughed. "Don't worry. I'll protect you. I'll throw Claire's biscuits at them. Guaranteed to knock 'em out cold." She clamped her hand over her mouth. "She's a love, and other than hockey pucks for biscuits, Claire is a marvelous cook."

Laura laughed in delight. "That's true enough. I guess Mitch is looking forward to your uncle's visit.

Must be important, for him to drive all the way out here."

Jill sobered. "All of this makes me a little edgy. Losing Susie, and my mom. I'm really glad Travis is only interested in working the ranch. It's hard enough knowing my brothers and uncles are always in harm's way because of their chosen careers. I couldn't stand it if my husband, the father of my children..." Tears clouded her eyes. "Sorry, being pregnant has my hormones out of whack. I'm not usually so emotional." Heaving a sigh to compose herself, she said, "Uncle Virgil could dig information out of a dried turnip. He's a good investigator."

"Mitch certainly looks up to him."

Jill's smile reflected the pride she felt for her uncle. "If you'll excuse me, I've got paperwork to finish before the twins get home from school."

Laura laid her hand over Jill's. "It's wonderful that your father took Aunt Philly to see the ranch. She's very special to me, and I hope she's enjoying the day."

Jill smiled. "It's me who's grateful for your aunt. Losing my mother was awful, but watching my father withering away from mourning has been heart-wrenching. I hope getting out today is the shot in the arm he needs to get back in the saddle."

Laura rinsed the dishes and set them in the dishwasher. She turned to leave, but Jill called her back. The narrowed eyes and serious scowl on the woman's face surprised Laura. She waited as Jill heaved a deep sigh. "There's only one way to say this, so I'll say it straight out. Mitch waited a long time to fall in love. When Susie was murdered, a light went out in my brother. That's why he left Texas and went to Maine.

To get away. To come to terms with the hate that was eating him alive inside." She paused as if trying to collect her thoughts. "One thing you need to know about us Carters is that once we give our hearts to someone, it's for a lifetime.

"I see the way Mitch looks at you, Laura. It thrills me to see him smile and hear him laugh again. If he's not all the way already, then it'd take a fool to see that he is at least falling in love with you. I don't see that from you. Your furtive glances are indifferent. If you don't share his feelings or don't think you can ever love my brother, then walk away. As much as I like your aunt, and appreciate her thoughtfulness, gather your belongings and leave this house. I want you gone by the end of the week. I don't care where you go, just get out of El Paso and leave Texas, because if you break my brother's heart, I *will* hurt you."

The feral expression on Jill's face let Laura know this woman was protective of her family, and her words were no idle threat. Leaving the kitchen and making her way up the stairs to her bedroom, she stood in front of the long mirror and looked at herself. She didn't like the person staring back at her—a bossy, opinionated, know-it-all woman who was afraid to open her emotions to a man who was kind, caring, and…and had been willing to give her up when he knew how much Bryan had loved her. But she hadn't really given her heart to Bryan, and now he was dead. She didn't want to revisit those old memories, but they were relentless. She leaned forward and touched the mirror. "Maybe there's something wrong with me. Maybe I'm not capable of love."

She wanted to punch the image staring back at her.

Chapter Twelve

Laura met Jill and Virgil Carter at the top of the stairs. She merely acknowledged Jill's nod. The Texas Ranger tipped his hat.

"Uncle Virgil, this is Laura Friday, a reporter and a friend of Mitch's from Maine. She and her aunt are visiting, but might leave at the end of the week." Jill cut a challenging look at Laura.

Laura didn't miss the emphasis placed on *the end of the week.* She offered her hand. "Mitch speaks very fondly of you and your brother."

He returned the handshake.

Jill said, "If I know Mitch, he'll insist you stay until he's pried every ounce of information out of you, Uncle Virge. He puts up a good front about being stronger than he is. He won't admit it if he's tired."

Virgil pecked his niece on the cheek. "Just like Marilee—always the mother hen. Where's Wyatt?"

"He's showing Laura's aunt around the ranch."

"Glad to hear it."

She smiled. "I'll bring a pot of coffee and some cookies."

Mitch was sitting up in bed, looking pale and gaunt, when Laura followed Virgil Carter into the room. He was a strapping man, whipcord tough. Gray hair at his temples added to the ruggedly handsome face. He bore the cleft chin and intelligent blue eyes that seemed to be a trait in all the Carter men. She estimated his age between fifty and fifty-five. He was intimidating, even to a woman who made her living interviewing all types of personalities. He seemed very businesslike and exuded an unapproachable aura. She guessed the bulge under his jacket was a sidearm.

He gave her a dismissive look and pulled a chair closer to the bed. "You look like you've been rode hard and put up wet. If you're not up to it, we can do this another day."

"Nope, I'm not sick or dying, not yet." Mitch pressed a hand against his shoulder when he tried to laugh. "Damn, it hurts."

Mitch's cell phone rang. Virgil handed it to him.

Looking at the caller ID, Mitch said, "Alma?"

Her voice, high-pitched, was almost yelling. "Just got a terrible phone call! He said, 'Tell Sheriff Carter the new marksman won't miss.' And then he hung up. Makes me pure sick to my stomach, Mitch."

"Settle down, Alma. Did the caller give a name?"

"No, but it was a man. He spoke real soft like, and with an accent."

"What kind of accent?"

"Don't know if it was Mexican or not. Definitely Hispanic."

"Did a number come up on the caller ID?"

"Sorry. All that showed was 'unknown caller.' Normally, I'd let the answering machine pick it up, but I had a feeling I needed to get this one. Wish I hadn't."

"You did the right thing, Alma. Where are Wes and Luis?"

"Both out on calls. You want me to bring 'em in?"

"Negative that. You know the drill. Write down

exactly what the caller said, date, time, sound of his voice. And Alma, go spend the weekend with your sister. I don't want to worry about you."

"Gotcha, Mitch. You need anything? I can always run it out to the ranch."

"Only thing I need is for you not to worry. I'll call Wes or Luis if need be."

He clicked off.

Virgil said, "What was that all about?"

Mitch's cell phone rang again. He pointed to the phone's screen and motioned his uncle to lean closer.

Caller ID—unknown caller.

A heavily accented voice whispered, "Next time we won't miss. Tell your *puta* her sweet ass is on the line, too."

"Who the hell is this?"

Disconnect.

"Any way to trace the call, Virgil?"

His uncle gave him a longsuffering look. "Unknown number? Not likely. Probably a throwaway cell phone. We've dealt with our share of those. The caller was definitely Hispanic. I caught enough to know it's not Mexican." He settled back in the chair next to Mitch's bed. "Lawmen make enemies. That's the reason I'm here. You have any idea who'd take a hit out on you?"

"Yeah, Navarre Àron. He still wants to settle an old score with me for making a dent in his human trafficking and drug operations, and for taking out two of his top captains."

Virgil's voice was gruff when he spoke to Laura. "Ms. Friday, how long do you plan to extend your visit?"

Her eyebrows arched. "Did the call involve me in some way?"

Virgil said, "Apparently. Do you know what the word *puta* means?"

She gasped as heat flared in her face. "He called me that? *Whore*?"

Mitch sat forward, his jaw taut with stress. His eyes narrowed. "How would Àron know about Laura?"

Virgil was silent for a moment. "I've heard Navarre's voice enough to know the caller wasn't him. And from the accent, I'd bet my prize Quarter Horse stallion our caller is South American. We've had wind of a new cartel from Columbia."

"*Las Serpientes Venenosas.*" The name slipped out before Laura could call it back. Trying to make light of interrupting, she shrugged. "I'm an investigative reporter."

Virgil nodded. She took his scowl to mean he didn't appreciate her interference. "Ms. Friday, I believe it's time you excused yourself. For your own safety, the less you know the better."

She crossed her arms. "Whoever *he* is called me a whore and made an implied threat. The more I know, the better I can protect myself and my aunt." She dared a glance at Mitch and hoped he'd back her.

"She's right, Virgil. She's the one who filled me in on the headless bodies cropping up all over New York."

"Suit yourselves. Don't say you weren't forewarned. Let's get down to brass tacks. Hugo Vargas is the supreme *capo*, leader, of *Las Serpientes Venenosas.* Otherwise known as *El Chapo*."

Mitch laughed as he translated. "Shorty!"

"Only his enemies call him that. Not his men."

Virgil's serious tone didn't change. "As far as Intel knows, Vargas's only major enemy is Navarre Àron, who is fighting him to keep control of the border and expand operations farther in the States and into Canada. We also know Vargas is young, about twenty-three, and intelligent and fearless, which makes him even more dangerous. We're slowly building a profile on him. Rumor has it he has ties to our country."

Mitch stared at his uncle. "How deep do his connections go?"

"Deep enough. American mother, wealthy, possible political ties all the way to the White House."

"Damn. I hate lying in this bed." He looked at Laura. "Call the physical therapist and set up an immediate appointment."

Virgil held up his hand. "Whoa, now. Don't go getting all rambunctious on me. I've been shot a couple of times, so I know what you're going through. If you don't follow Sam's orders, you'll lose the use of your arm. Need I remind you that this isn't your first go-round with being wounded."

Mitch winced as leaned back against the pillows. The entire right side of his body hurt. He felt older than his years.

"Listen to your uncle, Mitch. I also don't want you worrying about Aunt Philly and me. If it'll ease your mind, we'll leave Texas and go back to…" She stopped. Where would they go?

It was almost as if Mitch read her thoughts. "To where, Laura, New York? You said yourself there's nothing to return to in Maine. Besides, I'll feel better if you're here at the ranch."

"No, Mitch, I'm afraid my presence will only bring

more trouble. I don't know how I fit into all of this, or how this new gang found out about me." She clasped her hands together. "I admit, I am a little frightened."

"Then all the more reason to stay where there's safety in numbers. Don't you agree, Uncle Virgil?"

His face bland and noncommittal, Virgil lifted his eyebrows. He glanced at his watch. "I have to get back to the office. Think about what I said and allow yourself to heal properly. Unless you plan to hire a special deputy to chauffeur you around and tote a shotgun for you, a one-armed sheriff doesn't pose much of a threat. Keep your powder dry, nephew. And tell your dad I'll catch up with him later."

Mitch sighed. "Keep me updated."

Virgil Carter winked, gave a nod, and left.

"He's right about my returning to New York." Laura shrugged. "I feel as if I brought this trouble to you. Maybe I wasn't careful enough when doing my research on the headless bodies, or on this other outfit. I didn't know who the leader of *Las Serpientes Venenosas* was until your uncle told us."

Mitch pressed his sensual lips into a flat line. "Who's going to drive you to the airport? "

"What about Frankie Romeo?"

"Nope. I'll tell Travis to instruct the men not to drive you anywhere."

"I'll call a cab."

"And I'll have one of my deputies fetch you right back here."

He glared. She glared right back.

Then her voice went soft, her eyes cast down at her entwined fingers. "It's apparent your uncle doesn't like me."

Mitch didn't say anything for a minute. "Look at me, Friday. What matters is that I like you."

His blue eyes were dark and intent. His smile was slow and easy, and he held her stare until she became embarrassed. At that moment, an odd sensation fluttered her heart and weakened her knees. She was both hot and cold at the same time, and suddenly uncomfortable being near him. Yet she wanted to drink in the musk scent of his aftershave, to touch him, to have him touch her. It wasn't a sexual sensation but rather an emotion she'd never experienced. She drew in a deep breath and averted her eyes. "I-I think I hear voices. Your father and Aunt Philly have returned. If you need anything, call me."

He was still watching her with an odd half-smile as she fumbled her way to the door.

Chapter Thirteen

After dinner, when they were settled in the bedroom they shared, Phyllis twittered away about the buggy ride. "Beautiful country, Laura. We saw a herd of de-ah, and Wyatt drove the buggy right through a herd of cows. He's a nice man. Devoted to his family."

"You like it here, don't you?"

Phyllis was thoughtful for a moment. "Texas has a different kind of beauty, but it's terribly hot. You know the old saying, 'There's no place like home'? My heart will always belong to Maine, especially Cole Hahbah. Part of me longs to return."

"What about Mitch's father? You do like him?"

Phyllis sat on the twin bed, her back against the headboard with her knees pulled up, a book in her lap. She squinted over her glasses. The excitement of today's adventure ebbed as she looked at the tide of emotions on Laura's face. "Out with it. What's happened to upset you?"

Laura gave a brief synopsis of the day's events, including her conversation with Jill—except she omitted the part about Jill's threat to do her bodily harm—and meeting Virgil Carter. "Usually, I don't have problems making decisions. I honestly don't know what to do. Part of me thinks I should give up the notion of being editor-in-chief of the *Gazette* and go home to Maine. I've brought this trouble to Mitch, and with the threatening phone call, I've placed his family in danger." She interlaced her fingers as she also related how Mitch had laid it on the line about his feelings for her. "He's put the ball in my court, Aunt Philly. If we return to New York, or decide to rebuild in Maine, then I've lost him forever. I can't seem to think straight… Tell me, what would you do?"

Phyllis laid the book aside and went to sit next to her niece. She took Laura's hand into her own. "This isn't about me or what I would do. You just said, and I quote, 'Then I've lost him forever.' By Godfrey, Laura, I'm losing my patience with you. When are you going to get tired of using Jolly and Bryan's deaths as an excuse to hold Mitch at arm's length? So you made a rash decision. Do you think Jolly holds you responsible for his death? No! He'd say get on with your life. You are no more to blame for Cole Hahbah blowing up than I am. Bryan died. He'd probably tell you things happen for a reason. His death opened the do-ah for you and Mitch. You can't move forward with your life if you don't stop living in the past.

"And don't you dare look at me that way. Ayuh, I enjoyed today. It was refreshing to go for a buggy ride, to eat sandwiches by a creek, and be doted on by a handsome man…but don't even try to make this about me, or Wyatt. I don't like the heat or creepy crawly things like snakes, and Wyatt said himself that he doesn't take vacations. The ranch is too big an operation for him to leave. Besides, all he talked about was his wife. This is a man who will mourn his loss until his dying day. So there's no budding romance in the works there."

When Laura opened her mouth to speak, Phyllis

stopped her. “About this threat. I don’t like being in danger, so I agree with Mitch: we’re safer here surrounded by lots of people. Besides, we gave up the apartment in New York. What’s there to return to? And one last thing, there is a lot of love inside you just bursting to get out. Unlock your heart, Laura.”

Laura placed her head on Phyllis’s shoulder. She heaved a sigh. “You were in love once. What is love?”

Phyllis left her seat on Laura’s bed to return to her own, where she slid under the coverlet and propped up on an elbow. “Love is like riding on a rollah coastah. It’s exciting, exhilarating, and scary as hell, and like all machinery, it breaks down sometimes and takes work to put the pieces back in working ordah. Riding a rollah coastah with the right person makes it all the more fun. It’s up to you to decide if you are the right person for Mitch, because even someone blind in one eye can see how he feels about you.”

Phyllis reached to turn off the lamp and rolled over to face in the opposite direction.

Feeling totally dejected, Laura climbed into her own bed. She lay on her back with her hands folded against her chest and, in the dark, allowed silent tears to slide down the sides of her face. Weighing her aunt’s words, she deserved the scolding. Her ego deflated, she closed her eyes and dreamed of roller coasters—frightening dreams, dreams that had nothing to do with love.

Chapter Fourteen

The following week Phyllis had a doctor's appointment, and since Mitch's physical therapy was scheduled the same day, Laura volunteered to drive them. She used his personal vehicle, a black crew-cab pickup. "This is pretty cool. I like sitting up high, and man, this has all the bells and whistles. Very different from my little doodle bug."

Unsure of handling the powerful truck, she used caution when pulling from the long driveway onto the highway. Conversation was light, mostly small talk to pass the time.

"Friday, if you were a frivolous person, what is one thing you'd buy yourself?"

"That's just it. I'm not…frivolous. What about you, Aunt Philly?"

From the back seat Phyllis said, "If I were a person without money cares, I'd buy the city block in Cole Hahbah and rebuild my bookstore without the upstairs apartment and just live in a cute cottage on Lighthouse Road overlooking the bay."

Laura glanced in the rearview mirror at the melancholy look on her aunt's face. "That sounds wonderful."

Phyllis leaned forward. "Your turn, Mitch?"

He turned to smile over his shoulder. "Not until Laura takes her turn."

"Ayuh, Laura. There must be one frivolous thing you'd like to have."

Laura smiled. "Well, it's foolish, but when I was about nine I saw a picture in mother's photo album of an elderly woman wearing a cameo pinned to a lacy collar at her throat. For a long time it was my secret wish to own a real cameo. The old-fashioned kind, not a cheap imitation."

"Oh, ayuh, that was my mother, Estelle Hyer-Friday. Breaks my heart that all those memories were lost in the fire."

To lighten the gloom, Laura hastily said, "You're not off the hook, Sheriff Carter."

He glanced into the rearview mirror and winked at Phyllis. "I like to fish, and use worms for bait. Nice, fat, wiggly worms. What I'd like is a woman who enjoys fishing, and who doesn't squeal when she gets worm poop on her fingers."

The truck filled with laughter. Laura said, "That's it? You're kidding."

He shrugged. "It's all I've got for now."

Laura maneuvered the truck into a parking spot in front of Sam's medical office. She helped Phyllis out of the truck and walked her inside the building, then returned to help Mitch out of his seatbelt. Leaning in, her face was close to his, so close that her heart pumped overtime, and her cheeks flamed.

His voice reminded her of silk when he said, "Why are you nervous, Laura?"

"I-I'm not nervous. Hurry, or you'll be late."

"Will I?" His eyes held hers until she thought her heart would beat completely out of her chest.

"Yes. I've already been scolded by one uncle. I

don't want the PT tattling to Sam and giving him an excuse to reprimand me for making you late."

"Then I'll meet you in the lobby when I'm finished. Later, Laura."

The way he said her name caused her to feel uncoordinated, like she might fall into an abyss. "You have the number of the newspaper office, in case you and Aunt Philly finish early."

She slammed the truck door. He smiled again and walked away. The memory of his smile distracted her all the way to the *Gazette.*

****

His phone call said he needed her to pick him up right away. It was urgent. "What's happened—is Aunt Philly okay? Did you hurt your arm?"

"I'm fine. She's fine. Dad is on his way to drive her back to the ranch. I'll explain once you get here."

She glanced at her watch. Two hours had passed since she'd left her aunt and Mitch at the medical complex. The urgency in his voice pressed fear into her heart as she rushed out of the newspaper's parking lot. She cursed downtown traffic, and it seemed each red light took forever to turn green.

It was as if he had been watching for her. The moment she pulled up to the curb, he was standing there, his arm resting inside the blue sling. Laura slid from the truck and hurried to open the passenger door for him.

Thank goodness for air conditioning. Outside, she was certain the heat was melting the makeup off her face. The expression Mitch wore was grim.

"I'm not an invalid. You don't need to open doors for me." The angry pitch to his voice caused her to step back. The heel of her shoe bumped the curb, throwing her off balance. Mitch reached out to grab her.

"No! You might hurt your shoulder." Pain stabbed through her hip. She winced as she stood, using her hands to wipe dirt from the back of her slacks. "I'm okay." She tried to laugh off the fall.

"I didn't mean to snap at you. You or Sam should have warned me that PT hurts like hell. I feel like damaged goods."

A bead of sweat lined his forehead, maybe from the heat, maybe from the pain. She scolded, "Tough guy, huh? I told you to take a pain pill before we left the house. You didn't, did you?"

She waited for him to get in the truck, then strapped the seatbelt in place. "What's the emergency?"

Mitch heaved a heavy sigh and popped a pain pill into his mouth. "Virgil called. Wants me to meet him at the ME's office. Border patrol found a body and called it in."

She dared a glance at him. "A headless body?"

"Nope. This one is intact."

At his directions, she activated the left turn signal. "How much farther?"

"Swing a right at the next light, then three blocks. You'll see the sign."

"Why did your uncle call you? Isn't this a case for the Texas Rangers?"

"He'll fill in the details once we arrive."

She worried her bottom lip with her teeth. "He doesn't like me. I don't want my presence to upset him."

Mitch clenched his jaw, closed his eyes, and tried to will the pain medication to hurry and kick in. "One thing you need to know about Uncle Virgil; underneath his suit of armor is a soft heart. He's a good man. Once he likes you, he likes you all the way."

Laura harrumphed as she cast Mitch a doubtful look. She wheeled the truck into an empty parking space and grabbed her camera from the back seat.

Once inside the building, Laura said, "If you recall, I don't attend autopsies."

The sterile antiseptic odor roiled her stomach.

"Not my favorite kind of party either."

Virgil didn't crack a smile when he met them. "Ms. Friday, only authorized personnel allowed. There's a snack room with coffee and a couple of chairs down the hall."

Her expression faltered. She stared down at the white tile floors.

Mitch cradled the sling with his good hand. The edge was beginning to wear off the pain. "Virgil, if I have to deputize her, I will. She stays."

Virgil's steely-blue gaze pierced her. "No vomiting, no gagging, no fainting, and, most of all, no reporter questions."

She swallowed. Gads, she didn't want to witness the nude body of a dead man being cut open. Virgil Carter had issued a tough order. But Mitch had stood up for her. She didn't want to let him down, or embarrass him. As they walked down the long hallway she mentally chanted, *Don't faint, don't gag, and please-oh-please don't toss your cookies.*

The heels of their shoes clacked on the tile floors. Virgil filled Mitch in on the details. "The reason I called you in is I'm certain our corpse is Navarre Àron's brother."

Mitch adjusted the sling's strap to ease the pressure on his shoulder. "You think this is Hugo Vargas sending a message to Navarre?"

"That, and to all law enforcement. If this is Matias Àron, he was killed right under our noses and dumped in plain sight for our border guys to find him. Yeah, I think Vargas is thumbing his nose at us."

"How was our corpse killed?"

"There are ligature marks on his wrists to indicate he was tied up and tortured." He stopped at a door labeled Pathology Lab. "Here we are." Virgil opened a door and held it for Mitch and Laura to enter the cold, sterile room.

The overwhelming odor of medicinal fluids threatened to upend Laura's stomach. She pressed her hands against her abdomen. *I will not vomit. I won't.*

The nude body of a youngish Hispanic man lay on a metal slab.

She whispered to Mitch, "Should I take pictures?"

His statement was matter of fact. "Dr. Mercado, I've brought my own photographer."

The ME sighed heavily. "Suit yourself. Just don't get in my way. If you want to get up close and personal, there're extra hazmat suits and goggles in the drawer. Sometimes when I make the first cut, the body gases spew." He cracked a swarthy grin toward Laura. "Smell can knock an elephant to its knees."

Suddenly the room felt like a refrigerator, causing Laura to appreciate the hundred-and-five-degree temperatures outside. Virgil helped Mitch into the suit while Laura managed her own.

She stepped forward to snap several shots with her digital camera. The medical examiner spoke into the microphone suspended from the ceiling, detailing each of his findings. "Bleeding in the ears, which indicates brain trauma. Contusions to the chest, right and left rib cage, and abdomen. A five-inch bruise from his right upper cheek to the right ear, and fractures of the nasal bones and facial bones. The victim has bruises on his back, chest, abdomen, and both arms and legs."

He examined the bottoms of the corpse's bare feet. "No dirt or debris. With the depth of the ligature marks on the wrist, an educated guess is the victim was suspended with the feet off the floor during the assault. At this juncture, it can be concluded that his body was carried to the discovery site and dumped."

Mitch and Virgil stepped forward when the ME said, "Hmm, never seen this before. The mouth is stitched closed. Reminds me of how Amazonian headhunters sew the mouths of their victims shut before…" He swiped his finger across his throat to make his point.

Mitch made a rough sound in his throat. "Whatta you think, Virgil, is this Matias Àron?"

"Hard to tell with the way his face is all busted up."

Laura zoomed in and clicked. "Hey, is this guy really dead? I'm certain I saw his cheeks move."

The ME laid a hand on the corpse's cheeks, then snatched it back as if he'd been burned. "Holy shit!" He glanced at Laura. "Sorry, miss."

Virgil moved even closer. "I saw it move too."

Mitch said, "I've got a bad feeling about this…a real bad feeling."

The ME cleared his throat and continued his examination. He used the tip of the dowel to touch the heavy brown thread. "Looks like jute. The kind of twine used for tying packages. It's certainly not a thread for medical purposes." He pulled the metal arm of the large magnifying glass down for a closer look. "Stitching is definitely amateurish."

Mitch bent over the table. "Can you tell if he was alive or dead when the mouth was sewn shut?"

Mercado used the long slender dowel to point to where the twine interlaced in the holes. "Tiny specks of blood around the punctures. This leads me to believe the mutilation was performed post mortem."

Laura was certain everyone in the room sighed their relief together.

"No obvious defensive wounds." Speaking into the mic, Dr. Mercado also detailed the condition of the mouth.

"We'll need fingerprints to positively ID the victim." The tone in Virgil's voice indicated it was a command, and not a request.

"Way ahead of you, Lieutenant Carter. Took more than a few minutes to break the rigor of each finger. You'll have your prints by the time you're ready to leave my domain." Again he offered a satirical grin toward Laura. "Breaking the rigor to release the finger joints makes a popping sound. Much like popcorn. I like mine buttered. What about you, Ms. Friday?"

Mitch fairly growled his protest. "Cut the morbid humor, Mercado, and get on with it. We don't have all day."

The medical examiner merely shrugged.

Laura's stomach knotted, her breathing shallow. She had the sudden urge to flex her fingers.

After the methodical external examination, a hose

was turned on to wash the body. Mercado explained the procedure was to keep outside factors like dirt, fibers, and other debris from contaminating the internal organs. With precision he turned off the hose, then instructed Mitch, Laura, and Virgil to put on their goggles. He made a display of picking up a scalpel.

Laura was certain the exaggeration was for her benefit and wondered if her complexion had turned as green and sickly as she felt. Damn it all to hell. She was an investigative reporter. She'd seen more than her share of crime photos and crime scenes. She silently cautioned herself again: *Don't faint, or vomit, or gag!*

In spite of her mental pep talk, she felt herself sway, and just as she did, her hip collapsed from the pressure of continuous standing and she stumbled against the slab. She put her hand out to brace herself, giving her a close-up look at the victim's once handsome face. This was her undoing. She expelled a half-shriek coupled with a gasp. "It moved. There's something in his mouth."

Chapter Fifteen

Mitch reached out to catch Laura. She bumped against his wounded shoulder, and he flinched and groaned. Virgil stretched his arm across the couple as if protecting them from an unseen enemy. "Stand back."

Dr. Mercado backed away but leaned forward as close as possible and yet maintain a safe distance. It was there. He saw it, too. "I've never in my life encountered a…a living corpse."

Virgil fumbled with the safety clasp on his holster. He hefted the butt of his .357 Sig in case he had to pull the weapon. All observers watched as the corpse's left cheek bulged.

Mercado and his assistant both soldiered backwards. Mitch observed everyone's faces. Laura stood wide-eyed and fascinated. The ME and his morgue attendant both wore pale, tight expressions. His uncle stood like a sentry ready for war.

Before anyone in the room had a chance to relax, the cadaver's lips pooched out as if straining against the stitches holding its mouth shut.

Mitch tried to relax the tension in his body, hoping to relieve the throbbing in his shoulder. He wasn't sure why he was whispering. "Laura, for your safety, I'd like you to leave."

She edged closer. "Not on your life. I'm staying with you and Virgil."

Mitch's uncle gave her an unexpected pat on the shoulder and offered a weak smile. He stole a look at Mercado. "Doc, what's going on here?"

Mercado's voice quavered. "Honestly, I don't know. The body was found in the extreme heat of the day. I'm hoping it's gases from decomposition."

This time both cheeks bulged. Moving from side to side. Then, unexpectedly, the corpse's eyes opened. Laura clamped a hand over her mouth, the scream filtering between her fingers. "Oh, my God! He's looking at us." In spite of her intense trembling, she managed to switch the camera to recorder mode. "And m-maybe I can capture what's happening."

Mitch licked his lips. "Whoever killed this poor bastard put something inside his mouth. That's why it's sewn shut."

"Holy shit." Mercado's olive complexion had changed to pasty and pale. He made the sign of the cross over his chest. "I'm a few weeks away from retirement. In thirty-five years nothing like this has ever happened to me. What a way to end my career."

Virgil said, "One thing's for sure. We can't stand here all day trying to figure out what to do. The best plan of action is to act." He kept his voice as calm as possible. "Doc, you have the scalpel. You need to cut those seams."

Mercado's expression was wild-eyed; he was definitely scared shitless. "I don't think I can. No! I won't do it."

Virgil's tone was commanding. "Get hold of yourself, man. You'll do it. We need the autopsy results. Besides, whatever is in there has to come out and be destroyed."

The ME's scientific mind seemed to rectify itself. He inched toward the body slowly, very slowly. He blew out as if releasing his tension. "Okay, everyone, goggles on."

All attention was on the frenetic distortion of the cadaver's face, until Mitch stopped the ME with a near-yell. "Wait! Uncle Virgil, move that chair closer to the door, and then help Laura stand on it. Because of her bad hip, whatever pops out of this guy's mouth, I want her where she's safe but can make a quick exit." He looked at Laura. She nodded her understanding.

Dr. Mercado stood within arm's reach of the dead body, just close enough to the stitched-up lips that he could slip the scalpel's sharp blade under the jute. He blew out another breath.

"Okay, here goes. One…two…three." With his forceful upward slice, the cord separated. Mercado stumbled backward, bumping into his assistant, who yelped.

A dark heavy body with a triangular head burst free of its unwanted prison and hurled itself to the white tiled floor.

From the safety of her perch, Laura snapped frame after frame as the diamondback rattler slithered to a corner, then coiled, its tongue flicking, the rattles on its tail whirring. Laura was certain the creature's hooded eyes exuded pure evil.

Virgil whispered, "If I shoot the damned thing, we'll be wiping snake guts off us."

Mercado had scrambled to where Laura stood. Mitch said, "Give your lab coat to Virgil."

The ME didn't hesitate. He wadded the white lab jacket into a ball and tossed it to the tall Texas Ranger's waiting hands.

"What's your plan, nephew?"

"I have no desire to have guts of any kind on me. See if you can toss the coat over its body and then somehow scoop it inside that trashcan." He looked at the doctor. "Lift the lid off and have it ready."

"But it has contaminated gloves and gowns in it."

"Is any of it bio-hazardous?" Mitch practically yelled the question.

The doctor seemed to realize the inanity of his statement, and snatched the lid off.

"Let's pray this works." Virgil stepped forward. The agitated snake reared its head with an ominous hiss. The coat sailed through the air and settled over the reptile. As tall as he was, Virgil pirouetted like a ballerina, grabbed the container, and slammed it over the snake. He pressed a beefy fist on the upended bottom. In spite of the room's frigid temperature, beads of perspiration lined his forehead. "All we have to do now is figure out how to turn the can up, with the snake in it."

Mercado said, "I have some diethyl ether. It's a common solvent used in labs. Years ago, dentists used it to put patients to sleep. Maybe we can insert a tube under the trash can and I can gas the blasted thing."

Mitch and Virgil nodded their assent.

Mercado's hands trembled as he attached a long slender tube to a canister. He moved toward the trashcan. "Lieutenant Carter, I'm trusting you with my life. Whatever you do, lift the receptacle only high enough for me to slide the tube inside."

"How long will it take?" Laura remained in her position on the chair.

"I'm not a veterinarian, ma'am, but I'm shooting in enough to knock out a human. With any luck, it'll be a lethal dose." The doctor shuddered as he stooped.

Virgil eased the trashcan up less than an inch. The movement agitated the rattler. They could hear its tail whirring a warning.

Mercado scooted the long tube inside. He nodded, and Virgil lowered the can but not enough to put a crimp in the plastic tube.

Mercado said, "Everyone make sure you have your mask on. I don't want any of you passing out. Let's give this fifteen minutes. I'm not taking any chances."

The minutes seemed to drag by until the doctor said, "I did my part. One of you can lift the trashcan."

Virgil and Mitch exchanged glances until Virgil said, "Doc, you got anything with a long handle?"

"Yes." Mercado instructed his assistant to get a broom from the supply closet. When he returned, he handed the broom to Virgil.

Virgil tapped the side of the trashcan.

No one spoke.

No whirring was heard.

To be on the safe side, Virgil tapped again and was again rewarded with silence.

Drawing in a deep breath, Virgil said, "Man, I hate snakes. Doc, I sure hope you've put this one to sleep."

All eyes were on the lawman as he eased the trashcan up to expose the lab jacket. He used the tip of the broom handle to carefully lift the coat. "Well, I'll be damned. Doc, this is one for the record books. You've saved the day."

Virgil lifted the limp mottled body into a polyurethane garbage bag and tied a knot in the top.

Mitch seemed to rouse himself from a pain-filled daze. "I think I'm safe in saying this is definitely the work of Hugo Vargas."

Virgil agreed. "Yep, *Las Serpientes Venenosas,* living up to their name. Stuffing a poisonous snake inside a victim's mouth and sewing it shut. With this kind of calling card, Vargas is sending a strong message to his competitors."

Laura accepted Mitch's hand and stepped down from the chair. "Is it dead? The snake?"

"If it isn't, it will be. I'm taking it over to the vet's office to euthanize it for sure. We'll freeze dry it for evidence." Virgil smiled at Laura. "I admire a lady who keeps her cool under fire, Ms. Friday. You'll get me copies of the pictures?"

The compliment was small but powerful. She returned his smile. "Please, call me Laura, and yes, I'll email them to you."

Outside, the heat settled on them like a heavy blanket. Virgil opened the trunk of his black sedan and deposited the garbage bag inside. "If I wasn't still on duty, I'd buy all of us a couple rounds of bourbon. The two of you look done in. Go home. I'll keep you updated."

Virgil reached up and touched the brim of his hat in a salute.

Laura helped Mitch inside the truck and buckled his seatbelt. She held herself rigid as she drove toward the ranch. Mental exhaustion rode her hard. To break the silence, she said, "Discussion around the dinner table tonight will certainly be interesting."

Chapter Sixteen

The only sounds were the blood pulsing through his veins, its relentless roar inside his head, and the horse's footfalls against the hardened ground. With only the dim light of the moon peeking from behind puffy black clouds to guide him, the mountain's narrow trail grew steeper. He hunched forward to help the horse's leverage.

Foolish, he thought, trying to calm his racing heart. *Damned foolish.*

He was already doomed. There would be no forgiveness, no redemption from the contact he'd made with one of Hugo Vargas's capos. About to make a deal with the devil, the only thing that kept him from chickening out was the desire for vengeance that burned like a fire inside him.

The horse faltered up the steep incline. He dismounted and led the animal by the reins. The air thinned, and he sucked in a breath, blew it out slowly, and tried to calm his thoughts.

It's after midnight. Turn around. Go back to the ranch. No one will know. The air was cooler in the higher altitude. It wasn't the temperature that chilled him but the headlines, the detailed news story on the *Gazette*'s front page, and the gruesome pictures of a coiled rattler inside the forensics lab.

Practically out of breath from the climb, he was

relieved to reach Two Rock Peak. He leaned against a hard base of granite. In need of a smoke, he reached into his shirt pocket and removed a joint. Lighting it, he drew in deep, allowing the Mexican dirt weed to work its soothing magic.

What if someone asks where I've been? I can always say I couldn't sleep, and took a ride. Yeah, that's it. Lost in his dithering thoughts, the voice was so soft he almost didn't hear it.

"Ramirez de Ayala?"

His head snapped up. "Yeah."

A heavily accented voice spoke. "Anyone know you're here, *cholo*?"

He searched through the dark and saw no one. *Cholo*, a Chicano gang-banger. He didn't take offense. "No, I swear on my life."

A scrawny, bowlegged man sporting a goatee and wearing khaki cargo pants and a green shirt stepped forward. He held an AR-15 semi-automatic. "Bring the horse. You can follow me or ride in the mule." He pointed into the darkness. "Either way's no skin off my ass."

The moon moved from behind a cloud, making the snake tattooed on the man's neck visible. *Damn! There is no turning back now.*

Ayala tied the horse to the back of the ATV, and climbed in beside the goateed man. "How far?"

"You'll know when we get there."

"Where're you takin' me?"

No answer.

The ATV bumped over the uneven terrain. A half hour later, the vehicle stopped next to a black stretch limousine. Cattle bawled in the distance. They were on

Carter land. The driver motioned Ayala out. "Senor Vargas, he is inside. He is a busy man, so you no waste his time. *Comprende*?"

"Yeah, I understand."

Goatee man used a knuckle to rap on the window before he opened the limo's door. He motioned Ayala inside. A dim light lit the interior.

He'd heard Hugo Vargas was young. How could a kid have earned such a reputation of being the supreme capo of the Columbian cartel? He didn't look old enough to shave. Two things gave him the shivers: Vargas's piercing, callous eyes, for one, and the boa constrictor draped over Vargas's shoulder, for another. He stroked it much the way a lover might caress a woman.

"*Hablas español, hombre?*"

"*Si.*"

"*Bueno*."

The conversation proceeded in Spanish.

"What is it you want of me?"

"I work at the Carter Ranch, and—"

Vargas held up his hand. "Don't tell me things I already know. Get to the point."

Ayala took a moment to compose himself. "I want Laura Friday dead. Not just dead, I want her to suffer first."

Vargas steepled his fingers. "Ah, such hatred for the beautiful editor-in-chief of the *Gazette.* She wrote an interesting piece about me. I think my mother would like Señorita Friday. One can assume your need to request a vile act upon the woman has to do with your…brother?"

Ayala reached up to press the tic that had

developed under his left eye. How the hell did a young punk dressed in a thousand-dollar silk suit know about his brother? Hell, he even talked like an overly educated aristocrat. Maybe the rumor about his mother being a rich American really was true.

He felt sick to his stomach. "Yeah, sure. That's right."

"And what do I get in return for this deed?"

"I heard you wanted to expand into Noo Yawk. I can open a few doors for youse."

The boa slithered toward Ayala. He pressed against the plush leather seat. Vargas laughed at his fear. "Jazmin is as gentle as a puppy." He lifted the snake away.

Vargas's obsidian eyes glinted as he gave Ayala a sadistic smile. "Not good enough. In fact, you need me more than I need you." He handed a small box to Ayala. "I want to know what the sheriff and his Texas Ranger uncles know about Navarre Àron. I also want to know Mitch Carter's tactical decisions, and how much he knows about me. Plant the bugs, and next time we meet, I'll let you know my decision in regard to"—he cocked a perfectly manicured eyebrow, and a dimple flared in his baby-smooth cheek when he smiled—"my decision about the lovely Laura Friday."

Ayala simply nodded.

Hugo Vargas reached into a small refrigerator. He brought out a long-stemmed goblet and a bottle of Dom Pérignon and pulled the stopper. He poured a glass, and held it up to the light as if inspecting the liquid.

"Are you a coward, Señor Ayala?"

The question caught him by surprise. "Naw, not me."

Taking a sip of the champagne, Vargas said, "Pardon my not inviting you to share a glass. You see, from the tic under your eye, I believe you are a coward, and I don't drink with a candy-ass."

Vargas reached over and rapped on the window. Goatee man opened the door. Ayala knew he'd been dismissed, and he stepped out of the vehicle. His heart beat a tattoo against his chest.

Vargas spoke to goatee man. "*Ya sabes qué hacer si nuestro amigo me traiciona.*"

The dialect was different from Spanish Harlem, or Mexican, but the gist caused a chill to slither down Ayala's spine and settle in his bowels. "You know what to do if our friend betrays me." He shoved the box of spy bugs into his shirt pocket. Damn, he needed a toke of devil weed to calm his nerves.

Goatee man spoke to him in Spanish. He handed over the reins. Ayala said, "Thanks for nothing, pal. It's a two-hour ride back to the bunkhouse."

"Hey, hombre, don't even think about double-crossing Señor Vargas. It would be bad for your health. You could wake up with a diamondback in your bed."

Ayala's chest tightened to the point of physical pain. He swung into the saddle and touched a spur to the gelding's flank.

His emotions were still on overload when he arrived back at the ranch. He unsaddled his horse and turned it into the corral. Not wanting to answer a bunch of questions about where he'd been, he decided not to take a chance on awakening any of the sleeping ranch hands. Instead, he bedded down in one of the empty stalls. He set his phone to alarm an hour before Rob Carter, the barn boss, would arrive.

****

The alarm startled him out of a bad dream. It took a moment for him to remember why he had spent the night in a horse stall. He pulled his boots on, brushed straw off his clothes and out of his hair, then headed for the bathroom at the end of the barn. After relieving his bladder, he splashed water over his face. In fact, he stuck his head under the faucet and let the water cool his brain. Racking the dripping water from his hair, he looked in the mirror. The reflection scowling back at him was a man with dark circles under his eyes. Worry circles is what his aunt would call them. Yeah, he was worried, all right. He'd stepped neck deep into shit, and it was all his own doing. How the hell was he supposed to sneak into the main house and install spy bugs? He spoke to the face staring back at him. "Revenge isn't as easy as I thought it'd be."

Part of him wanted to hitch a ride into town, clean out his savings account, and buy a plane ticket to parts unknown. Forget Laura Friday, and, most of all, forget Hugo Vargas. He'd changed his name once and could change it again. Maybe he'd get a passport and disappear to some obscure little country no one had ever heard of. Yeah, that's what he'd do. Except, memory reminded him, between his checking and savings he didn't have enough money for plane fare, much less enough to apply for a passport. Damn…damn! The big cartels were ruthless, and they never let anyone renege on a deal, not to live and tell about it.

He walked out of the barn. The sky was clear and promising another Texas scorcher. The light in the dining room shone bright in the dawn light. A few of the hands were filtering out of the bunkhouse. The one nicknamed Porky called out, "Man, you trying to earn points with the boss by mucking out the stalls before the sun's up?"

Porky was the opposite of fat. In fact, if a good wind were to kick up it'd blow him away. Hollis Kent had an appetite that surpassed every hand on the ranch, but he never gained weight.

"Naw, couldn't sleep. Instead of tossing and turning, I decided to get a head start on today's chores."

Porky sidled up to him, and whispered, "Maybe we can get a little fishin' in. Heard Travis say him and Wyatt and ole man Sorrenson are driving over to Odessa to look at a couple of seed bulls. Miss Laura is driving her aunt and Mitch in for doctor appointments, and Jill has some kinda thing at the school for the twins." He clapped his hands together. "Hot damn, a little goofin' off will sure feel good. Whatta you say…you in?"

He thought for a minute. This was good news. The house would be empty. Perfect! "Not this time. I've already been put on warning once, for that fight I got into. Can't afford to lose my job."

Porky tucked his thumbs under his armpits and flapped his elbows up and down like a chicken flapping its wings. "Bak…bak…baaak."

This was the second time he'd been accused of cowardice. He wanted to put his fist in the cowboy's face. "Shut your hole, Porky, or you'll be eating your teeth instead of bacon."

"Aw, shucks. I'm just joshin'. Who put a burr under your saddle?"

Naw, he didn't have a burr under his saddle; it was

firmly stuck in the crack of his ass. He ignored the question and picked up his pace to enter the dining room.

A chuckle followed after him. He wasn't aware of the fiery brown eyes that watched him stride across the yard.

Chapter Seventeen

Tension ate at Frankie as he kept a close eye on the main house. Travis and Wyatt had pulled out shortly after seven a.m. Jill left with the twins thirty minutes later.

He cooked a large pot of colostrum for the calves whose mamas had rejected them, loaded the bottles, and set the bottles in the holders for the calves to suckle the liquefied powdery milk. Afterwards, he soaped all the saddles and then oiled them. He repaired harness while he waited and waited for Laura to drive her aunt and Mitch to town. Maybe a bigwig at a newspaper could set her own work hours. The more he thought about Laura, the more he hated her for what she'd done to his baby brother.

Finally, Mitch's truck pulled away from the house and rolled down the driveway. Frankie watched until it was out of sight. A glance at his watch revealed it was one o'clock. He left the barn and walked to the back entrance of the house. He didn't worry about it being locked. The Carters never locked the doors unless they planned to leave for several days.

He decided to plant a bug in Mitch's room first. He attached the device to the bottom of a lamp next to the bed. Next he moved to Laura's room and did the same thing there. He stopped long enough to pick up the large T-shirt that lay folded on top of her pillow and placed it to his nose. He inhaled deeply, drawing in her feminine scent. An ache grew between his legs, and he groaned. Maybe he'd give her a taste of his own form of torture before Vargas got to her. Shaking free of his thoughts, he hurried downstairs. Inside the great room, he turned in circles trying to decide the best places to hide the tiny listening devices. Then, his choices made, he moved into the dining room. Yeah, he was pleased with himself for thinking of the dining room, where lots of business was discussed. That done, he reached into the little box. One last device. Where to put it? Ah, he thought. Wyatt's office. He knew for a fact that Mitch and Wyatt often holed up in there when they wanted to talk in private.

Smug with satisfaction, and quite comfortable with being inside the house, he forgot he was on a covert mission. Just as he stepped through the front doors and onto the veranda, Jill's stern voice startled him. "Frankie, what are you doing inside the house?"

He blinked rapidly. *Oh hell! Shit!*

"I, ah, I needed to talk to Travis about…about, well, when I seen no one was home, I…"

"You know the rules, Frankie. When we're not home, the inside of the house is off limits. We trust all of our ranch workers to honor this policy." She fisted her hands against her hips. "Besides, you could've just as easily talked to Rob."

Frankie reached up and scratched his head. "I'm really sorry, Miss Jill. Didn't mean no harm." He sidled past her. "Won't let it happen again." He crossed his heart. "Excuse me. I'll talk to Travis later."

He ran down the steps as if someone had lit a fire under his boots.

****

Later that evening, the conversation around the dinner table was lively. Virgil Carter had surprised the family with a visit. "I'll tell you one thing." He pointed his fork toward Laura. "This young lady earned my respect yesterday. She kept her cool. Her only weapon was a camera, and damn if she didn't put it to good use." His compliment also extended to the article she had written and the pictures she had posted on the *Gazette*'s front page about the snake incident.

Mitch chuckled. "It wasn't funny when it was happening, but the look on Doc Mercado's face when that rattler exploded out of the cadaver's mouth is something we can laugh about now. It'll be the story of the decade."

Wyatt laughed into his napkin. "I would've messed my britches right then and there, and that's a fact." He held his coffee cup out for a refill. "I can tell you one thing, it's a mighty sick mind that can think up such as that." He cut a stern eye to his twin grandsons. His voice equally as stern. "Knowin' how you boys like snakes, don't either of you go gettin' any ideas."

Travis also looked at his twin sons. "You mind what your grandpa says. Otherwise, you'll never forget the punishment you'll receive."

Laura liked this family. She liked the way they respected each other's opinion even if they didn't always agree. She liked the genuine love they had for each other, and the way the family nurtured the grandchildren. This type of relationship was new to her, an only child with no close family, and very unlike her own childhood. Her emotions were at war as she listened and observed. One part of her desired this type of affection and camaraderie. Another part was scared to death to receive it.

Wyatt spoke up again. "Phyllis, as a cattle rancher, I'm a steak man." He scooped another spoonful of goodness into his mouth and spoke between chews. "But this here lobster pot pie is mighty tasty."

Jill agreed. "Thanks for supervising, Phyllis. Since it's passed Dad's taste bud test, I'll add it to my recipe box."

Her aunt's mood had been subdued ever since she'd received a letter and read it in private. This worried Laura. She appreciated the compliments that brought a flush and a smile to Phyllis's face.

Phyllis said, "Mitch, I had a letter from Maudine Perry today. She said to give you her best regards. Cole Hahbah is slowly being rebuilt. Maudie and the Historical Society are making sure the contractors abide by the plan Laura had laid out to keep all new construction authentic to the period each building was originally erected." She reached over and patted Laura on the arm. "I'm proud of my multitalented niece."

The round of applause and the gleam in Mitch's eye warmed Laura and helped lighten her own mood.

"That's not all Maudie had to say." Phyllis made a point of looking at Mitch. "You remember Cold Hahbah's sheriff, Roberta Gilman? Well, it seems her new husband has transferred to the B.A.U. as a field instructor."

Mitch raised his eyebrows as if the topic interested him. He answered the questioning expressions that had shifted toward Phyllis. "BAU is Behavioral Analysis Unit, located in Quantico, Virginia. It's a division of the FBI that uses behavioral science to figure out the profile of murderers. It's especially helpful in serial killings."

"And that's not all," Phyllis continued. "According to Maudie, Roberta submitted her resignation with plans to join her husband, but agreed to stay until the town council finds a suitable replacement."

Phyllis reached under the table and squeezed Laura's arm. Laura flinched at the unexpected touch. She looked at Mitch, who still wore a sling to support his arm.

The conversation had died. It was as if the quiet was waiting for someone to break the silence.

Jill stood and said, "Dad, Claire made your favorite, divinity fudge. It's from Mom's recipe."

Virgil coughed several times as if trying to dislodge an object from his throat. He, like everyone at the table, stared at his nephew.

Laura's stomach clenched. She knew her aunt's pronouncement at the dinner table was deliberate.

Kit said, "Uncle Mitch, did you do somethin' bad?"

Carson also said, "Yeah, when we do somethin' bad, everybody stares at us, too."

Laura felt like kissing the twins. Their honest questions seemed to penetrate the thick fog of expectation from Mitch.

Pain flickered across his face when he shifted the weight of his arm. "No, boys, I'm not in any trouble." Mitch used his good hand to pluck three divinity balls from the platter Jill placed in front of him. He held one of the confections and seemed to study it. "I'm sure the town council will do a good job of choosing a replacement for Roberta. Though I don't envy the new sheriff having to inherit Louise Highland for a secretary."

Phyllis and Laura chortled at the scowl on Mitch's face. Phyllis selected a piece of fudge. "That's the best part, Mitch. Louise retired, sold her cottage, and booked a trip with some university archeological group to dig for bones in Egypt."

Mitch shifted an irritable glance toward Laura. "Texas suits me just fine." He pushed from the table. "Virgil, if there're any breaks in the case of our two victims, keep me posted." He said goodnight and left the dining room.

His departure seemed to signal that mealtime was over. Virgil and Wyatt grabbed fresh cups of coffee, a couple more pieces of divinity fudge each, and ambled toward Wyatt's office. Laura helped clear the table, and after the dishes were loaded into the dishwasher and the kitchen cleaned, she said her own goodnights and went up the stairs to her room. Phyllis sat on the bed with a book. Laura didn't know whether to chastise her aunt or kiss her on the cheek.

"Did you deliberately mention Sheriff Gilman's resignation for Mitch's benefit?"

"Was it that obvious?"

Laura nodded and sighed. "He made his position clear. Texas is his home, Aunt Philly. His family is here. He will never again leave. When he was a deputy in Cole Harbor, he was a fish out of water…or maybe a cowboy without a horse. He did his job quite well, the citizens admired him, but he wasn't happy."

"Ayuh, true. What about you? Have you given thought to our previous conversation?"

Laura slid out of her slacks and pulled the blouse

over her head. “I have, and I’m at war with myself.” She grabbed the large T-shirt. “What about you, Aunt Philly? What are your plans?”

“My plans have nothing to do with you and Mitch.”

“I disagree. When we played that silly game, you said if you could buy one frivolous thing, you’d rebuild the bookstore and buy a cottage on Lighthouse Road. I saw the look on your face. You want to go home, don’t you, Aunt Philly.”

Emotions played across the older woman’s face. “Like I’ve said, Wyatt is a nice man, a real gentleman. It would take years for our acquaintance to grow into a deepah friendship, and at our ages neither of us has years.” She shrugged and extended her hands in a gesture of uncertainty. “Truthfully, El Paso isn’t exactly growing on me. The heat sucks the air out of my lungs, and the land is more brown than green. I understand about crime, but here with all that’s happened recently with headless bodies and poisonous snakes being sewn inside victim’s mouths, it makes me afraid.

“Plus, El Paso is overcrowded, and vast, and except for the people who work on this ranch, no one is friendly. It’s too far to ride my bicycle or walk to town. And look at this house, Laura. By Godfrey, it’s a memorial to generations of Carters, and I respect that. Where would I put my mark on it? I couldn’t.

“Do I want to leave? Ayuh. Do I want to return to New York? No.” She handed Maudie’s letter to Laura.

Laura’s eyes went to the sentence underlined in red. She skimmed over the words, then went back and reread them. She looked at her aunt. “The Buxton cottage… Is that the one with the wraparound porch, that sits on the point overlooking the bay?"

Phyllis nodded.

"But it's not on Lighthouse Road."

"Doesn't matter. It's a short bicycle ride into town, and a lovely, well-kept house, high enough to survive the winds from a nor'eastah, and there's a little beach just right for a morning swim. I called the realtor as soon as I read the letter, and made an offer. It was accepted."

"I—I don't know what to say. You're a grown woman with a mind of your own, of course. I just wish you'd told me before you made an offer."

"Laura, this has nothing to do with you and everything to do with me. I'm not asking nor do I expect you to choose between the editor-in-chief position, or Mitch, or even returning to New York. If you'd open your heart and let him in, the two of you could have a wonderful life here. Besides, I'll always have room for you and the entire Carter clan, should they ever decide to venture outside of Texas. I hope you know I didn't make my decision to upset you."

"How soon do you plan to leave?"

Phyllis tapped the cast on her arm. "As soon as this comes off, about four more weeks."

"What about physical therapy?"

"Don't worry yourself about that. I'll get plenty of exercise working to keep the gardens at the Buxton cottage beautiful. Which, by the way, I'm renaming as the Friday cottage."

Laura nodded and went into the bathroom. She turned the hot and cold taps on and stepped inside the shower. Her aunt's unexpected announcement left her awash in a sea of emotions.

Chapter Eighteen

Stephen Radcliff sprawled on the oversized brocade sofa in the oversized French Colonial mansion overlooking the Potomac River. The house smelled of take-out pizza and expensive perfume.

He wore tennis clothes and so did his mother, a stunning long-legged blonde with blue-green eyes. Other than the obvious chromosomes, the comparison ended there.

Senator Clarence Radcliff glared at his grandson as if Oedipus had materialized. He had many regrets in life. Stephen's father was one of them. Icy fingers of dread chilled the senator. He knew intuitively his grandson was as cruel and intellectually devious as the devil who had spawned him.

Stefano Hugo Vargas De la Paz, Jr., the son of a wealthy and powerful drug lord in Columbia, had swept into Lisa Radcliff's life like a storm. Both had been students at Caltech, Hugo majoring in engineering and Lisa in the fine art of finding a wealthy husband. Foregoing the approval of their parents, Hugo and Lisa had decided to keep their marriage a secret. Hugo graduated with a degree in chemical engineering. A brilliant mind wasted on the production of synthetic drugs. Highly addictive drugs. Drugs that killed people. Lisa dropped out of school the moment she discovered she was pregnant and followed her husband to

Columbia, South America.

Like the story of the Hatfields and the McCoys, the feud between Hugo Vargas, Sr. and his first cousin, Navarre Àron, escalated over a span of three decades.

What started as a small cocaine smuggling business had, over the years, blossomed into an enormous multi-national cocaine empire, with the elder Àron expanding the operation into Mexico. Vargas and Àron respected one another as family until Vargas brought in his son, Hugo, Jr., an expert in chemical engineering, who convinced his father and Àron they could fly cocaine in small airplanes directly into the United States, avoiding the need for countless suitcase trips.

But the success had a darker side. Stefano Vargas was incredibly violent, and his quest for power within the Colombian government led to a standoff between the cartel and the government, with Hugo, Jr. caught in the crossfire and dead before his fortieth birthday.

As the cartel began to self-destruct and the violence escalated, Hugo, Sr. had sent his grandson and daughter-in-law to Washington, D.C. to live with the esteemed Senator Clarence Radcliff.

As much as Radcliff had tried to influence meritorious and moral decency in his grandson, the fact remained that the sixteen years the young man had spent with his paternal grandfather had the greater influence. The boy had inherited his father's genius and suave good looks. Like his mother, Stephen was overly indulged. There was where the similarity ended. As much as Radcliff hated to admit it, he was certain his grandson teetered on sadistic lunacy.

Senator Radcliff slammed the *D.C. Times* onto the coffee table. "Unbelievable. I am no longer buying this fabrication that you are *not* the Hugo Vargas involved in these brutal acts of violence. Re-election is coming up, and I have a reputation to maintain. After all, I do chair the senate committee on Homeland Security. It is my money and influence that's kept you out of trouble ever since de la Paz sent you here to be educated. Kicked out of one good school after another, and for what? It was money wasted, that's for what. Twenty-three years old and never worked a day in your life! If it weren't for your mother, I would have sent you packing a long time ago." His face mottled with anger, the senator pointed a finger toward his grandson. "I'm warning you, Stephen. Garrett Carter is attached to Homeland Security. He's no one to mess around with. If he and his Texas Ranger brothers prove you and Hugo Vargas are one and the same, it will ruin me. As for you, with your pretty-boy looks, you wouldn't last a day in prison."

Lisa mewled, "Popsie, calm down. I'm afraid you'll have a stroke. There is no connection between my Stevie"—she picked up the paper and then tossed it back to the table—"and this criminal, Hugo Vargas. How can you even think such a horrible thing? Isn't that why we legally changed Stephen's name, so there would be no connection to his father's family? Perhaps this is a distant relative of Stefano's father in Columbia."

A tear squeezed from the corner of her eye. She sniffed. "Your father was a good man. A genius. He died too young."

Stephen Radcliff aimed venomous eyes at the elderly man who glared at him. "Careful, Grandfather. Making threats is bad for one's health."

He reached into the pocket of his crisp white shorts to answer the whirring vibration of his cell phone. Looking at the ID, he excused himself.

One hundred and sixty-eight seconds later, he returned and kissed his mother on the cheek. He offered his grandfather an arrogant lift of the eyebrow. “Don’t worry about your precious political reputation, Grandfather. I’m bored with D.C. and need a change of scenery.”

Lisa Radcliff’s breath caught, as if snagged on barbwire. “Again, so soon? You’ve only just arrived, and I’d looked forward to you escorting me to the welcome home party the Vice President is holding for his daughter. For the life of me I don’t understand why any young woman would want to join the Air Force. She’s a fighter pilot, you know. Oh, please, Stevie, darling, won’t you change your mind?”

“Not this time, Mother. Besides, whatever would she and I talk about? I have no interest in airplanes, and I’m certain she has no interest in herpetology.”

The senator glared. “I hope you’re taking that reptile with you. I can’t understand your fascination with snakes.”

Stephen Radcliff smiled, an undertone of threat lacing his voice as he commented, “There’s a lot you don’t know about me, Grandfather.”

He kissed his mother on the cheek. “To make up for not taking you to the party, I’ll book us a villa in Barcelona. Will that earn your forgiveness?”

Lisa sighed. She laid her hand against the side of her son’s face. “So much like your father. Handsome, and could talk me into anything. I already forgive you.”

Disgusted by the syrupy display, the senator strode

from the room, relieved his grandson was leaving and a little fearful of the boy's implied threat.

****

Mitch stood on the balcony that overlooked the pool. Laura floated on her back with her eyes closed and her arms spread wide. She seemed completely relaxed. He wondered what she was thinking.

He studied her with interest. Her short blonde hair reminded him of a curtain of gold. Beneath the dark lashes, he knew, were eyes the color of Texas bluebonnets, eyes that mesmerized him. He smiled idly at the picture she made in her modest purple bathing suit. His eyes drifted to the long scar that marred the perfection of her leg. A forever reminder of the day she was shot by a drug pusher, the day she almost died.

As if she sensed his presence, she stared up at him. He stared back with an odd sensation rippling through his body. He met her eyes, and for a moment all thoughts of headless corpses and cadavers with their mouths sewn shut disappeared for a matter of seconds.

"You're staring. Have I grown a third eye in the center of my forehead?"

"I was thinking that purple is a nice color on you." Silently, he mused that she'd be shocked to know what he was really thinking.

Laura lowered her feet and stood, the water coming to her chin. She moved her hands back and forth, swirling the water. "Thanks. I think."

He found himself tongue-tied and wanting to say things to her that he couldn't seem to find the words to tell her.

Silence again.

"Why don't you come down and join me? I know

you still can't get into the pool, but you could hang out with me."

"Sure. Give me a sec."

By the time he'd taken the stairs more energetically than he felt, he managed to make it to one of the pool chairs and sit until his head stopped spinning. He really did feel his age, and he wasn't healing as fast as he'd hoped. He continued to ask the physical therapist questions, and she would give him an insipid smile with the reassurance that he was making progress.

Some progress, he thought. At this rate, it'd be next year before he could go up and down the stairs without danger of passing out. He sighed heavily. A sharp pain jabbed his shoulder as he slumped into the chair. Front and back, his body was a mass of scars. Would Laura find his physique repulsive?

Thinking of soaking up some sun, and watching Laura's reaction, he tried to pull the T-shirt over his head. The wrenching pain stopped him. He worried about his lack of progress with mobility. As he leaned against the chair's cushioned back and closed his eyes, he made a mental note to discuss this with Sam.

****

Laura walked up the pool steps and grabbed a towel. She wasn't encouraged by the pallor on Mitch's face. The dark circles beneath his eyes heightened the pale, drawn look, and this worried her.

He sighed. "Mind lending a hand? I'm having a little problem lifting my arm to get my shirt off. Maybe a little fresh air and sunshine will help speed the healing process."

Laura toweled off. She leaned forward to gently roll the hunter green shirt with the El Paso Sheriff's

Department logo up Mitch's torso. She hadn't meant to gasp as she glanced at his chest and winced. Through the blond hairs that matted his well-muscled chest was a seamed scar. Under his arm was a matching red area where a tube to drain his lungs had been inserted during surgery.

Although the wound was healing, the unpleasant sight caused her to clamp her lip as the hot blush wended its way to the pit of her stomach.

"Dammit." He grabbed the towel she'd draped over the arm of his chair and covered his chest.

She sobered at once. The anger on his face was evident. "I'm sorry. It's just…I mean…" No matter what she said, the apology would sound lame. "I should have remembered how my leg looked when it was healing."

"Disgusting, huh?"

"I'm sorry, Mitch, really, I am."

He rubbed his hand along the heavy thatch of hair. "No, it's me who needs to apologize. I shouldn't have let my temper fire off like that."

Her blue eyes met his. He rolled his shoulder. "I guess I'm more self-conscious than I thought."

She flushed as she stared at the broad muscled chest and the mat of blond hair. "I suppose we're both a bit self-conscious. I'm not used to seeing half-dressed men."

He smiled and cocked an eyebrow. "The sun feels good."

"Uh-huh." She leaned in for a closer look at the wound. "I'm no doctor, but is it normal to still look that red?"

Mitch glanced down at his chest. "I was thinking

the same thing. I need to talk to Sam. I'm not healing as fast as I thought I would."

He drew in a breath. His skin prickled with goosebumps.

She watched the color drain from his tanned complexion. His eyes seemed to cloud before he closed them. "Mitch, what is it? Can I get you something?"

"Feeling weak as a newborn foal." He wobbled when he attempted to stand.

Laura put her arm around his waist to support him. "Let me help you to your room."

The nearness of him caused her heart to vibrate in her chest. She was tall, but the top of her head barely came to his chin, and she felt his breath flutter the hair on the top of her head. She struggled under his weight. His labored breathing while climbing the stairs to his bedroom worried her.

Inside the room, her hands involuntarily pressed against his chest. She leaned in against him. He sucked in a breath. She stepped back. "Oh, sorry. I did it again—hurt you—didn't I."

Large calloused hands captured both sides of her cheeks, tilting her face upward. "You have lovely lips."

"I-I do?"

His mouth hovered slightly above hers. She could taste his breath, feel the growing heat of his muscular body as they pressed closer together. The only sound as they stood next to Mitch's bed was the rhythm of her heart pulsating inside her ears.

"You're shivering. Are you cold?"

"Yes…no," she managed.

She closed her eyes and tried to conjure Bryan's image. It didn't come. Realization wafted over her. She was right where she'd wanted to be the first time Mitch had walked into the newspaper office in Cole Harbor. The emotion curling through her was not infatuation. No, it ran much deeper.

Mitch's mouth brushed lightly, ever so lightly, against her waiting lips. Her half-closed eyes riveted on his, she waited until his mouth crushed down on hers.

Without thinking, she wrapped her arms around him. He gathered her up so that her breasts flattened against his chest.

He groaned, and lifted his head. "Damn…this shoulder."

She looked into his eyes and hung there in suspended emotions. "M-my fault. Can I get you a pain pill?"

His hands slid up and down her long slender body. "No pain pill."

She delighted in the warmth and strength of him. He bent and kissed her again. This time with less restraint, and more hunger. So lost was she in the richness of his mouth savoring hers, she didn't protest when his hands found her hips and thrust them against the contours of his body. He groaned, and so did she.

A long-suppressed hunger rose inside her as her tongue danced with his. "Mitch?" She groaned against his mouth.

His voice rasped. "Shh. Don't fight it."

She wanted to keep kissing him. Passion acted as a powerful drug subduing her, causing her to cling to Mitch, to forget her scruples, to plead for him to lock the door, strip off every piece of her clothing, and whisk her into his bed.

Her body ached, craved emotional release.

From beyond the bedroom walls, Jill called, "Mitch?"

Like two teenagers caught in an illicit act, they broke apart at the sound and stood staring at each other in complete shock.

Jill called louder. "Mitch, Uncle Virgil just drove up."

"Yeah, okay."

Laura stared up at Mitch. She didn't know whether to be sad or happy about the interruption. "I'd better go."

She turned, hesitated, then turned back. "No regrets, Mitch. None."

He caressed the side of her cheek with his thumb. "I'm glad."

She tried to swallow the smile that had pasted itself to her face. This was not a secret she wanted to share with anyone.

Chapter Nineteen

The emotions involved in the kiss had promised to get out of control. Mitch was aching from head to toe, and not just from his injured shoulder. Licking his lips to savor the taste Laura had left on them, he looked down at the pulsating throb and groaned. His body was proclaiming its secrets to anyone with eyes.

There was an intimacy now between him and Laura. It was exciting and new, and he felt a fierce possessiveness for her.

Clad in pajamas, he was propped on the bed when his sister entered the bedroom, her uncle in tow. Mitch greeted them with a nod and a smile. She carried a tray. “Shame on you, getting rambunctious.”

Certain his body had once again betrayed him, Mitch grabbed a pillow and draped it across his lap, and was much relieved when his sister chided, “Actually, you don’t deserve cookies and coffee. Laura said you’d almost fainted, and she told me about the red puffiness surrounding the injury. I’ve already called Sam.”

Mitch looked at Virgil and rolled his eyes. Virgil merely smirked.

“I appreciate your concern, Sis.” Mitch looped his fingers through the handle of the cup and took a sip of coffee. It was then he noticed his uncle’s jaw tightening, the lines on his face deepening.

Jill stopped at the door and stared over her

shoulder, frowning at her uncle. "Do you have any idea who shot Mitch?"

"We're working on it, Jill. I promise we'll catch the scumbag."

She arched a brow at the depth of certainty in Virgil's voice. "I have to ask, and not out of curiosity but concern… Do you think the family is in any danger?"

Mitch exchanged looks with his uncle. Virgil shook his head. "Not likely. I say that because the shooter chose the rodeo, where he could remain anonymous. Whereas at the ranch, he'd risk being seen and even caught. Rest easy, Jill."

Mitch voiced his own concern. "What about Laura?"

Virgil set the coffee cup aside and sat up a little straighter, crossing one leg over his knee. "I don't know. We're taking every precaution, though."

The grit in Mitch's voice was unmistakable. "I don't intend to let anything happen to her."

"By the expression on your face, I guess it's time to excuse myself. Hope you're staying for supper, Virgil," Jill invited. "Got your favorite venison pot pie."

The Ranger winked at his niece. "Wild horses couldn't drag me away."

"Good. One hour." She added, "Bring the tray."

As soon as the door closed, his uncle said, "Just like your mother—bossy as hell." His smile reflected the affection he'd held for his deceased sister-in-law. "We have positive IDs on our two latest victims."

Mitch sat very still against his pillows. "Yeah, and?"

Virgil cleared his throat. "As messed up as his face was, fingerprints prove snake boy is who we thought—Matias Àron. Now, for our headless vic, forensics extracted semen and ran the sample through the DNA database. Got a ninety-nine percent hit that matched DNA from a pending rape case. Fabio Vargas Escobar."

Mitch used his good hand to rifle through hair in need of clipping. He blew out a low whistle. "Refresh my memory. Aren't these two families connected?"

"Yeah. Hugo Vargas, Sr., and Navarre Àron are cousins. Their mothers were sisters."

Mitch brushed cookie crumbs from his shirt. "That makes Escobar the nephew of both Vargas and Àron." He arched a brow. "Damn, what's going on, Virgil? Do we have a third party trying to horn in on territory by bumping off family members from two of the most powerful drug cartels?"

Virgil's fingers thrummed against his knee. "Maybe. Another possibility is these are vengeance killings within the family. The question is which family member or capo has the balls to take out both Navarre Àron's youngest brother, and the nephew of Vargas, Sr.?"

Mitch's eyebrows knitted into a frown. "The bigger question is what does this have to do with who shot me, and why? Is there a connection?"

"Don't forget, it was you who took down the senior Àron's brother. These cartels seem to take the 'eye for an eye' theory seriously."

Kit raced into the bedroom without knocking on the door, with Carson right behind him. "Mama says ten minutes to supper." The six-year-old scrunched up his freckled face. "Are you wearing your jammies to eat in, Uncle Mitch?"

Carson lamented, "No jammies allowed at the table even when you're sick."

Mitch smiled at his nephews. "Who made that rule?"

The twins chorused together, "Mama. She said if we can't wear regular clothes to the table, then we're too sick, and we have to stay in bed."

Mitch swung his legs over the side of the bed. "Well, fellas, I reckon I'll put on my regular clothes. Now scoot." He looked at his uncle. "'Preciate it if you'd help me pull this shirt over my head."

Once the shirt was off, Virgil grimaced at the angry red area. "Your shoulder looks mighty festered. If Sam doesn't get out here tomorrow, you'd better go to his office."

"Hurts like the dickens, too." Mitch suppressed a yelp when he lifted his arm. "Until it quits hurting, I'm sticking with buttoned shirts. Still don't have the strength to pull on my boots."

"Healing takes time, that's for dang sure."

The two men walked down the stairs and took their places at the dining table. After Wyatt graced the food, conversation began, first with asking the twins about their day at school. Then Travis and Rob gave updates on the new calves, the price of feed, and settling disgruntlements among a couple of the ranch hands.

After Jill excused herself to ready the twins for bed, Virgil said, "Travis, you and Rob notice any unusual activities on the outer ranges?"

The men looked at each other and shrugged. Travis seemed to weigh the question before he asked, "Anything going on we should know about?"

Mitch also sat a little straighter in his chair.

Virgil glanced around the table. “Mitch, ever since you came home from the hospital, I’ve had a mole on the ranch.” He held up his hand to signal no questions. “I talked it over with Morgan, and we both agreed the best way to keep tabs on you and the family was to place a man on the inside.”

This revelation brought raised eyebrows from everyone at the table. “I reckon it’ll be easy to figure out who he is.” Wyatt looked at his brother, then at Travis. “You hire any new men lately?”

“No, sir. Last man we hired was over a year ago.”

Virgil lifted an eyebrow, his expression serious. “I’m advising you to keep this confidential. Poking around and asking the ranch hands questions could blow his cover. I’ll not have the life of one of my agents compromised.”

Mitch shot his uncle a dry look. “There’s more to this than you’re telling. No sense keeping us in suspense.”

Virgil glanced around and then over his shoulder as if looking for an intruder. “A couple of nights before you were shot, our mole reported seeing a flash of light over toward the mountain range. Then a few nights ago, he reported movement in the same locale. Not wanting to risk discovery, he waited till morning to check it out. Sure enough, there were tire marks from two different vehicles, and hoof prints. He followed the tire marks, which led back to the highway. Thing is, the hoof prints led straight to the ranch.”

Up to now, Laura had sat quietly. “I saw it, too, that flash.” She went on to explain about standing on the balcony and seeing a glimpse of light off in the distance, and then an answering flash.

Mitch beat his uncle to the question. "Why didn't you say something?"

She shot him an impatient glance. "Because it was my first night on the ranch. Because I wasn't sure if it was something like St. Elmo's fire or some other natural phenomenon. Because it could have been my imagination. And when it didn't happen again, I didn't think it important."

Wyatt said, "Buck isn't for certain, but he thinks some of his cattle are being rustled. He's had tire tracks on his land, too." He slammed his hand down on the table so hard everyone jumped. "I'd like to think them horse tracks were made by one of the hands who needed to ride off insomnia. But if I find out he's setting this ranch up for cattle thieving, I'll personally peel the hide off'n him." He cast another look at his brother. "You got any idea who this lone rider was?"

"Nope, and neither does my man. When he knows, you'll know. In the meantime, keep a sharp eye, and keep your weapons loaded."

Unaware of the small transmitters hidden in inconspicuous places, and unaware of the dangerous eavesdropper miles away, more conversation filtered around the table.

Virgil's cell phone vibrated. He pulled it from the clip at his waist and looked at the red alert band streaming across the screen. He punched the button, lifted the phone to his ear with a brief, "Carter," and listened for a moment before exploding with, "Damn! ...When?...You know what to do...Yeah, I'm on my way."

His voice was tight with emotion. "Damn fuckers

killed one of my agents. This is the part of my job I dislike the most. I hate having to break the news to his wife. She's pregnant."

A loud knock sounded at the front door. Travis opened it to find Frankie Romeo on the porch holding a large box. "Pardon the intrusion. A UPS guy dropped this off a few minutes ago. Said he was running behind on his route and could I bring it to the house."

Travis took the box and thanked Frankie. He returned to the dining room and handed the package to Mitch. "Has your name on it. You order a new hat to replace the one the bull tromped on?"

Mitch shrugged. He looked at the label. "Odd, there's no company name or address." He grinned. "Come to think of it, I do need to replace that hat." He struggled with the knife. "I'm a bit awkward with my right hand, Rob. Mind opening it for me?"

His brother complied, and then pulled back the flaps. His eyes widened as he jumped back.

Mitch stood with such force he knocked over his chair. "What the hell! If this is a joke, I'm not laughing."

Laura touched her hands against her cheeks and screamed. Phyllis rose to place her arms around her niece. "What is it? What's inside the box?"

Travis ran out the door and snagged Frankie by the arm to nearly drag him inside the house. "Whaa…what'd I do?"

Mitch practically yelled the question, "Are you certain a UPS driver delivered the box? Did you see the truck?"

"Well, it was brown, and the guy was dressed in brown. I didn't pay no particular attention, you know."

Frankie looked inside the box. "Oh, shit! Is it alive?" He practically body-slammed the wall trying to get away from the snake.

Mitch reached inside the box and lifted the coiled but dead rattler. To his surprise, the creature's body undulated and the tail gave a sluggish rattle. "Oh, hell." He dumped the lethargic reptile inside the box and slammed the flaps over the box. "Rob…Travis…take this thing outside and kill it."

Wyatt stood with his revolver ready. "Must be sick or drugged. Don't think I've ever seen a rattler that slow-moving, except mebbe in the winter."

Mitch agreed with his father. "Why would Vargas send me this kind of message? Until now, my department didn't have a beef with him."

Virgil spoke through his teeth. "Quinton Meadows didn't deserve to die, and I sure as hell hope those sick bastards didn't sew a rattler inside his mouth. If this gang wants to act like rabid wolves, then we'll treat 'em as such. No mercy!"

He yelled for his nephews to return the carton. "I'll have the lab dust it for prints. Mitch, call Morgan. Fill him in. No more pussy-footin' around. If Vargas wants war, I'll give him hell."

****

A malicious snarl formed on Hugo Vargas's lips as he listened to the spy bug activated by the Carter family's dinner conversation. He lifted the boa draped over his shoulder and placed it inside the glass container. He slammed his fist against the wall and in Spanish spewed a string of cuss words. "Jose, I did not order a hit on the Ranger, nor did I order the package sent to the Carters. Only one of my cousins would do such a thing, to save his sorry ass while pointing the finger at me."

Vargas paced around the room. His ebony eyes narrowed. "Get in touch with that bastard Frankie Ayala or whatever the hell he calls himself. If he wants me to take care of the woman, he'll need to do more than plant bugs in a house."

Goatee man said, "Ayala is a coward, *jefe*. I seen it in his eyes. I say we get rid of him before he rats us out."

"Yeah, he comes on like a human Rottweiler when he's really a turtle who will hide in his shell when trouble comes." Hugo's cell phone beeped, and he answered, his voice a falsetto of cheeriness. "*Hola? Bien, abuelo*." After he greeted his grandfather and inquired about the old man's health, Hugo listened. "It is true, Matias is dead, and before you ask, not I nor one of my capos killed him. Someone is copying my signature by sewing a rattler in my cousin's mouth." He pressed the phone to his ear. His breathing deepened as he listened to the terse but wheezing voice.

"No, Grandfather, I swear on Grandmother Elena's grave, I did not kill Matias." A strange smile tangoed across Hugo's face. What harm was the lie? Let the old man die in peace. A little help from his grandfather's nurse and the vial of venom she would inject into his IV, and as Hugo Vargas' only heir, Stefano Hugo Vargas de la Paz, III, would inherit the title of *el lìder supremo* and control of the Columbian cartel. And then there was the sweet and innocent Mariposa Benitez, daughter of Columbia's *el Presidente*. Once he proposed marriage, and then she produced a son, with this power he would annihilate his uncle, Navarre Àron, take over all of Mexico, and march through the U.S. and into Canada. He would be king.

Hugo's euphoria crashed when he remembered that someone had sent a sedated rattlesnake to Sheriff Mitchell Carter.

Who, besides his uncle, was his enemy? An image of Senator Clarence Radcliff flitted through Hugo's mind. He dismissed the thought as quickly as it appeared. His maternal grandfather didn't have the balls, even if he weren't definitely afraid of snakes.

Chapter Twenty

Sleep had evaded Laura. She contemplated refusing the position as editor-in-chief and returning to Cole Harbor with her aunt. Texas was turning out to be even more dangerous than New York. She had lain awake considering what kind of life she would have with Mitch if she remained in El Paso. Crime and duty would always be at the forefront. Then there was her career of running a newspaper. Would she always feel threatened every time a crime story made the paper's front page?

In three weeks, El Paso had become a den of danger—the attack on her aunt, the headless body, Mitch's vehicle attacked by a crazy bull, a sniper trying to kill Mitch, and snakes… A shiver wracked her. She reached to pull the coverlet to her chin. Was this the kind of life she wanted to live? The answer came easily: No!

After surviving a gunshot wound and witnessing the death of her best friend, hadn't she changed her name and relocated to Cole Harbor to live a more peaceful and safe life?

But even there… She tucked the bedspread tighter as she recalled falling into a grave and finding the skeletal remains of a woman's body, and then the struggle with the man who had tried to kill her. Was there no safe place?

To ward off the troubling tickertape thoughts, she closed her eyes and focused on the kiss she and Mitch had shared earlier in the day. Warmth traveled from her cheeks down to the core of her womanly apex, kindling an erotic stirring. She released a heavy sigh and resisted the urge to pleasure herself.

"You're not asleep. What's wrong, Laura?"

"Nothing and everything, Aunt Philly. Every time I close my eyes, I see images that I don't want to see."

She heard the sheets rustle and sensed her aunt had turned to face her. Phyllis said, "After what happened at dinner tonight, if I ever had any doubts about returning to Maine, those doubts are long gone." Phyllis propped on an elbow. "The selfish part of me wants you to return to Cole Hahbah with me, so we can pick up where we left off before the town exploded. The practical and loving part of me understands that becoming editor-in-chief of the paper is a major lifetime opportunity for you. It's your time to shine. I also believe you and Mitch have a future together. I saw the way you looked at him tonight. Whatever is blossoming between the two of you has my blessings."

Laura's heart jolted. "I have lots to think about, Aunt Philly."

Not wanting to pursue the topic, Laura said goodnight. Thoughts of Mitch and of the position of a lifetime had discontent simmering in her veins.

****

At her desk previewing tear-sheets, Laura picked up the receiver when the phone rang. "Laura Friday."

The voice was low and muffled, as if he spoke through a handkerchief. "Hello, Laura Schofield."

A chill wafted over her, and the hairs on her arms

stiffened. Laura's breath hung in her throat. She sat up very straight in her chair. No one knew her by that name anymore. "Who is this?"

"You will pay for what you did to my brother."

She didn't know what to say.

"Did you hear me, Laura Schofield?"

She spoke, her voice heavy with alarm. "Who was your brother?"

He laughed softly. "In due time. Are you prepared to die, Laura Schofield?"

She swallowed hard. Her hand shook. She gripped the receiver to keep it from slipping out of her hand. "I'll ask again, who is this?"

His voice hardened. "Your worst enemy."

She listened, but the threat caused her very being to plummet down around her. With all the bravado she could muster, she said, "I am under the protection of the Texas Rangers and the El Paso sheriff."

The voice laughed. "Old news, Laura Schofield. You will never know when or where I will strike, and if the sheriff gets in the way, oh, well..."

Chills prickled her skull and skittered to the soles of her feet. "You are a coward."

"No, Laura Schofield, I am a man who plans to avenge his brother's murder. The death you caused."

He hung up.

Laura cradled the receiver. She tried to lift the mug and had to use both hands to keep coffee from sloshing over the edge.

"Hey, Laura, you finished with those tear-sheets? We have a deadline to meet."

She swallowed, got to her feet, picked up the cup of cold coffee, then set it down again.

"Give me twenty minutes."

She wanted to go home. She wanted Mitch to wrap her in his arms. She wanted to feel safe.

The hours dragged by. Every phone call, every person who walked into the lobby, even the vehicle that backfired on the street sent her nerves into a tizzy.

The moment she parked Mitch's SUV in the drive and entered the house, indecision weighed on her. Tell Mitch…don't tell Mitch…tell her aunt…don't add to her aunt's already fearful frame of mind.

In a quagmire of indecision, she hesitated at the base of the stairs. She had to deal with this. She had to protect herself and her aunt.

****

"Laura?"

She hadn't seen him seated in the man-sized recliner, a book in his lap. Her face was pinched and pale. Mitch lowered the footrest and stood. "What's wrong?"

She flinched. Drawing in a deep breath and blowing it out slowly, she shrugged one shoulder. "I received a disturbing phone call at work."

He quirked a smile. "Let me guess. My would-be assassin called to say he'd hired a shooter with better aim."

Mitch watched the way Laura knotted her hands together. The mask of fear covering her face caused his joke to fall flat.

She shook her head. "No, actually"—she seemed almost afraid to say the words—"it was from someone who called me…Laura Schofield. I haven't used that name in years. How would the caller know?"

Mitch stood and pulled her into a hug. She

stiffened a bit. He kissed her with restrained emotion. She nestled against him. He held her closer, her breast pressed firmly against his chest. The touch aroused him, and he shifted so she wouldn't feel his bulge. He truly wanted to comfort her, not provide sex. At least not right now.

Laura spoke against his chest. "He said he was my worst enemy."

Mitch winced when she placed her hand against his chest and pushed away from his embrace. Using the back of her hand, she wiped the tears from her eyes. "Where is Aunt Philly?"

"She went with Jill and Claire to help decorate for Saturday night's dance." He used his good arm to guide her toward the kitchen. "C'mon, let's get you something stronger than coffee, and secondly, to avoid prying ears, let's take this to my dad's office."

Settled in a chair and facing Mitch, she sipped the rum and cola he had poured. Keeping his voice calm and casual, he said, "Tell me about the phone call."

Laura spelled out the details, withholding nothing. "I don't know how he…whoever he is…would know where to contact me. Especially at the *El Paso Gazette*."

"Did he call your cell phone?"

"No. That's just it, he called the office number."

"Think, Laura, how did his voice sound?"

She cocked her head to one side, as if listening. "I don't know. It was muffled, like he had a cloth over the mouthpiece, but"—she hesitated—"but, there was something I thought I recognized, yet I can't quite latch onto it."

The anguish on her face tugged at his heart. "Can

you recall any particular stories you reported that dealt with trials, or death sentences, or…" He stood to walk around the desk, and his hand brushed against Wyatt's antique candlestick phone, knocking it to the floor.

"Shit." He bent to pick up the phone, thankful it wasn't broken by the fall. That's when he spotted the tiny round cylinder that had landed near the toe of Laura's shoe. He pointed to it and then lifted a finger to his lips to signal—silence. And without hesitation he dropped the small drum into her glass. With a plop, the listening device sank to the bottom of her unfinished drink.

Her voice was hushed when she whispered, "What is it?"

"A bug. A listening device." Shocked at finding the gadget, and taken completely by surprise, Mitch was engulfed by a black storm of anger. "Where there's one, there are more. No telling how many are in the house." He wanted to laugh, and cuss, and punch the wall. "Whoever planted this has guts."

He motioned for Laura to give him her cell phone. He removed the battery cover, then checked his own for a minuscule listening device. Laura slid the phone inside her purse. "Who would do this?"

"I can't answer that, but when I find out, there's hell to pay. For sure, it's someone who has access to the house, and knows when we come and go."

"What about the mole your uncle spoke of? Could it be him?"

"It's possible, though I can't think of a reason why he'd need to listen in on our conversations. Besides, there aren't any new men on the ranch. One of the hands would have come to me or dad, or even Travis and Rob, if they'd seen a stranger skulking around the house. This leads me to believe it's someone we know and trust."

A tight knot of irritation settled in his chest. He extended his hand toward Laura. "Let's take a stroll down to the barn."

Outside, and a distance away from the house, he opened his phone and dialed his uncle. No pleasantries passed between them. Mitch got right to the point. "The house is bugged. Found one by accident when I knocked over Dad's 1910 candlestick phone. The device was probably stuck to the bottom and got knocked loose." He listened. "What the hell is happening, Virge?…Yeah, sure. I understand."

Mitch tried to smile when he looked at Laura. It didn't quite work. "There's another headless body. Virgil's got his hands full."

A gust of hot wind kicked up a dust devil, sending Mitch and Laura toward the house. On the porch, he bent close to her ear and whispered, "It's up to us to find the bugs. No talking. Look under lamps, the telephones, run your hands under the coffee tables."

"What if I find one?"

"Stick it in your pocket. We'll dispose of them all at once."

His thumb stroked her cheek, and he whispered, "We'll get through this, together. Let's do this before the family gets home."

He picked up a note pad and scribbled, then pointed to himself. *Living room, dining room, and bedroom.* Then he pointed to Laura and again scribbled. *Kitchen and bedroom.*

She nodded her understanding and walked through

the door he held for her. Mitch lifted a lamp next to the recliner he'd relaxed in. He glanced at Laura and gave a nod, and his hand came away to reveal a tiny circular device. Just as he'd advised her, he slipped it into his front pocket.

The search lasted for more than an hour, until it ended in Mitch's bedroom. Laura added her cache to a small plastic bag Mitch had found in the kitchen pantry. Eleven little bugs.

Laura held number twelve in front of her. Without rhyme or reason, she placed it on the floor and stomped on it, then calmly picked up the flattened cylinder and dropped it in the baggie. "Whoever was listening, I hope I burst his eardrum."

Mitch zipped the bag shut. He walked into his bathroom and lifted the lid on the toilet bowl, then dropped the bag of bugs into the water. He looked at Laura. "Don't call anyone unless you use your cell." He also cautioned her to discreetly check her aunt's phone.

This was getting tedious. He hated the idea that someone was spying on him, especially when people wanted to kill him. He tried not to think about Laura being in jeopardy.

Her face was solemn when she spoke. "Life shouldn't be this hard. What if…"

Mitch looked at her. His heart seemed to burst with the need to protect this woman. His hand slid into hers, locking their fingers together. He leaned toward her parted lips. He caught the floral tones of her perfume. He felt her tension. The elements were personal and powerful. His hands moved again. Now they found her hair, gently feathering it back. His fingers ran from her temples down the taut lines of her neck.

He pulled her down to the bed, and she fell without protest. There was only Laura, no listening devices, no assassins. Just her sensual mouth drawing closer and closer…

"…and in breaking news, live from Ciudad Juarez, Sebastian Vargas assumes the office of mayor after his cousin, Alejandro Lopez, was tragically gunned down. It is reported that Lopez was linked to the infamous Navarre Àron, leader of the Mexican drug cartel. A spokesperson for the Drug Enforcement Agency in the United States reports that Vargas may have ties to the South American cartel. Sources point to Vargas as allegedly ordering the hit on his cousin. It is no secret about bad blood between the two families, each wanting to control a burgeoning drug trade throughout the U.S., but Vargas denies all allegations."

As if catapulted, Mitch sat up and grabbed the television remote to up the volume. He pointed toward the screen. "Did you see him? I know that guy."

Laura seemed to push the words out through stiff lips. "Who?"

Mitch scooted to the end of the bed and leaned forward, his finger inches from a face in the crowd. "That guy! Sebastian Vargas, the new mayor of Juarez, which is a hub of drug trafficking." Mitch ran a hand through his hair. "Holy shit, and six ways to Sunday, he'll turn the entire state of Texas into a drug empire."

Laura squinted for a better look. "Ooh, noo! I've just had a horrible thought."

Mitch looked at the concerned frown marring the lines on her beautiful face. "What?"

"The man who shot you… Do you think Sebastian Vargas ordered the hit, or maybe pulled the trigger himself?"

Mitch blinked, not fully comprehending her meaning. She hastened on. "Because if you saw his picture in the newspaper or on television you would…"

Mitch seemed to drift off, as if thinking. "Yeah, because back then his name wasn't Sebastian Vargas. It was Julio Lopez. A cold-hearted bastard. He was a field boss in one of the migrant camps. We arrested him for stripping the hide off a worker who was too sick to work. Then as further punishment, Lopez forced the poor devil's wife and children to watch."

Laura's mouth dropped open. "Why isn't he in prison?"

"Bastard lawyered up. His work visa was revoked and he was deported. That was about five years ago."

"So he's back and calling himself Sebastian Vargas. A drug lord setting himself up as mayor by killing his relative. This is a crazy coincidence that he's on television."

She cast a worried look toward Mitch. "If he's smart enough to work his way out of the migrant camps and into a political office, he'll suspect you've seen him."

Mitch puckered his lips and nodded.

The thought slapped her like a connecting hand. "Oh, dear. Just when I thought things couldn't get any worse, now this happens. These people are unethical. They don't care who they hurt—not even the school children who get hooked on the drugs these monsters push."

Mitch sighed. " 'Monsters' is a good word. I won't tell you the things these cartels are capable of doing."

She looked hard at him. Her voice subdued, she

said, "I've covered muggings, stabbings, fires, people who've taken swan dives off bridges. I've seen bodies in various states of decomposition. There's not much that shocks me."

For a moment it seemed she had drifted away to another time and place. He'd seen that stare in the eyes of the men he had served with in Iraq, especially after returning from combat. He studied her, thinking how deeply Laura was embedding herself into his heart. "Laura?"

Her eyes refocused. She sighed. "It doesn't mean we don't continue to carry those memories around like extra baggage for the rest of our lives."

He stood and folded her into his arms, resting his chin on top of her head. "As much as I loved my wife, there were certain subjects I couldn't share with her. It's different with you. In a sense, you've been through combat, too, and survived. I feel like I can talk to you about things I couldn't share with Susie, my sister, or my mom. You're different from most women. I admire you for that."

Laura turned in his arms, her head on his chest. "He's going to come after you again." The worry in her voice was obvious. "He'll know there's a chance you saw him on the news."

Mitch held her tight. "Yep."

Sitting around the dining table that night, Mitch recounted to the family how he and Laura had found the listening devices and scoured the house in search of more. "We found twelve. I hope that's all there were. As a precaution, Virgil is sending a man to sweep the house."

Phyllis reached over and gripped Laura's hand as

her niece explained about the call she had received. Laura looked at her aunt. “I’ve wracked my brain and can’t think of any story I’ve covered to bring about this kind of threat. Aunt Philly, for your own safety, and since you’ve already decided to return to Cole Harbor, maybe now is as good a time as any.”

“By Godfrey! I will not leave until Mitch or his deputies or his uncles find this maniac and put him out of commission. I have enough gray hairs in my head. Returning to Cole Hahbah while still worrying about you will only add more.” Phyllis crossed her arms over her chest. “I’m staying until the cast comes off, and that’s my final word.”

Wyatt wadded his napkin and tossed it against his empty plate. “Who in the hell would have the *cojones* to come into this house and take the time to find just the right places to hide the bugs?” A vein bulged in his neck, evidence of his anger. “Has the whole damn state of Texas gone crazy to the point where a man can’t have privacy in his own home?”

He leaned forward on his elbows and cast a squinted eye around the table. “Keep your guns close. The only way to kill a rattler is to blow its head off.”

Jill placed her hands to her face. “I had totally forgotten until now. Frankie was in the house.” She explained about coming home and catching him leaving through the front door, and about his lame excuse of needing to see Travis.

Mitch’s gut clenched. “I think we should have a chat with Frankie. Rob…Travis, one of you go get him, now.”

Rob exchanged glances with his brother and shrugged. “Sorry, Mitch. It’s his weekend off. He usually goes out of town for a little sportin', if you catch my drift."

Chapter Twenty-One

Hugo Vargas' lips twisted into a wry grin as he eavesdropped on the Carters' conversation. He looked at goatee man. "Life is good, *mi amigo*. With Sebastian as Ciudad Juarez's new mayor, we are—as the sheriff says—'building an empire.' "

"*Si, jefe*. What about Ayala? What if he spills his guts about you?"

The smile on Hugo's face disappeared. He stroked the yellow boa draped across his shoulder. "Sloppy of him to get caught by the Carter bitch. Also sloppy of him to make the threatening phone call to the reporter bitch's workplace." He took a long throaty drink of bottled water as he mulled the situation. "It's too bad we can't erase the entire Carter clan. I've taken quite a liking to their ranch. Very strategically located. Don't you agree?"

His henchman stroked his goatee, pulling the gray hairs to a point. "*Si, mi jefe*." Through a yellow-toothed grin he said, "What you want I should do about Ayala?"

Hugo contemplated the answer. "I could say 'off with his head,' and blame it on my cousin, or…" He lifted his eyebrows. "You could sharpen your needle and practice your stitching skills. But not yet. Let's see what the good sheriff and his brothers have in store for our amigo."

Goatee man acquiesced. "As you wish, *jefe*. All the

same, if Ayala spills his guts, I will have my sewing kit ready."

Hugo's cell phone rang. He smiled at the caller ID. "*Hola*, Maria. Is my grandfather's health improving?"

"It saddens me to say you must come immediately to Columbia to arrange for your *abuelo*'s funeral. He asked for you in his last moments."

Though he spoke in sorrowful tones, Hugo's eyes sparkled with triumph. "I am heartbroken to hear this devastating news. I will leave tonight, and Maria, you will be amply rewarded for…taking care of my grandfather."

He phoned his pilot and gave instructions to ready the Lear jet. His next call was to Washington, D.C. "Distressing news, Mother. I must leave for Columbia at once. Grandfather Vargas has died."

Lisa Radcliff pouted into the phone. "Oh, my darling boy. He was a wonderful man. I know how much you adored him. Do you wish me to go with you? Of course, I'll need a new black dress, though black really doesn't become me."

"No, Mother. You have parties to attend, and I have no idea how long it will take to settle grandfather's affairs."

"Of course, dearest. Come to D.C. when you return. We'll do lunch, and you can tell me all about the funeral, and the will."

The will. Of course.

His mother was a self-serving bitch with the IQ of a mosquito. A party-hearty girl addicted to booze, facelifts, and money. The perfect example of a mother. Nothing like his grandmother Elena, who had loved him unconditionally but had died too young.

****

Commending himself for placing fourteen bugs inside the house and one inside Mitch's SUV, Frankie Romeo pressed the wireless earpiece and listened to the Carters. But his breath now constricted in his throat. After hearing about Vargas' delayed plans to snuff him out, and now with the discovery of the listening devices and Jill's confession about him being in the house, Frankie knew his ass was about to be ripped a new one. He beat his forehead with the heel of his hand.

He looked up at the sky. "Don't you worry, little brother. I'm gonna make this right." At least Vargas leaving the country was a point in Frankie's favor.

He shifted the beat-up Dodge truck into gear and pulled from the safety of a stand of trees and onto the highway. Driving toward his girlfriend's apartment, he formed a plan.

He reached forward and jacked up the radio's volume to his favorite rap song. Belting out the lyrics and swaying to the beat of the music, he relaxed. The road ahead of him was void of traffic. He took this as a good sign. Caught up in his own elation, he didn't notice the vehicle rapidly gaining on him until his head whiplashed forward. The unexpected force caused him to swerve off the road. He overcompensated, sending the truck into a spin. Nausea replaced exhilaration as he brought the pickup to a halt and watched two men, with assault rifles aimed and ready, approach him.

Goatee man shouted, "Ayala, get out of the truck. Hands in the air."

"W-what's this all about? I did what Vargas wanted. I placed the bugs in the house."

"You were careless, *amigo*."

Frankie dropped to his knees, the palms of his hands pressed together as if praying. He pleaded, "Don't kill me. I'll do anything you say, just…please don't kill me."

Goatee man signaled with the rifle barrel. "*Silencio*. Get in the truck." In Spanish, he instructed his partner to follow in Frankie's truck.

Frankie mewled, "W-where are you taking me?"

"You will know when we get there."

"I don't understand. It's not my fault the sheriff knocked over the old man's telephone. Otherwise, the bugs wouldn't have been found. Hugo Vargas is a young punk. He owes me."

Goatee man shrugged as he offered a yellow-toothed grin. "You no want to die? I have a job for you. Do it good, and maybe *mi jefe* lets you live. Maybe not."

"Vargas wants to control Spanish Harlem. He needs me. I have connections."

Like a lightning bolt, goatee man backhanded Frankie. Blood spurted from his nose. His mouth filled with blood.

Goatee man laughed at the cowed expression he had elicited from his passenger. "Fernando Ramirez de Ayala. You weren't jack-shit in New York. A punk even the gangs no wanted." He hawked a wad and spat out the window. "Now you call yourself Frankie Romeo and you're still a piece of Chicano shit."

Frankie sleeved away the blood that dribbled down his chin. He stared at the man with mute appeal. *Fuck you, man. What the hell do you know about me? Nothing! Calling me a piece of shit. You don't even have a real name: Goatee man! Bah-baaah. Yeah, let me get my hands on that slug chucker you're holding, and then we'll see who is a piece of shit. Yeah!*

His heart thumped and his breath hung in his throat when the goatee man turned onto a dirt road. Frankie's bowels reacted like he'd taken a double dose of laxative. He knew where they were going.

****

By evening Mitch's temper had settled down. His shoulder was another story. He sat on the edge of the bed, flanked by his sister and Laura, a thermometer in his mouth. He grimaced when Jill removed the bandage to expose the mottled red flesh. "It's festered," Jill lamented. She removed the thermometer.

Laura watched with concern. "What is it?"

"One hundred one. Sure sign of infection."

Laura frowned. "It's too bad Sam couldn't come tonight. I'll drive Mitch to the hospital in the morning."

"Good. The twins have a soccer game. I'll pick Mitch up after the game."

"Great, Jill, that'll work. The former editor left a backlog of paperwork. I plan to work late, so don't wait supper."

"I'm sure Wes or Luis will be happy to pick Mitch up and drive him to the jail. There are probably cases they need to discuss with him. That way he won't have to sit around waiting on me, unless, of course, Uncle Sam Houston decides to admit him to the hospital."

Mitch glanced from woman to woman, his annoyance apparent. "Hello? I'm right here. The two of you act as if I'm not in the room. Damn it all anyhow! I can drive myself to see Sam." He stood and grabbed his shirt. "Don't need mollycoddling like I'm an invalid." He continued to fuss. "I'm a war hero with two Purple

Hearts, not some weak namby-pamby…" He lifted his arm to slip it into the shirt sleeve, and it felt as if shards of glass stabbed his shoulder. He sank to the bed. "Damn, I'm kinda woozy-headed."

"That's it, big brother. In bed. Laura, get his pj's."

Laura stepped to the bathroom and returned with his pajamas and a glass of water. "You heard your sister—in bed. All that huffing around and being overly active, you've probably undone the past three weeks' recuperation." She uncapped the bottle of pain pills and dropped one into his hand.

The ache in his arm escalated, increasing his foul mood. "Oh, hell, get out of here and leave me in peace. One mother hen is bad enough. Two mother hens hovering over me is two too many."

He changed into his pajamas and climbed into bed. In truth, he liked the attention from the two women he loved most in the world. Especially Laura.

Before he drifted off into a pain-free slumber, he dialed his office.

"El Paso Sheriff's Office. Alma speaking."

"How's my favorite secretary?"

"I'm your only secretary. That is until December. We're missing you around here, Mitch. How's the arm?"

"Could be better. Is Wes or Luis in?"

"Sure thing. You take care, you hear?"

Mitch listened to her say, "Wes, Mitch on line one."

Seconds passed. "Howdy, Mitch."

"I need a favor, Wes."

"Hey, you name it, you got it."

"Some pissant called Ms. Friday's office and

threatened her life. She didn't recognize his voice—in fact, said it sounded muffled, like he was speaking through a cloth. It's got her pretty spooked, and I can't say as I blame her. In the morning, she's driving me in to see Sam about my shoulder. I'd take it as a personal favor if you or Luis or even Alma could check on her throughout the day."

"Happy to, Boss."

"'Preciate it. Got anything new going on?"

"Well, might be nothing, but out toward the old Horse Hole Ranch, someone reported seeing unusual buzzard activity. Luis went to check it out. I'm telling you, Mitch, I hope to God we don't find another headless body."

"That's two of us, Wes." Mitch filled his deputy in about receiving the UPS package with a half-conscious rattlesnake inside. "Did you see the news report about Alejandro Lopez being shot?"

"Oh, yeah, and by his own relative. Bad blood between the two families."

"I'm thinking Julio Lopez aka Sebastian Vargas is the one who put the hit on me. He knew if I saw him on television I'd come after him."

"Yeah, and I'll bet he's the one who called the office with the threat to pop a cap on you."

Mitch drew in a deep sigh. The pain pill had begun to work its magic. "You ever thought about retiring, Wes?"

"Almost every day. I've got two kids and a pregnant wife. What's happened to El Paso, Mitch? It used to be a safe city."

"Assholes like Navarre Àron and Hugo Vargas is what happened. I hate seeing our fair town held hostage between warring drug cartels. You know, at the dinner table last night, Dad said the only way to kill a rattlesnake is to shoot its head off. Somehow, we've got to cut the heads off the two main snakes."

"Count me in on the action. I don't want to think about what drugs can do to the kids in our schools. Hold on, Mitch. Alma just signaled that Luis is on the other line."

Mitch sank against the pillow. His hand wanted to let the phone slide to the bed. He forced himself to keep his eyes open.

"Mitch…Mitch…Dammit! You're not going to believe this." Wes was yelling into the phone.

"Hold it. Calm down. What?"

"We have a dead Ranger."

"The hell, you say! Where did Luis find him?"

"In a clump of trees where the Horse Hole butts with your property line. Luis said it looked like he was camping out. Even had surveillance equipment. Shot in the back, he figures."

"Virgil had a man posted to keep an eye on the family. We didn't know who he was or where he was. Damn. Any identity?"

"Yep. Jack Lundy. Nothing appeared stolen. Luis said he was probably shot from a distance with a high-powered rifle."

"Yeah. If Luis found the spent casing, I'll bet it matches the one you found when I was shot. And the bullet will match the one Sam dug out of me."

"You want me to notify your Uncle Virgil?"

"If you would. I'll see you tomorrow, Wes."

"Take it easy, and don't worry. We'll keep a watchful eye on Ms. Friday. She's a nice lady."

"Thanks. I think so, too."

In the morning, against his wishes, Laura placed her hand between Mitch's shoulder blades and gently guided him away from the driver's side of the SUV. "Keep on, and you'll be in worse shape than you are now."

He argued, "I'm perfectly capable of driving with one hand."

She frowned as she leaned in to strap the seatbelt in place. He grimaced. "I feel like an invalid."

She offered a sympathetic smile. "It won't be long and you'll be back to work. But it's not like you're recuperating from a bee sting." She rushed around to the driver's side and slid behind the steering wheel.

They rode in silence. He stared at the passing scenery. "I guess I'm impatient." He glanced at her and smiled. "Not that I haven't enjoyed watching old westerns with Dad, listening to the twins talk about their days at school, and watching you in the pool. I like the way you fill out that purple bathing suit."

She flushed and laughed. "Thanks…I've enjoyed being with you…and your family."

He pursed his lips. "Do you think you could get used to being around me and my family full time?"

She caught her breath.

She was so busy staring at Mitch she didn't notice at first that the truck following them had sped up to run next to Mitch's SUV. "Mitch, is this guy…"

Before she could get all the words out, the driver swerved, ramming against the left front fender, forcing her off the road. The heavy SUV tilted on its wheels, almost flipping on its side before settling on all four tires and rolling to a stop.

Laura held the steering wheel in a death grip. Mitch had no time to open the glove compartment and reach for his pistol before one man had yanked the door open while another pointed a semi-automatic weapon at Mitch's head.

"So, Senorita Friday, our boss took exception to the article you wrote about him. He'd like to meet you."

"If you mean that scumbag posing as an honest citizen, and the new mayor, he can kiss my…"

The man wagged his finger and flashed a pearly grin. "Aah-aah-ah. Be nice."

The second man gave Mitch a benign look. He spoke with a thick Hispanic accent. "You one lucky hombre. *Mi jefe* no happy you still alive, Sheriff." He shrugged. "But, hey, at this range, I no can miss." Using the rifle barrel, he signaled for Laura and Mitch to exit the vehicle.

Mitch slammed the door back with all the strength he could muster. The first man brought the barrel down hard across Mitch's right arm. "Resisting could be bad for your health, Sheriff. If you wish to live another day, I suggest you cooperate."

The two men conversed in a language Mitch didn't understand. He spoke fluent Spanish, both Mexican and Yaqui, and he was well-versed in Farsi. The language didn't sound French nor German. It was obvious the tall reedy man with cat eyes was the more intelligent of the two.

The short stout man poked Mitch's shoulder, bringing a pained grunt. The tall man tied Laura's hands behind her back.

She was instructed to get in the back seat of the quad cab truck. "Not until you tell me where you're taking us."

The tall man laughed as he ran a thumb down her cheek. "Feisty. I like that, but don't worry, pretty lady. No harm will come to you…yet."

Mitch reached inside his pocket. With his left hand, he punched in the number for a distress call. He hoped either Wes or Luis were in range.

The fat man yelled as he grabbed Mitch's arm. "Ay, what you doing, *hombre*?" He reached into the pocket and brought out the phone. "Ay-Chihuahua, I should kill you right now." He dropped the phone on the ground and crushed it with the heel of his boot.

Mitch bit hard against his lip to keep from crying out when his arms were jerked behind his back. Both he and Laura were blindfolded, then pushed into the rear seat of the quad cab truck. He always knew at some point in time he would die, but he hoped right now wasn't his or Laura's time to wind up in a ditch on a desolate dirt road.

As the vehicle sped down the highway, Mitch figured they were headed toward the border, or someplace close to Ciudad Juarez. He was outraged to be caught with his guard down. He'd been too absorbed in his own pity instead of keeping a watchful eye for unusual activity, when he knew someone was targeting Laura, he chastised himself. He hoped the emergency signal had gone through before the goon destroyed his phone.

The discomfort in his shoulder grew more unbearable. All the surgery, all the painful physical therapy to regain full use of his arm—gone, down the drain. He fought the chills threatening to chatter his teeth. His fever had returned. He whispered, "Laura,

I'm sorry."

She didn't answer as she rubbed her leg against his. He remembered the gag the fat man had placed over her mouth. Fury rose up inside him, but he had to stay calm, remain rational. To keep Laura and himself from being killed, maintaining sensibility was essential. He tried to relax, to clear his mind, to think of a way to escape. He called on his military training to help him mentally detach from the situation. No matter what happened to him, keeping Laura safe was his main objective.

Chapter Twenty-Two

The truck dipped into deep ruts and vibrated over ripples in the surface it traveled. Mitch knew they drove on a dirt road. He tried to keep track of time. He and Laura had left the ranch at nine a.m. He figured twenty minutes had passed before they'd encountered the enemy. It was difficult to judge time while blindfolded. How long? An hour, two? From the gnawing inside his stomach, his best calculation was around noon. He almost wanted to laugh. Didn't his stomach realize that concern over dying took precedence over food?

With each jarring rut the pain in his shoulder mutated into agony.

He hadn't recognized either man. One, definitely Hispanic. The other, a blend of European and possibly Andean. Whoever these men were, they belonged to the powerful and dangerous cartel run by the elder Hugo Vargas, though rumor had it the grandson had inherited his grandfather's love of reptiles and the old capo's penchant for cruelty, and that young Vargas would someday inherit the title *Capo Supremo.*

The truck ground to a halt. The door opened. Hands grabbed him. The first thing Mitch noticed was the contrast between the air-conditioned vehicle and the blast of heat that greeted him. Rough hands pushed him forward. He stumbled and was lifted, then led.

He assumed the dwelling they entered was without

electricity when he heard a match strike and caught a whiff of sulfur. The blindfold was removed. In the glow of lantern light, he was relieved to see Laura standing next to him. Her hands still bound, she wore an expression of resignation. She worked her jaw and licked her lips when the gag was removed, and then blinked as the blindfold dropped from her eyes.

He exchanged glances with Laura, allowing his gaze to linger, knowing this might be the last time he ever saw her. The ache tugging at him had nothing to do with the pain in his shoulder.

The tall man instructed the squatty guy, "Put them there," and indicated two cane-backed chairs.

From the obvious lack of use, Mitch figured someone had cautioned the men to keep their names quiet. He decided to test his theory. "Which Vargas ordered you to keep your identities secret—the ole man himself, Vargas senior, or his ass-kissing illegitimate nephew, Julio Lopez?"

The fleeting looks confirmed his suspicions. The men belonged to *Los Serpientes Venenosas.* A shudder wracked through Mitch. He didn't want to think about what the future held for him and Laura.

"Since your names are a secret, I'll call you Mutt and Jeff."

His comment brought confused stares.

"You know, after the famous comic strip characters? Now, Mutt, he was like you, tall and lanky, a dimwit who loved to bet on the ponies but always lost his money. His opposite, Jeff, was short and bald, and resided in an insane asylum. The only thing the two clowns had in common was their love of horseracing. You see, Mutt and Jeff were almost too stupid to live."

Tall man kicked the chair legs out from under Mitch, sending him crashing to the floor. He drew back his foot as if to kick Mitch. Laura screamed, "No! His shoulder hasn't healed from where you shot him."

Squatty man hissed, "*El Jefe*, he say no hurt more."

Laura snarled her plea. "Then help him up, and if he must be tied, please retie his hands in the front."

Mitch cursed his injury. He grunted when the squat man's calloused hands lifted him from the dirty floor and shoved him into the chair. At this rate, even if he did live, it would take twice as long for his shoulder to heal, and a lot more grueling physical therapy. Hell, why was he thinking about his shoulder when he needed to concentrate on an escape plan?

Tall man ordered his partner to retie Mitch's hands in the front. The surge of blood shooting down both arms and into his fingers caused Mitch to squeeze his eyes shut and suck in his breath. He mentally cursed these *narco traficantes*. "Tell me, Mutt, do you and your lackey, Jeff, deal in just drugs, or humans, or maybe both?"

Tall man gritted his teeth. Mitch knew he was succeeding in pushing the guy's mental buttons. At the same time he cursed his own stupidity for allowing these thugs to capture him, to capture Laura.

Laura said, "Why did you bring us here?"

Tall man spared her an indolent look. "Julio Lopez is the illegitimate son of our *jefe*'s youngest sister. As Sebastian Vargas, he is the esteemed mayor of Ciudad Juarez and is to be respected. He is coming to deal with your sheriff. You, señorita, are a bonus."

He moved close to Laura. "Sebastian has instructed that no harm is to come to you. He is bringing with him an associate with a laptop and webcam so you can do what you do best, report the news. You will retract the lies you told about the honorable mayor."

She met his smug glare. She didn't smile, or flinch. She kept her voice quiet and emphatic. "I report the truth. Do you think Sheriff Carter's uncles will let you get away with kidnapping us? They will hang you up by the thumbs and castrate you."

"And do you think to frighten us, señorita?" Tall man looked at her with malevolent pleasure. He stood erect, grabbed his crotch and thrust his hips forward. "I will have the pleasure of tasting you first, for the benefit of the viewers."

Mitch lunged forward. Squatty man slammed the rifle butt against Mitch's bad shoulder, then used his foot to shove him back into the chair. Mitch gasped through a haze of pain. He spoke between breaths. "By all that is holy, touch one hair on her head and I will personally break your neck."

Tall man apparently thought that hilarious. "Ooh, I am so afraid."

A door slammed. Squatty man peered through a broken window. He spoke in Spanish. "They are here."

Goatee man entered, with Frankie Romeo ahead of him. As if they were sharing a mind meld, Mitch and Laura cast questioning glances at each other, then at Frankie. No one spoke.

A cell phone rang. Were it not for the dire situation, Mitch thought it almost comical to watch the four drug lizards checking their phones to see whose was ringing. Tall man answered his phone, and his face formed a frown as he listened, then changed to a shocked expression. He made the sign of the cross over his chest. "*Madre de dios! Si*…I understand."

Mitch listened while tall man communicated in Spanish. He was glad no one knew he understood every word. "That was Alejandro. Plans have changed. *El Jefe*, Hugo Vargas, is dead. We are called to the hacienda in Columbia immediately. A new *jefe supremo* will be named after the funeral."

Goatee man smiled. "Young Hugo will be our new *capo*. He is one smart hombre and is no afraid to spit in the enemy's eye, but smart enough to charm the rattles off a serpent."

Tall man sneered. "He is a spoiled punk. His cousin, Alejandro, will spank junior's butt and send him crying to his rich American mama."

The two gunmen squared up to each other. Squatty man stepped in between them. "Now is not the time. You can kill each other when the new *capo* is named." He pointed toward Laura and Mitch. "What we do with them?"

Goatee man turned to Frankie and spouted orders. "You sold your soul to the devil." He reached down, pulled a pistol from his ankle holster, and directed, "Now prove your loyalty to young Hugo and he maybe let you live for failing him. If they try to escape…kill them." He grinned a yellow-toothed grin and made a hissing sound. "Do not fail. You know how *mi jefe* likes his *serpientes*."

Frankie's tanned face changed to a pasty pallor as he stuck the pistol in his belt. "When will you return? What do we eat or drink?"

"Cistern in the back. Canned food, there." Goatee man pointed to a shelf nailed to a wall. "We return in one week."

Frankie protested, “Are you crazy? One week? We’ll die out here.”

Tall man gestured the other two men toward the door. He cast a sardonic smile toward Frankie. “We will give you a good funeral.”

As soon as the door closed, Mitch said with cold contempt, “Frankie, don’t tell me you’re a mule. After all my family has done for you? To think you’re using our ranch to transport drugs, for chrissake. You sat at our dinner table!”

Frankie pulled the pistol from his belt and waved it in the air. “Shut up…just shut up, and let me think. I don’t want to hurt you, Mitch.” His gun hand trembled until he had to steady it with his other hand as he aimed toward Laura. “It’s her fault. All her fault.” He backed to the other side of the room and slid to a squatting position. “Don’t talk, either of you.”

Sunshine leaked through cracks in the roof, striping the dirty floor with brilliant gold. Laura studied the dust motes that danced in the shafts of light. The stale air worked on her nerves. She was utterly drained. Her arms and legs were heavy from being bound. When she looked at the man slumped against the wall, his legs splayed wide, the revolver resting against his knee, she felt nothing but contempt.

No sounds. Not even the wind blew.

After an hour of silence, Laura glanced at Mitch. His head sagged so that his chin rested against his chest. She knew he was still in pain. The day and the rough treatment had taken its toll on him. Blood stained the front of his shirt. She was filled with love and anguish for him and roiling anger at the men who had caused him such agony.

More than dust hovered in the air. She sensed Frankie watching her. She ventured a look in his direction. He studied her, a peculiar expression in his eyes. Bristling with anger, she cleared her throat. "It was you who threatened me, wasn't it, Frankie?"

No answer.

Her voice rang with irritation. "I don't even know you. Why do you glare at me with such hatred?"

A distant look came into his eyes. Then he seemed to refocus on her. "You killed my brother."

A shudder ran the length of her. "That's ludicrous. I've never killed anything in my entire life. Not even a cockroach."

Mitch rallied from his stupor. His gaze shifted from Laura to Frankie. "Why would you make such an accusation?"

Frankie rewarded them with a high-pitched little laugh that sounded more hysterical than bemused. He waved the gun in the air. "Oh, what the fuck, we're all gonna die anyhow. My name is Fernando Ramirez de Ayala, and I'm from Spanish Harlem, Noo Yawk. My kid brother's name was Romeo Ramirez de Ayala. He was my only brother. Do youse remember him, Ms. Schofield?"

Drooping with exhaustion, she closed her eyes and did a mental search of names and crime stories, and came up empty. "Refresh my memory, Frankie."

He spouted off the words as if he'd spent years memorizing them. " 'Another lowlife off the mean streets of Noo Yawk. Although Romeo Ramirez de Ayala deserves the electric chair, he will spend the rest of his life incarcerated on Riker's Island, placing yet another tax burden on our law-abiding citizens.'

"My brother was barely seventeen years old when an inmate shoved a shiv into his heart. You stood on the courthouse steps and before all the world you called him a sociopath, an incorrigible baby-faced killer."

Laura sat erect. Shocked and taken completely by surprise, she said, "That was almost ten years ago. The jury found him guilty; the judge passed the sentence. I merely reported the news. You said yourself he was killed in prison."

Frankie came to his feet. He sprang at Laura, grabbing her face in his hand. He squeezed her cheeks together, and relished the tears that filled her blue eyes. He wanted to hurt her, to punish her.

Mitch leapt from the chair so fast he nearly fell. Frankie pointed the revolver at him. "Sit down. I'm the boss here."

Mitch settled. The burst of energy had zapped his waning strength. His voice rasped with the need of water. "Tell me what happened, Laura. Maybe hearing it again will help Frankie realize you're not to blame for his brother's death."

She sucked in a shuddering breath to steady herself. "Romeo was the youngest person ever sentenced to Riker Prison. He was given ten life sentences with no probation." She drew another deep breath. "The day before Good Friday, he walked into a high school and opened fire, killing five teachers, including the principal, plus ten students, and wounding countless others. His reason: he was having a bad day."

Mitch's voice was calm. He spoke with authority. "I've known you for three years, Frankie. Until today, I never suspected you had a mean bone in your body. I've seen the way you've nurtured the calves rejected by their mamas. Ten years is a long time to harbor hatred against anyone, but surely there must be some rational part of you that knows your brother entered that school with the willful intent to commit murder. No one forced him to kill innocent people. Think how the parents of those dead kids have suffered; never to celebrate another birthday or Christmas, or to see them graduate or get married. You're not your brother, Frankie. Untie us. We'll get through this together." He looked at Laura. "Given that the only crime you've committed toward Laura is using bad judgment, I'm sure she won't press charges. But placing listening devices in my house, and holding us hostage, and with a deadly weapon, is aiding and abetting a gang of drug mules. That's a federal offense. Help us out of here and to safety, and I'll do everything in my power to get you a light sentence."

The sun's heat had intensified, making the small adobe house feel like an oven. Frankie scrubbed a hand across his face. It came away wet from the sweat. He laughed. "Man, don't you know where we are? We're in Mexico. The only thing around is sand, cactus, and miles of nothing. Look at you…bleeding. You wouldn't last a mile in this heat, and neither would she."

Chapter Twenty-Three

In spite of the air-conditioned office, Senator Clarence Radcliff loosened the tie at his neck and wiped his face with a clean white handkerchief as he sat in his office contemplating the report he held in his hands. He already knew from his daughter that his grandson had flown to Columbia.

He opened his desk drawer and withdrew the bottle of antacid tablets, popped two in his mouth, and waited for the relieving belch to come.

A knock sounded, and the door opened. His secretary said, "Director of Homeland Security and FBI Director to see you, sir."

Radcliff tore his gaze away from the report. The dreaded hour had arrived. "Give me five minutes, then send them in."

The young woman nodded and closed the door.

Radcliff straightened his tie. He had always suspected this day would come. Now it was here, and he was nervous as hell. He'd spent thirty years in the political arena, building a reputation for being tough on crime, keeping the borders safe, working on immigration reform, and grooming himself to make his bid for the presidency in the upcoming election, and a snot-nosed, spoiled maniac was about to bring it all down around him.

He rued the day he had allowed his daughter to talk

him into giving her son the Radcliff name.

The door opened and the secretary announced, "Director of Homeland Security Garrett Carter and FBI Director James Buchanan."

Radcliff stood. "Jeri, would you bring us some fresh coffee?"

Carter held up his hand. "None for me, thanks." FBI Director James Buchanan also declined. Carter waited until the secretary closed the door before speaking again.

Radcliff focused on the plastic rectangle pinned to the breast pocket of Carter's dark gray suit jacket. Yes, ID badges were important. He extended his hand as an invitation for the men to sit. His nerves tap-danced on his overly-inflamed ulcer.

Carter released the button at his waist to open his jacket. He sat and crossed one leg over the other, revealing a western boot, black with an ornate silver toe tip. "Let's cut to the chase, Clarence. You know why we're here."

The senator cleared his throat. He reached for the metal carafe and poured a glass of water, drew a long swallow, then returned the glass to the tray. "I've read the report, but I do believe I need further clarification of the alleged accusations. My good name and reputation is at stake."

Buchanan said, "Clarence, how long have we been golfing buddies? Long enough for you to know I don't put up with bullshit. So far, the media hasn't gotten wind of this. When they do, we all know you can kiss your career goodbye."

The senator's chair squeaked as he leaned forward. He needed to tell his secretary to call maintenance. He sighed as he steepled his fingers to pat their pads. "Does the President know?"

Buchanan shrugged. "Not yet."

Carter's brows furrowed together in a deep frown. "You chair the committee for Homeland Security. Why in the hell did you think you could keep this a secret?"

Radcliff shoved back his chair and stood. He raked a trembling hand through snow-white hair. "God only knows how much I hate that boy. Hate him and fear him at the same time. He's my daughter's son, but I feel no loving connection to him, or compassion for him. Does that make me some kind of heartless monster?"

Buchanan was loathe to answer the question. He flicked an imaginary piece of lint from his black slacks. "The only monster is Stephen Radcliff."

The senator bemoaned, "I can't tell you how many times I've wanted to confide in both of you that I suspected he was involved with the Vargas cartel. It's difficult for me to believe he is capable of sewing snakes into the mouths of victims." He grimaced. "Although the kid did keep a yellow boa in the house. Let it slither anywhere, as if it had the run of the place. Gave me the sheer willies to think it might find its way into my bed."

The senator paced back and forth. "Still, Stephen is only twenty-three. Surely being involved with his paternal grandfather is a passing fad. You know how young men need heroes. I'm certain he'll see the danger in it and come to his senses, for his mother's sake."

He stopped pacing and looked at the resolute faces watching him. Life seemed to be slipping through his fingers. It had been a good life. One he wanted to continue. Hell, he was sixty-five and had at least twenty more productive years ahead of him.

He heaved a deep sigh as if having difficulty breathing. "James, or you, Garret, maybe one of you can pull some strings and get Stephen into the military." The senator waved his hand. "If it weren't for his criminal record, I would have already persuaded him to enlist. A stint in a combat zone might knock some sense into him."

Buchanan said, "Clarence, we have positive proof that your grandson Stephen Hugo Radcliff and Hugo Vargas III are one and the same person." He placed a miniature tape recorder on the desk and pushed play.

Senator Radcliff buried his face in his hands as he listened to the voices on the wiretap announcing his grandson as the supreme leader of the South American cartel, and the cheering voices in the background, followed by what sounded like firecrackers. *Viva el jefe supremo. Long live the name of Hugo Vargas.*

Groaning out loud, the senator said, "What are your plans?"

Carter and Buchanan looked at each other. Carter's voice was matter of fact. "The only way to kill a snake is to cut off its head."

The senator paled. "Do what you have to do. Don't tell me. I'd rather read about it in the paper."

Buchanan thrummed his fingers against his knee. "You do know the plan is to eradicate your grandson?"

"Like I said. I'll read about in the newspaper, and for my daughter's sake, I'll put on the best heartbroken face I can muster."

Garret Carter and James Buchanan stood. After a moment of silence, Carter said, "I suggest you submit your letter of resignation immediately, Clarence. We're shutting down Hugo Vargas' entire operation. The Texas Rangers and the Border Patrol in both the Southwest and along the Canadian border are awaiting orders. Transportation Security for all major airlines has been alerted, as well as the larger private airports. We fully expect casualties." He continued, "There's no way we can gag the media. You know that as well as any of us. Cite health issues as the reason for resigning, but do it within the hour. Clean out your desk. You might even buy a plane ticket as far away from D.C. as possible. That's the best we can do to save your hide, Clarence. But know this—you are under investigation for possible collusion. For old time's sake, I hope you in no way aided and abetted your grandson. If so, friendship or no, I will see to it you go to prison."

The senator nodded his understanding. He placed his hand against his chest to ease the crushing pain. He felt clammy and was certain the tie around his neck was choking him. The beat of his heart thundered in his ears. He tried to speak, but his tongue refused to work, and then the world spun out of control.

Garret Carter knelt beside the senator where he had fallen and started chest compressions while Buchanan dialed 9-1-1.

Five hours later a press conference was held to announce the death of Senator Clarence Radcliff.

Chapter Twenty-Four

Laura watched Frankie Romeo pace the worn floors of the old wooden shack until she wanted to scream. He looked very nervous as he mumbled to himself and waved his arms about. Mitch had often spoken highly of the young man. Surely there was a smattering of decency hiding inside him. She decided to appeal to his sense of honor.

"If killing me will bring you peace, then do it, but please don't let Mitch die."

"Laura, no," Mitch groaned.

When Frankie didn't respond, she decided on another tactic. "May I ask you a question, Frankie?"

"Like I could stop you?"

"Why didn't *you* kill me? Why get involved with Hugo Vargas?"

Frankie gave her a long-suffering look. "Fair enough. For ten years I lay awake at night thinking of ways to make you suffer, to make you beg for your life before I ended it. Truth is, I'd pretty much forgotten about you, until three weeks ago when you showed up at the ranch with Mitch. All the hatred flooded back. One weekend I'd had a little too much tequila and shot my mouth off to a man whose name isn't important. He said for a small favor he could make you disappear, but first I have to do him the favor. He said I would make lots of money." Frankie guffawed. "I figured it had to be more than what I make as a ranch grunt. So I agreed. All I had to do was go to the border, look in a special spot for the cocaine, then get it to another mule. When I went to collect my money, I was told that was a test to prove I was trustworthy, but to earn a hit on you, I had to…"

Mitch lifted his head. "To do what, Frankie?"

"Sebastian Vargas wanted you taken out. I couldn't do it, Mitch. I couldn't pull the trigger on you." Frankie buried his face in his hands and drew a sobering breath. "But it was me that told him you'd be at the rodeo. I did sell my soul to the devil—to the Vargas Cartel. Sebastian is crazy, especially when he chews the coca leaves. He is a man without a heart, and Hugo plays with those damned snakes like he's some kind of invincible god."

"Why didn't you come to me, Frankie? I'm the law. I could have helped you."

Frankie sighed. He looked at Mitch. "Do you know who Hugo Vargas really is? He has several names. Stefano Hugo de la Paz Vargas is one, and he's also known as Stephen Hugo Radcliff. No matter how much evil Hugo does, his American grandfather is a senator and will protect him."

Laura gasped. "Surely you're not referring to Senator Clarence Radcliff? Why, he has an impeccable reputation for being hard on crime."

Frankie raised his eyebrows and offered a smug look. "We cannot choose our relatives." He shrugged. "Now I am a mule, an accessory to murder, and will take the blame for kidnapping a law officer and a newspaper reporter. I don't know Hugo or Sebastian's plans after they return from Columbia. But I think they will return hoping to find us dead, and if not, they will kill all of us. You, Ms. Schofield, they will torture, because they are lustful animals and you are a beautiful woman, and they do not honor women. They will kill you, Mitch, because you are a lawman, and they have no respect for the law. They will kill me because…because I stole five million dollars' worth of coke, and because I am going to help you escape. But you must promise me amnesty. I'll need a passport with a new identity, a plane ticket, and an armed escort to see me safely seated in first class."

Laura sat as still and as straight as she could, waiting for Mitch's reply to Frankie's demands. In the waning light, she twisted until she could see the outline of his face. His beard had sprouted to more than a five o'clock shadow. His cheeks seemed sunken, and when he turned to look at her, his eyes were glazed with fever. She prayed he would agree to whatever Frankie said without placing any conditions on his requests.

Her patience worn thin, she gave Mitch a harsh look. "I don't know about the two of you, but it's getting dark, and there are creepy-crawly things in the dark. The sooner we leave, the better. Besides, I'm hungry, I'm thirsty, my fingers have lost all feeling, and I have to pee. So, dammit, Mitch, will you please give Frankie an answer?"

Mitch gave a long hard stare. His face hardened. "I hate drugs, and drug dealers." Then his face smoothed out like an ironed cloth. "If you'll testify in a federal court, I'll get you in a witness protection program and make sure no one finds you unless you slip up. Ball's in your court. What'll it be?"

Frankie reached into his pocket and flipped open a

switchblade. Laura held her breath as he approached her. Certain he intended to slit her throat, she almost wet her pants when he slid the blade through the nylon rope that bound her ankles and then sawed apart the cord to release her hands. He said, "The outhouse is around back."

He cut Mitch loose and helped him to the bed that had sagging springs and a vermin-chewed mattress. "Rest while I gather up supplies."

He grabbed a Mason jar, ran outside, and knocked at the outhouse door. Laura answered, "I'm not finished."

Frankie ground the words, "Hurry up. There's a glass jar on the ground by the door. Fill it with water from the cistern."

Inside the cramped structure, the foul odor caused Laura's stomach to roil. She gagged as she maneuvered her slacks over her hips and crouched over the hole cut in the center of the wooden bench. She looked around desperately for toilet paper. A bondage and sadomasochism magazine lay partially open at one side. She cringed as she ripped a page full of explicit photographs of women to complete her toilette. She held her breath against the stench until she was almost certain she would pass out, pulled up her pants, and threw the door back with such force it banged closed before she could step out. Muttering a curse, she hoped the noise hadn't awakened any poisonous creatures. She searched the ground before she stepped out.

She raced to the cistern with the glass jar. It took a couple of moments for her to figure out how to extract water from the contraption, but she finally succeeded. Tightening the lid, she hoped a gallon jar of water was enough for three people on a long hike. They were probably miles from civilization, but now was their best chance for escape. She didn't want to die. She wanted to grow old with Mitch, and for the first time in her life she wanted a baby. She gave herself a mental scolding: now was not the time for her maternal clock to start ticking.

Inside the shack, she grabbed the canned goods Frankie had gathered and crammed as many as she could fit into her oversized Gucci bag. As she was rearranging the items to make room for the jar of water, her fingers touched a smooth surface. Her heart fluttered. She swallowed hard. Dare she mention her find? Not fully trusting Frankie, for the time being she decided to keep her discovery a secret.

Mitch's voice startled her. "The desert is cold at night. We'll need these blankets."

She slung the strap over her shoulder. Her artificial hip protested the weight. Mitch struggled to stand. He grabbed the purse. "C'mon, let's get the hell out of here."

She and Frankie followed him through the door. In his weakened state, she saw Mitch struggling with the weight. This was going to be a painful journey for him. She looked at Frankie. "Do you know which way is the border?"

Laura looked at the sky and was thankful for daylight savings time. Stars were still a dim dot in the pale blue cloudless sky. She figured they had at least three hours before dark.

Frankie ground his teeth together as he scanned the expanse. "I didn't pay attention. We were on a highway. We turned on a dirt road. It seemed like we hit every bump and rut. Couldn't travel very fast. Then we came to a broken-down gate. Another lifetime of riding, and we arrived. The rest is history."

Mitch, too, scanned the surroundings. "Were the mountains on your left or right when driving in?"

Frankie thought for a moment. "On the right."

"Good. That means you were heading south. As long as we keep the mountains to the west of us, on our left, we'll head north, and hopefully to the highway. Let's stop talking and start walking."

They walked for a long time, through scrubby undergrowth and across a dry creek bed. They cut a wide swath to avoid a diamondback rattler, its tail whirring an ominous warning. The sight and sound caused her to rethink living in Texas.

Mitch had begun to shiver. Laura knew the ordeal was draining his strength. She relieved him of the purse. "Any idea how much farther?"

Mitch coughed. He stumbled, and Laura cried out, "Frankie, catch him!"

Mitch heaved a sigh. "Miles and miles."

She groaned out loud. "It didn't seem to take that long to get here in the truck."

"Yes, it did." Mitch forced out the words. "Between the highway and the rutted pig trail, I'd say we traveled at least an hour, maybe two."

Her voice was incredulous. "B-but that's approximately ninety miles. It will take us forever to reach the border."

Frankie lamented, too. "Yeah, unless we can steal a car. Which ain't likely in the middle of nowhere."

She worried they wouldn't make it that many miles. Mitch's gait had slowed to a snail's pace. The trip and the rough physical treatment had taken its toll. She hoped the damage wasn't irreparable.

"We have to stop. Mitch needs rest, and food. Frankie, can you build a fire?"

"I wasn't never into Boy Scouts, you know, but I'll see if I can scare up some wood."

Laura hesitated. She stared at him, unsure if she trusted him to not run off to save his own neck.

He stared back at her.

"If you betray us and Mitch dies, I will use every resource available to me to hunt you down and make sure you suffer an unpleasant death."

"Trust is a two-way street, Ms. Schofield."

"Stop calling me that. She ceased to exist three years ago."

Even in the dark his smirk was visible.

She looked at Mitch, but he was lying on the ground, so exhausted he was unable to move. "Mitch Carter is a man of honor. If he lives through this, he'll get you in that witness protection program. I hope you're a man of honor, too, and won't run out on us."

"I'm not as bad as you think I am. I'll gather as much wood and brush as I can, as quickly as possible. You have my word."

As he turned to leave, Laura spoke. Her voice filled with kindness. "I'm sorry about your brother. Truly."

"Yeah." The word was derisive as he faded into the darkness.

Laura sat on the ground next to Mitch. She placed her hand on his forehead and wished there was water to spare to cool his fever.

Instead, she gathered him into her arms, holding him close, hoping to keep him warm.

He sighed. “I’m sorry, Laura. It should be me protecting you.”

She nestled into the planes of his body. “All that matters is that we’re alive, and we will make it to the border. I promise.”

He brushed her temple with his lips. “Hurts my pride. You saving me. My mother would have really liked you. I like you.”

They were both silent for a moment.

“Mitch, a while back you asked how I felt about you. You said it was the last time you’d ask.” She collected her bravery. “I’m not saying this because we might die tomorrow, I’m saying it because I know without a shadow of a doubt that I never want to let you go. I don’t know what love is, but if it’s feeling like my world will come to an end if you’re not in it, then I more than like you.”

She felt giddy and wanted to giggle like a foolish school girl. If this was love, she wanted to wallow in it as long as Mitch was with her.

He laughed in her ear. “You are a special woman.” His good hand slipped around her back and dipped into the waistband of her slacks and down the curve of her hips. She moaned as his mouth found her lips. They pressed together in an agony of need, oblivious to the sights and sounds of their surroundings.

“Oh, damn.” He groaned and rolled to his back, wincing as he met her eyes. “Damn this shoulder.”

She fought down a long-suppressed hunger that threatened to undo her. “It’s okay, really. We’ll have plenty of other times.”

He smiled and kissed her softly. “That’s assuming we last until then.”

"We will. You're the sheriff, and good guys always win."

She sat up, drawing her knees to her chin. "Shadowed reunion."

"What?"

"This has been a shadowed reunion. Since the day we met in Aunt Philly's hospital room it seems a dark shadow has loomed over us."

He chuckled.

"It's not funny. Why are you laughing?"

"Because it sounds like the perfect title for a book." He patted the ground. "Not exactly the luxury suite at a fancy hotel, but for now it's the best I can offer. I promise to behave myself."

As the night deepened, the temperature grew colder. Wrapped in thin blankets, Mitch and Laura huddled together. She spoke through chattering teeth. "Where is Frankie? So much for expecting him to keep his word."

"Maybe he got lost. Give him the benefit of the doubt." Mitch's stomach rumbled. "Is there anything in that bag to eat that doesn't require a can opener?"

She sat up and pulled the large purse closer. She gasped. "Oh!"

"What is it? Scorpion?"

She pulled the old-fashioned flip phone from the bottom of the purse. "It's Aunt Philly's. I discovered it earlier and decided it was better that Frankie didn't know. I don't know why she put it in my bag, but, bless her heart"—Laura pressed the On key, the pre-programmed tune played, and the screen lit—"it works. Oh, thank goodness. It's ten o'clock, though it feels like midnight."

Mitch sat up. "Dial 9-2-7. It's the emergency code for lawmen. Let's hope we're in range for a strong signal."

Laura did as she was instructed. Her heart sank. "No signal."

"Don't worry. We'll eat whatever we can open and doesn't require utensils, then get some rest. In the morning we'll walk. The farther we walk, the closer we'll come to being able to make a phone call and getting rescued."

She turned off the phone to preserve the battery. "Okay."

They shared a can of Vienna sausages, thankful for the pop-top. Laura refrained from mentioning that Frankie had not returned. A distant noise aroused her attention. "Did you hear that?"

The blast was followed by a second, and a third, and then a rapid exchange. Mitch frowned. "That's gunfire. Sounds like a Beretta semi-automatic. That's what Frankie has."

"It's far off."

"About a mile, maybe."

Laura caught her bottom lip between her teeth. "Do you think he's signaling because he's lost?"

"Sound carries for miles across the desert at night," Mitch said, listening some more. "Vehicles! At least two."

"Maybe your emergency signal went through before that thug smashed your phone." She wrapped her arms around him and hugged. "There's no reason for anyone to drive around at night in the desert. We're saved, don't you think, Mitch?"

"If the sound was coming from the north, I'd be

inclined to agree with you. Right now, I think we'd better get the hell out of here." He stood and grabbed the bag of food. "You carry the blankets."

"How will we know where we're going?"

He fastened bruised-looking blue eyes on hers. "I've always been fascinated with the constellations. We'll find the Big Dipper and then follow the North Star."

In sharp contrast to the day's heat, the night air was damp and cold. She looked at Mitch. To her frightened mind he seemed to loom taller than he had before, a solid wall of power, in spite of the agony of his shoulder. A lump welled in her throat. It had been hours since they were abducted. Surely Virgil Carter and the rest of the family were searching for them.

She hoped.

Chapter Twenty-Five

Virgil and Morgan Carter were identical in every way. Looking at them was like seeing a reflection in a mirror—imposing height, broad shoulders, piercing blue eyes, deep crevices that gullied down their cheeks, and scowls that could intimidate the worst offenders. Add to the mix a third and similar face. Garret Carter stood shoulder to shoulder with his twin brothers. All three had pulled their black suit jackets back to hitch behind holstered Colt .45s.

Victor Ortiz tugged a handkerchief from his back pocket and wiped his sweaty brow. He was certain the rumbling in his stomach had little to do with the burritos and tequila he'd eaten for lunch. What he wanted now was a siesta, and to rid his office of these gringo lawmen. He shifted his eyes from one to the other of the two taller men. He blinked. How many tequilas had he consumed? He must be seeing double.

Giving the men his strongest glare, he cleared the squeak rising in his throat. "You gringos come to my country and accuse me of drug trafficking. You assume all Mexicans are drug pushers. Do I, Victor Ortiz, deputy mayor of Ciudad Juarez, look as if I deal in drugs?"

Virgil addressed the man in flawless Spanish. "I will repeat that we are not here on drug-related business."

"Ai-yee! So you wish me to believe two of your citizens are missing, and you think they are in my country?"

Virgil's patience was wearing thin. He wanted to grab the fat faggot by the string tie and twist until the man's eyes popped out of their sockets.

Morgan stepped forward. His top lip curled into a snarl. "We have evidence that our nephew, Sheriff Mitchell Carter, and his companion, Ms. Laura Friday, were abducted and driven across the border."

Ai-yee, how many of these damned gringo hombres were there? "So these people are here illegally. Then I will notify the proper authorities, and when they are found we will put them in jail."

Silently, Virgil called the man a fat toad. He interjected, "Look, we're not here to provoke a diplomatic upheaval. We just want to find our people and take them home."

Garret took his turn. He too addressed the man in Spanish. "*Estados Unidos América* Senator Enrique Martinez's niece is married to Che Rivera, who is one of Mexico's presidential candidates." He added with a cold smile, "You seem like an intelligent man, *amigo*."

Ortiz mopped his face again. "I see you have interesting connections, *señor*."

All three brothers smiled nonchalantly. The mayor glared at them.

"So"—Garret's deep voice belied his impatience—"can we count on you to assist in helping find our kidnapped citizens?"

Ortiz's mind worked overtime. This whole situation could come tumbling down around him if he mishandled it. Especially since he'd received word that the new mayor, Sebastian Vargas, was due to arrive any day. Ortiz didn't know who he feared more—Vargas or Che Rivera. These Texas Rangers could cause him a lot of trouble if one of the village peons blabbed that he had entertained them in his office.

Ortiz pushed away from his desk. Grinning so that his yellowed teeth showed, he was suddenly affable. He raised his hand as if taking a sworn oath. "You have my solemn promise that I will do everything within my power to find them."

"Pepito!"

A young man holding an electronic tablet rushed in. "Yes, Uncle…I mean, Mayor?"

In a show of exasperation, Ortiz threw up his hands. "Ai-yee! My nephew has the intelligence of a donkey." He glared at the young man. "These gentlemen are federal law enforcers looking for two of their citizens who they believe were kidnapped and brought into our country. I wish you to go among our people and make inquiries to ask if strangers have been seen."

The lad stood wide-eyed. His eyes riveted on the giant twin brothers and the big guns on their hips. Ortiz barked, "Why are you standing there like a *estúpido burro*." He clapped his hands together. "*Rapido!*"

"Oh, *si, si*." The boy saluted. "Right away."

Virgil said, "I don't think you quite understand, mayor. Our visit is a courtesy to you. My brothers and I intend to conduct a search. With your permission, of course."

Still smiling from ear to ear, the mayor reached out his hand in a gesture of friendship. "Of course, *señores*."

Ai-yee! The Americans didn't know where they were. They had no compass to find their way to the border. Too bad. They might die in the desert. After all, it was very cold at night, and there were wild animals who lived in the desert. Anything could happen.

****

In the waning light, Frankie ambled along, his eyes riveted to the ground, wondering why he'd ever left New York. He hated everything about Texas—the heat, shoveling horse shit, sharing a bunkhouse with twenty farting, snoring guys, the low wages—in fact, he hated most everything about his life. He replayed Laura's words about his brother. Yeah, in retrospect, what sane human being walked into a school and snuffed out innocent lives, and for no good reason.

He shivered as he bent to the task of collecting wood. He didn't want to die in the desert. The temperature was frigid, and Mitch was fragile from the new injury to his shoulder. Frankie's stomach rumbled with hunger, and he worked to conjure up saliva to moisten his dry mouth.

A coyote yodeled in the distance. Another answered. Yeah, that was another thing he hated. The only wild animals he liked were the ones that lived in zoos. He picked up another piece of dried mesquite. Caged animals. His brother had been an animal that needed to be in a cage. Where had that streak of insane meanness come from? Maybe people were just born bad. He wondered if he shared those same depraved genetics. Frankie heaved a sigh. What drove him to steal cocaine from a drug cartel and think he'd live to grow gray hairs?

"Stupid…stupid." He repeated the word. Then out

of sheer frustration for his situation he shouted, "Stuuupiiid!"

The coyotes howled again, this time sounding closer. Shivers rippled both inside and outside of Frankie's body. He gave a fleeting thought to Mitch and Laura's safety.

Forget them. Forget the witness protection program. He'd hidden the cocaine and had memorized its exact location. With twenty kilos, and street value over sixty thousand per kilo, he could live like a king from the greenbacks it would bring.

Hearing the sound of vehicles, he scanned the darkness. No headlights. Suspecting what that meant, he dropped the wood, and ran like the hounds of hell were nipping at his heels.

He had to save himself. Had to!

Two jeeps using parking lights for visibility skidded to a halt, sending up a shower of dirt. Assault rifles aimed at him. A heavily accented voice called out, "You are Frankie Romeo?"

"Who wants to know?" He sounded more confident than he was.

A pair of low-beamed headlights switched on. The figure that approach reminded Frankie of a prize fighter. He put the man in the middle forties. Hair mussed from the wind. Dressed in starched camouflaged khakis. A faded scar that ran from his chin and ended at his ear added to the evil expression.

There was nothing about this man's demeanor that implied "model citizen."

"How do you know my name?"

"I know everything that happens in my country. I know you are connected to the Vargas cartel and are in the employ of my long-time enemy Mitch Carter." He pointed to the more recent scar, still raised and red at his temple. "Once Sebastian was my brother. Now he is a traitor, which makes him my enemy."

Frankie stammered, "I don't know what you're talking about. Me and my friends were camping. We needed firewood. I got lost. I-I don't know any Sebastian Vargas."

The man reached out and placed a vicious slap across Frankie's cheek. "Don't play games with me. Do you know who I am?"

Frankie rubbed the sting on his cheek. He shook his head in denial.

"Perhaps you have heard of me from that young snot Hugo Vargas. I am Navarre Àron. You dare steal from me? I have business associates breathing down my neck. You don't get me that five million I owe those hombres, and they'll have my head." Àron leaned forward. Frankie nearly gagged from the man's fetid wine breath. Àron laid another slap across Frankie's cheek. "Get me my five million, or I'll make the devil look like a Sunday school teacher."

Frankie's bowels leaked into his shorts. For a reason that escaped him, the term "dead man walking" filtered through his mind. Yeah, that's what he was, a man getting ready to walk to his death. Once he told Àron where to find the cocaine, Frankie knew his life was over.

These were evil men, these rival relatives, Vargas, who sewed live rattlers in his victims' mouths, and Àron, who severed heads from bodies. A shudder wracked Frankie. Neither was a good way to die.

There was no one to mourn his death. What was it

the priest used to say? "If you don't change your ways, Frankie, you'll end up in a coffin with no one to cry over you." He'd been thirteen then, and now at age thirty he wished he'd listened. He wished he'd found a good woman to settle down with, and had a houseful of kids. He uttered a prayer asking God's forgiveness, and regretted there was no priest to hear his confession.

He shifted his body into rigid awareness as he reached around to grab the Beretta tucked inside his waistband.

****

Laura had faced death before. While fear constricted her heart, so did resolve and the will to live. Maintaining control kept her from panicking. She had no illusion of control tonight. She could die, and Mitch had never heard her say she loved him. Deep down, she knew he was waiting for those three little words. Her fears held more power, because the fears weren't just about her, they were about *them.*

She had to tell him.

She had to survive.

"Laura?"

"I'm okay, Mitch."

"We can take a minute to rest."

She didn't know how Mitch managed to keep going as she watched him drop the expensive purse to the ground. Laura wanted to laugh at the ridiculous price she had paid, and on sale, thinking, *What a bargain.* Its bright yellow leather was now coated with a film of dirt, the silk lining a bed for canned goods and a jar of water. Owning the bag had seemed so important while she'd stood inside Bloomingdale's convincing herself that she deserved to reward herself.

The moonlight revealed a dark stain on Mitch's shirt. She touched her fingers to it. They came away moist. She sniffed. Blood. Mitch's wound had opened, and he was bleeding. "You're right. We both need a breather."

She removed the bottle of water from the purse and unscrewed the lid. She lifted it to Mitch's lips. "You're burning with fever. How far do you think we've come?"

Mitch took a stingy sip. He heaved a sigh as he sank to the ground. "Two miles, maybe."

Laura took her own tiny sip. She rummaged inside the bag and gave a gleeful, "Aha! I knew I had one." She held up the metal fingernail file. Grabbing a can of tomato soup, she jabbed at the lid, and jabbed again, and again. "It worked." She handed the prize to Mitch. "Here, take it. There's another can." She repeated the act, then held the tin forward to clink against Mitch's. "We'll pretend it's gazpacho. Cheers!"

Mitch smiled. "You are a treasure, Laura Friday."

"And you are my hero. I love you, Mitch Carter, and before the stars in the sky, the cacti, and the lizards, I truly love you."

"Those words are music to my ears. I wish I had the energy to hold you in my arms, and the strength to make love to you."

"When we're safe and your shoulder is healed, we'll make up for lost time. I promise, and I never break my promises." A weight of doubt burdened her heart. If Mitch didn't get to a doctor soon, there might be no future for them.

They finished their light meal in silence, each seemingly lost in their own thoughts. Laura rarely cried, which made the tears burning her eyes all the more frustrating. "Do you think Frankie is dead?"

"Most likely."

"Who?"

"Can't say for sure. Maybe Vargas ordered a hit on Frankie. But this is Àron's stomping grounds. If it was him, I don't know what grudge he'd have unless…Vargas set Frankie up."

"Set him up for what reason?"

Mitch thought for a minute. "Maybe Vargas knew Frankie stole the coke. Maybe he put the finger on Frankie and arranged for Àron to pull the trigger."

She closed her eyes. "I'm so sick of crime. Sick of reporting it. Sick of depravity. I miss writing trivial articles about who won Cole Harbor's Fourth of July pie-baking contest, and writing about you rescuing Nadia Cruex's cat from a tree."

He gave her a half-smile. "Yep, I know how you feel."

She sipped her soup and watched him. Exhaustion rode hard on his handsome face, and she knew from the way he spoke through gritted teeth the pain in his shoulder was probably unbearable.

She tried to smile but it didn't quite work. "Do you think, whoever *they* are, they're looking for us?"

"If they were, we'd be found by now." He struggled to his feet. "Let's put some more distance behind us. Maybe in the morning we can find a shady spot and rest for a couple of hours."

He picked up the bag and looped the strap over his good shoulder. His legs buckled, and Laura caught him. "Okay?" she asked.

He nodded.

She wrapped her arm around his waist and helped support him as they resumed walking unsteadily across the desert.

Chapter Twenty-Six

Victor Ortiz splashed cologne over his freshly shaven face. He frowned at his jowled reflection as he straightened the bolo tie in anticipation of the arrival of the new leader of the South American cartel, Hugo Vargas III, the one about whom the stupid peons whispered the humiliating title *El Chapo*. What the young *patrón* lacked in stature was compensated by his enormous penchant for cruelty. Revulsion rippled over Ortiz.

Hugo was coming to see the prisoner Sebastian had hidden in an abandoned shack in the desert. Navarre Àron's young nephew and cousin now held power, and he, Victor Ortiz, had sent his best enforcers to capture Àron. It would be an interesting visit, though he himself much preferred remaining in the village. He abhorred violence and feared retribution.

Victor slicked back his greasy hair. He had a fat wife who no longer satisfied his sexual appetite but was a good cook. He had six hungry children to feed and a mistress who made him feel like a young stud. All made demands on him and his paltry salary. A man had to choose where to place his loyalties, and Ortiz considered himself an ambitious but cautious man. He thought about the phone call and the steely voice relaying the message, "Anyone who renounces allegiance to the young *patrón* can dig his own grave, but first he will dig the graves for his *familia*." The voice had laughed and then said, "The Vargas Cartel is marching through Mexico. Declare your loyalty and live, or prepare to die."

"Uncle?" Pepito came to the door. "They are coming. It is a convoy."

Ortiz extracted a cigarillo from his pocket. Unwrapping the cigar, he jammed it into the side of his mouth. "How many?"

"Four."

"Go to the church, Pepito. Today is a good day for praying. Do not come back to the office unless you are summoned. Though you are a worthless nephew, I promised your mother to keep you safe."

Ortiz made the sign of the cross as he gathered his waning courage. He feared the worst would happen if his new *patrón* found out about the American *federales*. He had only agreed they could look for their lost citizens, he had not actually given them permission, but if Hugo and Sebastian didn't believe him…oh, well.

Ortiz and Pepito turned to the door. Two men stood there, one tall and lean, with long thick black hair hanging to his waist, Indian, but not Yaqui. The other was short and mustached, with olive skin and beady black eyes, and grinning.

"*Hola, cómo estás!* I am Victor Ortiz, the mayor of Ciudad Juarez, at your service, and who are you, may I ask?"

The short man said, "They call me *hombre de cabra*. My partner is Incendio."

Goat Man? An odd name. Hanging from his waist was the most vicious-looking knife Ortiz had ever seen. And *Fire*. These were men to fear.

Goat man said, "Come. *El Jefe* awaits."

"*Un momento*. My nephew, Pepito, he is not so smart. Slow in the mind." Ortiz made the sign for crazy and rolled his eyes. "He will only be a nuisance."

Goat man gave a sadistic smile. "Boo!" And laughed when the young man cowered behind his fat uncle. "We have no need for a frightened *ratón*. Shoo, mouse."

Incendio snatched the cigarillo from Ortiz and stuck it in his own mouth. He flicked open a cigarette lighter, inhaled, then smiled as if enjoying the cigar.

Goat man said, "*El Jefe*, he no like to be kept waiting. You will ride in the second car."

Ortiz walked outside into the bright sunlight. He pulled the sunglasses from his shirt pocket as he approached the black Escalade with tinted windows.

He glanced up at the clear blue sky. Off in the distance buzzards circled like miniature black airplanes. It was an omen. A helplessness rose in his chest.

****

The Carter brothers' vehicle scuttled across the sand, their weapons drawn and ready. The GPS showed a building. Using caution, the brothers parked the Jeep a quarter of a mile from the structure.

Garrett expressed his aggravation. "Damn desert. Miles of nothing. I thought we'd at least spot some sign of Mitch and Laura by now."

Virgil and Morgan seemed to share the same thought. Virgil held up his hand in a signal to halt. He whispered as he pointed to the circling vultures. "I'm almost afraid of what we might find inside."

Morgan wore a grave expression. "I'm with you, Brother. The jitters in my stomach are working overtime. If it's bad, I don't know how we'll break the news to Wyatt, or the elder Ms. Friday."

Garrett looked as if he wanted to say something, then changed his mind.

Walking parallel to each other, they approached on cat-silent feet. Garrett and Morgan flattened themselves against either side of the sun-bleached shanty's door. There was no response to Virgil's repeated knocking.

Virgil signaled for his brothers to go around back. He pointed to his mouth, then held up ten fingers and folded each one, to show that he would count to ten, announce himself, then enter.

Two solemn nods indicated their understanding.

Morgan and Garrett jogged around to the back, keeping low beneath the line of windows. At exactly ten seconds, Virgil shouted, "Texas Ranger Virgil Carter. Drop your weapons. I have men stationed around the house."

He positioned himself where he could watch the doorknob. When nothing happened, he kicked the door and it fell off its rusted hinges. The thud as it collapsed onto the floor sounded like a gunshot. Morgan and Garret burst through the rear entrance ready to discharge their Colt .45s. The small living area was clear.

As soon as the three entered the one-room structure, they smelled it. Vomit, alcohol, blood.

Garrett called out, "Mitch…Laura!"

The bed with sagging springs was shoved against a whitish clay wall. Dried vomit coated the holey mattress.

Morgan lowered his weapon. "I'm not sure what I expected. It certainly wasn't a bloodbath."

Garrett glanced around. "Dear God."

Blood had splattered across the entire white wall. Darker red arcs covered the ceiling in a montage of patterns. Some blood had trickled to the floor, drying in puddles of dirty pink.

"I'm afraid to think about what happened in here." Virgil was glad he'd missed breakfast that morning. "No one could survive this."

Morgan heaved a heavy sigh. "I spotted a privy around back. It can't smell any worse than this, so we might as well check it out."

Guns ready, three grim faces approached the outhouse. Morgan placed a swift kick on a particularly obstinate buzzard that refused to get out of the way. The wooden door was shut. A sandy rut at the bottom indicated an animal had tried to dig its way inside. Blood was obvious against the ground. Lots of blood. The stench doubled Garrett over and caused him to gag.

"I'm gonna tell you right now"—Virgil holstered his .45—"there's nothing that scares me. Not even the devil himself, but right now, I'm almost sick to my stomach, afraid of who we might find inside."

Morgan's voice was low and serious. "Want me to do it, Virge?"

Virgil shook his head. "Let's do this." He grabbed the knobbed handle and yanked the door wide open.

Garrett nearly dropped to his knees. He huffed out, "Sweet Jesus."

In one corner, Navarre Àron's mutilated body slumped against the wall. Next to him, sitting on the shit hole, his hands tied to a rotten rafter, was Victor Ortiz's naked body, his dead eyes bulging as if witnessing the horrors that were happening, his mouth sewn shut, his cheeks puffed and moving from side to side.

Almost all the blood had drained from Àron's body. His head sat oddly on his neck, and Morgan used the barrel of his revolver to turn it. He yelped when the head toppled from its resting place, rolled to the floor, out the door, and landed with the gaping eyes staring at the sky.

Morgan coughed to clear his throat as he reached down to grab the head by the hair. He set it on the wooden seat, next to the body. "Garrett, go get the Jeep. We'll use the satellite phone to contact Che Rivera. This is a definite crime scene, and Che's the only one I trust to see we don't spend the rest of our lives in a Mexican prison. This looks like the work of Hugo Vargas. I'll bet a year's pay a rattler is sewn inside Ortiz's mouth."

Virgil's stomach knotted. "Not a bet I'd want to take."

Garrett said, "Since I'm Director of Homeland Security, and since Senator Radcliff is dead, we'd better contact the President. We'll need support from our guys, too."

****

Laura awoke shivering with cold. Mitch had collapsed about an hour after they'd heard the gunshots. She touched her hand to his forehead. Delirious with fever, he mumbled incoherent words.

She reached inside the bag and searched for the cell phone. Flipping it open, she prayed for service. The little chime of music played. She punched in the number for the Carter Ranch. Nothing. No service. In frustration she tossed the phone back into the purse.

"Thirsty." Mitch rasped out the words.

She opened the Mason jar and supported his head as she lifted the water to his lips. "Just a sip. I'm sorry, I wish you could have more. Surely tomorrow we'll see a house, a ranch, a person."

He reached up to wipe the tear that glistened on her cheek. The words came out as if it were an effort for him to speak. "We'll make it. I know my family is searching for us."

She sipped enough to moisten her throat, then returned the jar to its nesting place. Settling against Mitch, she pulled the blankets closer around them. She wanted to believe him. She blinked back the tears. They were not for herself but for him. The wound in his shoulder was filled with yellow pus and had an odor. She worried about gangrene. His fingers were swollen to the point he couldn't flex them. Mitch would die if he didn't get medical treatment soon.

She gazed up at the sky until she spotted the Big Dipper and remembered what Mitch had said about walking in the direction of the North Star. How far was it to the border—one mile, fifty? Considering the alternatives to dying, she figured she could travel faster without him. It was up to her to find help. She longed for civilization, for a hospital and a doctor.

She folded Mitch into her arms, listening to his labored breathing. She had selfishly allowed this good man to leave Cole Harbor, to walk out of her life. She wasn't ready to let him go again.

In a few hours it would be daylight. She had to make a decision—stay and watch Mitch die, or try to find help and hope he would still be alive when she returned. She dragged herself through the usual brain-sweep, trying to quiet her mind.

She didn't know how long she'd slept, or what instinct caused her to awaken. What she did know was the heat had seeped into her bones and chased away the chills. Last night's goose bumps were replaced by a sheen of sweat.

A sound in the distance caused her to sit up and throw off the blankets. She listened. Maybe her imagination was playing tricks on her. She stood, shaded her eyes, and strained her ears.

The sound of a vehicle. Her elation was rapidly replaced with panic. What if Vargas had returned to find them? She searched for a weapon. Sand, only sand and dried brush. A Jeep approached through the shimmering waves of desert heat.

She rummaged inside her purse and wrapped her hand around the fingernail file. She would not go down without a fight. She sat next to Mitch, shielding his body with hers, and waited in breathless fear.

Chapter Twenty-Seven

Sun spots danced in front of her eyes, making it difficult to see. She shielded her eyes with one hand and clasped the fingernail file in the other. If it could open tin cans, then it could surely pierce a heart, or gouge out an eye.

A hand reached toward her.

She drew back her arm, ready to fight to the death.

"Laura?" It was a deep, slow voice.

The man went down on one knee. Her vision cleared, revealing two more men who knelt, their hands reaching for Mitch.

"Virgil," she managed, weeping. "Oh, thank God. Mitch said you would come. They hurt him. Those bastards kept hitting him in the shoulder with a rifle. And…and"—she sniffed—"I think they must have killed Frankie."

Virgil smiled grimly at her. "We found Frankie."

By the frown on his face, she knew, but still asked, "Alive?"

"'Fraid not. Time enough for you to fill us in on what happened. What about you? Are you hurt?"

"Exhausted, bitten all over by bugs, but other than that, I'm okay."

Mitch opened his eyes. He managed a weak smile. "'Bout time you showed up. We were heading toward the border. I couldn't walk any farther."

"Don't you worry about that, nephew. We've got a helicopter waiting to give you a free ride."

Morgan popped a flare. Seconds later, the womp-womp of a helicopter sounded overhead. Morgan covered Mitch with the blanket to shield him from the blowing sand as the copter landed.

Morgan and Garrett raced toward the big metal bird and lifted down the stretcher.

Laura held Mitch's hand to her breast. "We're going home."

Before being loaded into the helicopter, Mitch looked at his uncles. Too sick and weak to speak, he offered a thumbs up and a smile.

The pilot secured Mitch, then reached down to grab Laura's uplifted hands. Virgil clasped her around the waist to boost her inside. He shouted over the engine noise, "We've notified your aunt and Sam and Wyatt that you're safe. They'll meet you at the hospital. We have some unfinished business to wrap up before we leave Mexico. See you in a couple of days."

Laura nodded her understanding. She placed the protective earphones over her ears, settled in the seat, and strapped on the safety harness. The pallor on Mitch's face worried her.

****

The helicopter landed at the El Paso hospital, and Sam Houston Carter and two nurses raced to lift Mitch and the stretcher to the ground. He was transferred to a gurney and rolled into the hospital.

Tearful and anxious faces greeted them in the emergency room waiting area. Aunt Philly grabbed Laura, sobbing.

Sam instructed the nurse to take Laura straight to a

room. "I'm okay, Sam. Just hungry and exhausted. Don't worry about me. Take care of Mitch."

"We're sending him to x-ray, and then we'll prep him for surgery. The shoulder looks bad." He patted her hand. "We'll keep you overnight as a precaution. We've also arranged for your aunt to stay in the room with you."

Laura looked at Wyatt. "Virgil said he and Morgan and Garrett had to tie up loose ends in Mexico."

"Yep, I've talked to 'em. You get some rest, young lady. We'll let you know when Mitch is out of surgery."

****

Ten days later was like déjà vu as Laura and Wyatt followed Sam as he pushed Mitch in a wheelchair, repeating the scene that had happened not so long ago. The trio strolled out of the elevator and through the lobby to the waiting SUV. Mitch's younger brother Rob stood next to the open door.

Wyatt locked down the chair's wheels so Mitch could stand. With his arm in a sling that was strapped tight around his waist, he needed Sam's help to steady him as he stood.

"Let me remind you, nephew, you've had a shoulder replacement, not to speak of nearly succumbing to gangrene. You're lucky we didn't have to amputate." Sam's forehead wrinkled into a frown. A no-nonsense squint framed those famous Carter blue eyes. "Fair warning—with all the damage to muscle and bone, I can't guarantee how much range of motion you'll get back, but for the next couple of weeks, I'm ordering you to keep that arm immobilized and not lift anything heavier than a piece of toilet paper."

Mitch scowled as he stepped up on the running

board. He used his left hand to grip the safety handle. "I'm beginning to feel like a damned invalid. When can I go back to work?"

Sam merely smirked. "Just like the rest of us, full up with Carter stubbornness. In about ten days. Light duty, and that's only to answer phone calls, read reports, and boss poor Alma around."

At the aging secretary's name, everyone chuckled. Mitch smiled. "Knowing Alma, she'll do the bossing, and try to drown me in green tea." He grimaced.

Sam issued a reminder. "With your arm in a sling, you won't be able to drive."

Laura spoke as she leaned in to fasten Mitch's seatbelt. "Don't worry, Sam, I'll take care of the transportation."

****

They arrived back at the ranch to be greeted by two exuberant twins and the rest of the family. Kit and Carson each latched on to one of Mitch's legs. "Boy, Uncle Mitch, we thought you were a goner."

A guffaw bubbled out of Mitch. "Out of the mouths of six-year-olds." He reached down with his good hand to tousle the blond heads of his nephews. "Well, boys, I'm glad to be home."

Jill ushered everyone inside the house. She looked at her brother. "I don't know whether to be mad at you for putting a scare into all of us, or hug the daylights out of you."

When Mitch opened his arm, she stepped in and gingerly squeezed. "Laura will help you upstairs while Claire and I finish supper. Virgil, Morgan, and Garrett are back from Mexico. It's been a long time since the family was together. So rest up, brother. I expect a lively conversation around the dinner table tonight."

That night proved to be a joyous occasion. A sadness tugged at Laura's heart. Aunt Philly had confided that now Mitch was home, Laura was safe, and the purchase of the cottage in Cole Harbor had been finalized, it was time for her to leave Texas.

Jill's voice interrupted Laura's reflections. "If you boys plan to go fishing with your uncles tomorrow, finish your dessert. It's past your bedtime."

The twins shoved last bites of pecan pie cookies into their mouths. Kit said, "Uncle Mitch, me and Carson been thinking."

Mitch smiled at his nephews. Love tugged at his heart as he looked at them and at his sister's growing belly. In a few months there would be another Carter-Conroy in the family. He wanted children, too, and he wanted them with only one woman.

He smiled at his nephews. "Sounds serious. Thinking about what?"

Kit and Carson surveyed everyone at the table. Their heavy sighs were simultaneous. "Well, we been thinking. Would you and Grandpa, and Uncle Virgil, Uncle Morgan, and Uncle Garrett be mad if me and Kit didn't want to be lawmen?"

Before anyone could answer, Carson interjected, "'Cause it's dangerous." The young boy looked at his father and then his granddad. "We'd rather be ranchers like Daddy and Grandpa."

Mitch's breath hitched in his throat. He watched his dad sneak the napkin up to wipe a tear before it dribbled down his cheek. His brother-in-law, Travis, seemed surprised at his sons' declaration, and at the same time curious to hear Mitch's answer.

Mitch laid his fork on the table. He gauged his answer. "Ranching is an old and honorable profession. Just like being a lawman is an honorable profession, and you're right about it being dangerous. It makes me proud to know you boys want to carry on the ranching tradition in this family. But…"

A hush filled the room as if everyone hung on that one word…But.

"But what, Uncle Mitch?"

"There's more to ranching than riding horses and working cows. It's more than planting hay and mending fences. It's hard work. To run a successful enterprise, you have to have book smarts. You'll need a college education, that's for sure." He leaned closer to the table. "There's something I want you boys to always remember: I'm proud of you. Now, the only thing that'll make me mad is if you don't out-fish your grandpa tomorrow. So scoot. Off to bed."

Jill mouthed, "Thank you," as she herded the twins out the door heading to their house.

With the coast cleared of innocent ears, the conversation began. Virgil said, "Which brings us to the highlight of our visit."

Alternating between Morgan and Garrett, the brothers detailed the gruesome discoveries at the shack in the desert.

A shudder wracked Mitch. "Yeah, Laura and I know that place. That's where we were taken. I'm ashamed to admit that my lawman instinct let me down where Frankie was concerned. Still, if it hadn't been for him having a change of conscience, I'm afraid we'd all have ended up like Navarre Àron and Victor Ortiz."

Laura toyed with a piece of cookie crust. "What

about Frankie? They didn't…I mean, he wasn't…"

"Tortured?" Virgil shook his head. "No, he managed to take down several of Àron's men before he died. When we found Àron, he had a bullet wound to the gut. We believe Frankie put it there. Otherwise, there's no way Hugo Vargas or anyone else would have captured him. As for Frankie, we found him and two of Àron's flunkies in a ditch. He was riddled with bullets. Rest assured he didn't suffer. Those were probably the shots you heard. Especially since you said it sounded like a gun battle."

Mitch fussed with the sling. He cradled his bad arm to relieve the tension from the strap pressing against his neck. He sighed. "That leaves Hugo and Sebastian to deal with."

Morgan reached for another pecan pie cookie. He took a man-sized bite and chewed thoughtfully. "Man, I could pack away about a dozen of these." He washed the cookie down with coffee. "Actually, there is an almost happy ending to this story, Mitch. We contacted our friend Che Rivera." He glanced at his brother, Garrett. "You know Che's fiancé is Ava Mendez."

Garrett smiled. "Her father is Jorge Mendez, Texas's state representative. He's a good man. If Che is elected president of Mexico, we'll see another good man in office. Finish telling Mitch what happened."

Morgan smiled. "After we related our find and that we believed Vargas either committed the murders or ordered them done, Che put together a search party—a helicopter search-and-destroy party, no less. It was enough that the current president was on Àron's payroll, but with him out of the way, it meant Vargas would assume control of the drug trade, human trafficking trade, and all other illegal activities. Che's political platform is to get tough on crime and create a safer Mexico."

Virgil took over. "Four black SUVs were spotted traveling toward our borders. Che ordered his pilot to do a fly over, just for a look-see. Che said the retractable sun roofs on all four vehicles opened and the helicopters were fired upon, at which point Che gave the order to return fire. RPGs took out all four vehicles. Hugo and Sebastian Vargas's bodies were among those identified. There were no survivors."

Mitch tsked. "So he's dead?"

Morgan assured, "Oh, yes, quite dead. With Àron and Vargas out of the way, I assure you we have dealt a deadly blow to both drug cartels."

Mitch moaned as he stood. "I think I can rest easy tonight." He thanked his uncles again for coming to his and Laura's rescue, and for sharing their news. "You fellas better catch some shuteye if you plan to rise and shine before the twins. I can assure you those two little scamps will out-fish you and brag about it."

Chapter Twenty-Eight

Upstairs in his room, Laura helped Mitch remove the sling and slide his shirt over his heavily bandaged shoulder. In fact, she helped him completely undress and slip into pajama bottoms, leaving his chest bare. A yearning filled her, along with feelings she had never experienced with Bryan. The memory of him was now only a fleeting moment. What she felt for Mitch was so powerful it was almost painful. Death had nearly claimed him.

He bent to her mouth. "Have I told you," he whispered against her lips, "that I'm madly in love with you?"

She smiled into his kiss. "Well, not exactly madly in love."

"Well, I am, totally."

She linked her arms around his neck, careful not to press against his sling. She said, her voice a bit shy, "I love you, too."

His smile grew wider. "Would you sit on the bed, please?"

She cast him a curious glance and did as he commanded.

He knelt on one knee. He took her hand into his and kissed the palm. "I wanted to do this in private." He sucked in a breath and blew it out. "Laura Friday, would you do me the honor of becoming my wife?"

Her heart beat a rapid tattoo against her chest. She took his face between her hands and kissed his eyes, his nose, his lips. "Yes…yes…yes!"

He wobbled as he stood, and nearly collapsed onto the bed. Beads of sweat lined his forehead. His breath came in gasps. "I so want to make love to you."

"There's nothing I desire more. But not tonight, and not until you can hold me in both arms without wincing in pain."

"It's against my better judgment, but I want to do this right, for both of us."

She walked to the bathroom and returned with a glass of water. She uncapped the little brown vial and shook a pain pill into his hand. "Do you mind if I pick the place for our honeymoon?"

He swallowed the pill and drained the glass. "Anywhere except the desert."

She laughed. "I suppose we should set a wedding date first."

He glanced down at his arm and frowned. "What about next week?"

She ordered him to lie back while she pulled the duvet up to his chest. "Too soon. I don't want a big wedding, but I do want one to remember, and that means you in a nice cowboy tuxedo that isn't adorned with a blue arm sling." She bent and kissed him.

He reached up and caressed her breast. "I guess waiting has its rewards." He didn't mean to grimace as though the pain had begun to wear on him. "Laura?"

She had turned to leave when he called her back. "Virgil told me how you nearly attacked him with a fingernail file. You were brave out there." He looked at her lovingly. "I'm proud of you."

She laughed self-consciously. “Showing up when they did saved me from having to make the toughest decision of my life—to leave you and try to find help”—her voice cracked with emotion—“or stay and watch you die.”

His eyes reflected his own emotions. “We make a good team, you and me.”

The hunger and love in his eyes were all she needed. She blew him a kiss and slipped out the door.

Laura floated on air as she headed to the bedroom she shared with her aunt. Phyllis looked up from the romance novel she held. “By the look on your face, I’m thinking something wonderful must have just happened.”

Laura pulled the blouse over her head and slipped the jeans down her hips. She tossed the garments in a chair and grabbed her pajamas. “Mitch asked me to marry him.”

Phyllis squealed and clapped her hands like a happy child. “And…and?”

“Well, of course I said yes.” Laura did a little happy dance. “We haven’t set a date yet.”

Phyllis cocked her head in a slight nod and laid the book on the night table. “I’m happy for you, and I don’t mean to put a damper on your wonderful news.” She fidgeted with her fingers.

“You’re leaving, aren’t you?”

“Ayuh.”

When Laura started to protest, Phyllis held up her hand. Whatever Laura intended to say died in her throat.

“You’re safe. Mitch needs you. I have a cottage to furnish. The truth is, I want to go home.”

"The cottage is really a house. A huge house. Do you plan to ramble around in it all alone?"

"Not at all. I've enlisted Maudie's help. I'm turning the Friday House into a bed and breakfast. Maudie will work her magic with her wonderful baking skills, and I'll use the marketing information you taught us to promote the B&B." Her expression pleaded for Laura's understanding. "Texas isn't for me. As much as I've enjoyed the Carters, and Wyatt, Maine is my home."

"When are you leaving?"

"Saturday. Wyatt will drive me to the airport."

Laura's voice was emphatic. "Five days! I'm going with you."

"Now listen to me, young lady. You just said yes to Mitch's marriage proposal. He needs you. Plus, what about your editor-in-chief position at the *Gazette*?"

"I'll work it out. I'm going with you, and that's final." She flounced into bed, pulled the covers to her chin, and turned out the light.

After breakfast the next morning, Laura joined Mitch in the den. He stirred her blood with a craving she couldn't ignore, and she didn't know if she could stay true to her declaration of waiting for his shoulder to heal before making love to him.

She refilled his cup. "Any day in September. I've picked the month, now you pick the date."

When he cast a puzzled frown toward her, she smiled. "Have you forgotten that you proposed last night? I think in two months both your arms should work just fine."

His deep blue gaze drifted over her. "September 16th. It was my mom's birthday. I'd like to think she'd be with us on that day."

Laura's eyes misted. "I'll make sure my bouquet is filled with her favorite flowers."

"Texas bluebonnets."

She smiled and nodded her agreement, then drew a deep sigh. Setting the date and deciding on flowers was easy. She hoped he'd understand what she was about to say. "Mitch, I'm resigning from the *Gazette*. In my short few weeks as editor-in-chief, I've discovered that running a big newspaper isn't what I desire."

"But you ran the *Harbor Gazette* and loved it."

"It was a small operation, and I did love it. I only had to answer to myself, and I didn't have to worry about out-scooping a competing news rag, or getting my ass chewed by New York corporate if I didn't make sales quotas."

"Okay, I can buy that. My concern is this: once we're married, what will you do to keep from getting bored? A bored housewife equals an unhappy wife."

She placed her hands on her knees and thought for a moment. "Maybe I'll be too busy raising a houseful of little Carters"—her smile was emphatic—"whom we will not name after famous people."

Mitch laughed, then sobered. "What else, Laura? I can tell by the way you're worrying your bottom lip that something else is bothering you. Does it have anything to do with my going back to work? I'm a lawman and will remain one until circumstances dictate otherwise."

She huffed a sigh. "No, Mitch, it's not your returning to work or your chosen career, though I can't say that I look forward to the day one of your deputies knocks on the door to tell me you've been injured or worse. I don't ever want to relive what we've just survived."

She watched his jaw tighten as he spoke. "Okay, then what's eating at you?"

There was only one way to say it, and that was straight out. "Aunt Philly is leaving in four days, and I'm going with her."

He sat forward, sloshing coffee on his pants leg. "Leaving! Did I have a brain fart? Didn't we just set a date for our wedding?"

Good heavens! She arched a brow at the depth of irritation in his tone. "Oh, crap, that didn't come out right, did it? Let me start over. You have weeks of physical therapy, plus you're returning to work next week. Aunt Philly plans to turn the cottage into a bed and breakfast. She's not old, but she's no spring chicken, and neither is Maudie. Those two women need help. I'm at loose ends and need activities to fill my days while you continue to heal. It might as well be in Cole Harbor. It's only for two months, Mitch. I'll even enlist Jill and Claire via Skype to help me plan the wedding. Please don't let this turn into our first lovers' quarrel."

He set the cup aside and patted his knee. "Come here."

She obligingly obeyed, and shyly looked up at him through lowered lashes. He captured her mouth in a slow drugging kiss that sent her heart soaring. Oh, how she loved him. Needed him. She buried her hands in the thick softness of his hair. His manhood pulsed against her thigh, and heated need shot through her like liquid fire.

He left her mouth, trailing kisses down her neck.

She moaned in sweet ecstasy as his lips made a sensual path along her breast, firing her blood to a raging inferno.

The giant grandfather clock standing guard in the corner of the room chimed eleven times. The sound was like throwing water on a fire. Laura scooted from Mitch's lap. Her breaths came in little pants. "I think I need a cold shower."

Mitch grinned. "Me, too." He held up his sling. "Except for this, I'd join you."

She ran a trembling hand through her hair as she licked her swollen lips. "Does this mean we're okay?"

Lust shimmered in his blue gaze. "We're more than okay as long as you promise to say 'I do' on September 16th."

Chapter Twenty-Nine

The warm afternoon sun beat down on Laura, relaxing her, making her drowsy. There was nothing like Maine at the end of August. Not too hot nor too cool. She inhaled the crisp sea breeze. So different from Texas's hundred-degree weather. She adjusted her sunglasses and gazed out over Cole Harbor's bay and smiled at the white sails dotting the pristine teal water. Harmon Taylor motored by in his whale-watching boat loaded with tourists. He sounded the horn and waved. All the tourists waved, and she greeted them with a return wave and a smile.

Dressed in shorts and a sleeveless top, she stood ankle deep in the water, relishing the teasing waves lapping against the calves of her legs. This was paradise. In a week she would board a plane back to Texas. She was happy, she'd told herself for the past two months.

The plans for her wedding were coming along without a hitch. Skyping with Jill and Claire and discussing decorations and food for the reception was fun. She and her aunt had ventured into Bangor and spent the day shopping for just the right wedding dress. Not a gown, and nothing too fancy. A knee-length white shift with a scooped neck and short capped sleeves, with a chiffon lace overslip adorned with beading and sequins. Chic without being dowdy.

She was marrying a man who loved her, with a huge family who had adopted her as their own. Everything was perfect. So what was wrong with her? Maybe she was one of those women designed to throw away every opportunity for happiness. This idea upset her. She kicked the water, sending up droplets that glittered like diamonds in the sun. Her eyes filled with tears. She loved Cole Harbor. From the first moment she and Phyllis had driven into town, it felt like home, even when they had both cried after seeing the vacant lot where the Friday Sisters Bookstore and the *Harbor Gazette* had once stood.

She and Phyllis and Maudie had immediately rolled up their sleeves to begin the spit polish work and shining renovations to bring the 1940s cottage back to its former glory and convert it to a bed and breakfast. The old garage had been transformed into a honeymoon suite separate from the main house, for privacy—the ultimate honeymoon getaway. It was already booked for a wedding on the lawn overlooking the bay, and a party of twelve guests. Wistfulness plucked at her heart. This is where she'd like to host her own wedding. That was an impossible dream. Too much planning had gone into hosting it at the Carter ranch.

She waded out of the water and grabbed her sandals to trudge up the steps that led to the yard bursting with color from a variety of flowers. She held out her left hand, the ring finger bare. Mitch had promised to surprise her with the perfect wedding band.

"Oh, Mitch, I love you so much it scares me." He owned her heart, yet she knew a portion of her heart would always remain in Cole Harbor. She let out a woeful sigh.

She rinsed off her feet before walking up the steps and through the screened sunroom. Inside the sitting room, she stopped to admire the rattan furniture with bright floral-patterned cushions that reminded her of Hawaii. In the main room's check-in area, Aunt Philly sat on a tall stool with the phone to her ear. From the tone of the conversation, she guessed it was with a client as Phyllis said, "Don't worry. Everything is all arranged, just the way we've discussed. Ayuh, we can certainly make the cake." She scribbled as she talked. "If you can give me a description of the decorations and how many layers. Lovely. Ayuh, Maudie Perry is a genius when it come to baking and icing decorations." She paused. "Don't worry, it's our secret." She hung up the phone, smiling to herself.

"What's your secret, Aunt Philly?"

Phyllis jumped as if she'd been shot and placed a hand over her heart. "S-secret. Oh, ah, th-the future sister-in-law of the bride wanted to make sure I didn't let slip about the…ayuh, the cake."

Laura thought she had never seen her aunt so flustered, but chalked it up to having startled her. "What about the cake?"

At the expression on her aunt's face, she winked and smiled. "Don't worry, my lips are sealed."

Phyllis sighed. "Oh, nothing fancy. Four layers, alternating chocolate and yellow cake. White icing." She fluttered her hands. "Like I said, nothing Maudie can't handle. And they've asked if I'd arrange for a photographah."

"Look no further. Right up my alley."

"By Godfrey, that won't do. You'll be far too busy helping Amy Osmond serve the guests and supervising the activities while I help Maudie with the food."

"Calm down, Aunt Philly. I can do both. It isn't like you to be so rattled." Laura laughed.

"Everything has to be perfect right down to the last detail. The future of Friday's B&B depends on the reputation of first impressions. Isn't that what you said when you held the marketing classes last summah?"

"I remember—building Cole Harbor's reputation on tourists' first impressions. I never dreamed those words would come back to haunt me."

Phyllis hugged her niece. "You'll be leaving in a week. I'm really going to miss you."

Laura's sadness equaled her aunt's. "Planes fly back and forth from Texas to Maine every day."

Phyllis offered a sad smile as she turned to answer the telephone again.

****

The evening of September 3rd, Phyllis hugged the tall, ruggedly handsome man who stood in the middle of the B&B's living room. An entourage followed him. She jumped up and down in silent glee as she grabbed him by the arm and led him to the entrance of the sunroom where Laura sat with her bare feet propped on an ottoman, her head bent over a book.

Phyllis squeezed his arm, grinning from ear to ear, and then made a little shooing motion with her hands. As he eased forward on silent feet, Phyllis was joined by Maudie. The two elderly women stood with hands clutched to their hearts, while the others also watched.

The man cleared this throat. "Laura Friday, will you marry me?"

Laura's mouth fell open and the book slid to the floor as she stood. He held a small red velvet box in his hand, which she ignored as she put her hands to her cheeks. "What are you doing here?"

He opened his arms and she filled them.

"Oh, Mitch, you already know the answer. Yes, a million times, yes."

The Carter clan came in with a bit of shoving. The room was suddenly very crowded, and everyone stood rather awkwardly in the middle of the sunroom, and nobody said a word for a moment until Wyatt broke the silence. "Don't just stand there gawking at the girl. Show her the ring."

The moment of awkwardness ended, and it seemed everyone gabbled at once. Mitch opened the red velvet box. He lifted out a rose gold engagement ring, the diamond centered inside a flower shaped like a miniature bluebonnet. He slid it onto Laura's finger. "Now it's official."

The Carters let out a big Texas whoop.

She extended her hand for everyone to see. Two exuberant twins burst forward and wrapped their arms around her. They looked up at her with toothless grins. "Can we call you Aunt Laura instead of Miss Friday?"

She returned the hugs, and tears fell. "You betcha."

Mitch gave his father a thumbs-up.

Claire helped Maudie and Phyllis serve refreshments while Jill propped her swollen ankles on an ottoman. Mitch said, "Laura, you know everyone here except…" He motioned a stranger forward—a man who bore a strong resemblance to Mitch, Wyatt, Rob and the four uncles. "I'd like you to meet my other brother, Tully, Chief Petty Officer, United States Navy."

She extended her hand and offered a smile. "I'm

honored to meet you. Mitch speaks of you often and fondly."

"Yes, ma'am, and you're a whole lot prettier than my ugly brother described."

She blushed. "Am I missing something? The wedding is in two weeks, in Texas, right?"

Wyatt laughed at his soon-to-be daughter-in-law. "Jill had a hankering for one of them gen-u-wine lobster rolls. Mitch said the only way to get one was to come here." He pointed at his daughter's swollen belly. "She also said I needed a vacation. Claire pointed out that the whole family needed a vacation. Mitch had pamphlets scattered all over the dang house trying to make up his mind where the two of you should spend your honeymoon, so we had a family meeting and decided instead of having the nuptials on the ranch, and ya'll going off to some foreign country for a celebration, we'd bring the wedding and the honeymoon to Cole Harbor."

Phyllis also shared the laughter. "I can't tell you how many phone calls we've made back and fo-ath doing the planning and trying to keep it secret from you. Besides, I think it fitting the first wedding at the Friday B&B should be yours."

Jill's eyes were filled with soft affection. "Don't be mad, Laura. I guess we really did fool you while doing all those Skypes."

Laura was overwhelmed and filled with love. "You mean the entire time we were converting the garage to a honeymoon suite and decorating it, it was really for me? Oh, my gosh, Aunt Philly, you are truly a wonderful scoundrel."

Mitch excused himself, then returned to the room

with a small square white gift box tied with a red ribbon. He laid it in Laura's lap. "My wedding present to you."

She offered a puzzled look. "Another gift?"

She picked it up as she glanced at the expectant faces around her. "Are you all in on some kind of big secret?"

Only wide grins answered her.

She untied the bow and lifted the top. Her puzzlement grew. She didn't know what to think. She blinked to make sure her eyes weren't playing tricks on her. The depth of the object lying nestled on a cotton bed caused her breath to stop in her throat. She looked at Mitch. "It's a sheriff's badge. I don't understand."

Sam Houston Carter cleared his throat. "As the doctor in this family, may I elaborate? Mitch loves the law. In fact, he'd never be happy punching cows, and with an arm that has limited range of motion, he's not much good at shoveling horse manure…"

Mitch interrupted. "What my long-winded uncle is trying to say is that I'm Cole Harbor's new sheriff. The night Phyllis announced that Roberta Gilman had resigned and was moving to Quantico, I had no intention of ever leaving El Paso, but circumstances often create unexpected life changes." He glanced at a nodding Sam, then continued. "El Paso needs a sheriff with two good arms. Wes Rojas was an excellent deputy. He'll make an even better sheriff. Truth is, I've dodged a lot of bullets and lived to tell about it. I'm ready for a quieter type of law. That is, if you don't mind spending the rest of your life as the wife of a small town sheriff."

Laura hugged him, not bothering to hide the

brightness in her eyes. "Best wedding present ever."

****

The wedding was a social event held on the B&B's back lawn overlooking the bay. Everybody showed up, even people who weren't actually invited. Beneath a cerulean sky, Mitch and Laura said their vows at the altar, kissed, and were pelted with rice. Claire acted as the photographer and captured the images. Laura tossed the bouquet, and everyone doubled over with laughter at Kit's dismayed six-year-old face when the spray of Texas bluebonnets landed in his lap.

Harmon Taylor danced with Laura. He gave a hearty congratulations to Mitch. Rob and Travis broke out their guitars, and with Morgan on the violin and Virgil with a harmonica, they accompanied all the voices singing old cowboy songs and modern country ones long after the bride and groom slipped silently into the night.

Mitch lifted his bride and carried her over the threshold of the honeymoon suite. "Are you up for one more gift?"

"At this rate, you're going to spoil me rotten."

"Hold out your hand."

She obeyed.

He placed a key in it.

"What does it open?"

"I'll show you tomorrow."

"Let's bargain. Hmm, how about sex for the answer to the mystery of this key?"

His mouth curved into a smile as he wrapped her in his arms. He was ready to taste her sweetness. "Deal. The key fits the front door to our new home—the lighthouse cottage."

Tears replaced the words she wanted to say. She pulled him close and slid her arms under his shirt, against his back, feeling the rough edges of the scars that had nearly stolen his life. These were marks of his bravery, and she was glad he was alive to live out his days with her.

He felt her hands, felt their gentle stroking, and he relaxed as he guided her to the bed. They left pieces of clothing in a trail on the way. Once she was lying there, his kisses covering her, he nudged her legs apart and lowered himself so they fit against each other almost as closely as possible.

She arched up, feeling the swell of his manhood, feeling his hunger. “Please, Mitch,” she whispered, shifting even closer. “Please…”

The hardness of him entered her, his mouth covered hers, and she moved with him, lifting to the sudden urgency of his body. The tension in her grew and grew until it exploded in a hail of white heat that enveloped and consumed her.

She heard the quick sharp movements of their bodies against the crisp white sheets. Her body followed his, grinding itself against his hips until she felt his heat burst inside her. He groaned hoarsely and shivered again and again, pressing down into her with all the power of his craving body.

She clung to him. Her lips on his chest, on his throat as the furious waves of passion crashed over them, leaving them breathless and spent.

He lifted his head, his breath coming in short spurts. “I’m sorry. I couldn’t hold back.”

“I think neither of us could hold back. It was perfect.”

She held his gaze while her hips rotated under him. “Let’s do it again.”

He drove into her with a white-hot passion. She rode the crest of heat, reveling in the torrent of unimaginable delight. And then it came, like suddenly being dropped from a great height. She wanted to cling to that silvery pleasure for as long as possible.

She wept.

“Did I hurt you?” The worry in Mitch’s voice was evident. Cradled against her, he rubbed his hands up and down her back.

Still joined with him, she whispered breathlessly, “Just the opposite. I never in my wildest dream knew it was like this.”

He kissed her forehead gently. “You are beautiful.”

“So are you.”

He got up slowly. “How about a nice warm shower?”

“Together?”

“It’s what husbands and wives do.”

She laughed with pure delight. “Want to try for three in a row?”

Now it was his turn to laugh. “Woman, you are insatiable. If you kill me, at least I’ll die happy.”

****

Halloween night Laura gave out the last of the candy. She ached all over and had thrown up twice that evening. She had lost her breakfast every morning for a week. Certain she had the flu, the next day she made an appointment to visit Dr. Ken Musuyo. Not wanting to worry Mitch, she went alone.

She smiled to herself as she left the doctor’s office and walked toward the courthouse. She greeted Mayor

Shipley when he said, “Nice having Mitch as our sheriff.”

“The new gazebo is beautiful. Martha did a wonderful job with the redesign.”

“Ayuh, I’ll tell her you said so.”

Amy Osmond had graduated high school and was attending community college while working part time as Mitch’s secretary. She looked up from the computer screen and greeted Laura with a smile. “Morning, Mrs. Carter.”

“Amy, I thought we agreed you’d call me Laura.” She lifted her eyebrows, and returned the girl’s smile.

Amy glanced at her watch. “Time for school.” She called out, “See you tomorrow, Sheriff Carter. Bye, Laura.” And she was out the door.

Mitch rose, pushing away from his desk. “Hello, gorgeous. Ready for lunch?”

She sat in his chair and leaned back, placing her feet on his desk, her hands behind her head. “Can’t go to lunch today, and maybe not tomorrow, or at least not until I get over having morning sickness.”

His expression changed from puzzlement to serious to delight to uncertainty. “Morning…sickness…as in…we’re having a baby…morning sickness?”

She lowered her legs to sit straight in the chair. He knelt in front of her. “You’re certain?”

She nodded. “See what fooling around will do? Yes, I had a test, and Ken confirmed that we’re pregnant.”

He kissed her with gentle tenderness. “You don’t think I’m too old to be a dad?”

Her mind flashed to wonderment when he pressed his cheek to her belly. “Our child will be lucky to have you as a father."

He pulled back, an uncertain scowl on his face. "You're not going to be like my sister and crave chocolate-covered cherries and sardines, are you?"

"No, but I could go for a thick chocolate milkshake and a large order of fries, and a lobster roll."

His smile turned serious. "Some journey we've been on, huh?"

"Yes, it's been quite a journey."

He took her by the hand and led her out the door. His mind was filled with dreams—of the coming child, and of his future with this very special woman.

A word about the author…

Romance with a Twist…Expect the Unexpected is the promise award-winning author Loretta C. Rogers gives to readers. Once an avid horsewoman, she now travels with her husband on their motorcycle. She enjoys hearing from readers and encourages them to contact her at:

www.lorettacrogersbooks.com

Thank you for purchasing
this publication of The Wild Rose Press, Inc.

If you enjoyed the story, we would appreciate your
letting others know by leaving a review.

For other wonderful stories,
please visit our on-line bookstore at
www.thewildrosepress.com.

For questions or more information
contact us at
info@thewildrosepress.com.

The Wild Rose Press, Inc.
www.thewildrosepress.com

Stay current with The Wild Rose Press, Inc.

Like us on Facebook

https://www.facebook.com/TheWildRosePress

And Follow us on Twitter
https://twitter.com/WildRosePress

www.ingramcontent.com/pod-product-compliance
Lightning Source LLC
Chambersburg PA
CBHW060527260626
47161CB00003B/796
* 9 7 8 1 5 0 9 2 0 3 2 2 2 *